I hadn't coun... ...n a second man.

He grabbed me th... ...room, his hands c... ...
But my adrenaline was flowing, and this time I attacked first. I drove into him and shoved him backwards, catching him off guard and knocking him against the desk chair. He staggered back and fell – bringing me down with him.

His body broke my fall and I sprawled over him, aware my advantage would last no more than a breath. I grabbed a knife from the strap around my thigh and pressed it to his throat.

"You have ten seconds to tell me who the bloody hell you are and what you're doing here." Then, for effect, "And you should know I'm not afraid to use this."

He lay solid and unmoving beneath me, not fighting as I'd expected, barely breathing. Then came his voice, low and raspy – and devastatingly familiar.

"Madre della Madonna…Nadia?"

He'd found me, just as he'd vowed to do.

Available in April 2008 from Mills & Boon® Intrigue

Veiled Legacy
JENNA MILLS

MILLS & BOON
Pure reading pleasure

First published in Great Britain 2008
by Harlequin Mills & Boon Limited,
Eton House, 18-24 Paradise Road, Richmond, Surrey TW9 1SR

© Jennifer Miller 2006
THE MADONNA KEY series was co-created by Yvonne Jocks,
Vicki Hinze and Lorna Tedder.

ISBN: 978 0 263 85955 3

46-0408

Harlequin Mills & Boon policy is to use papers that are
natural, renewable and recyclable products and made from
wood grown in sustainable forests. The logging and
manufacturing processes conform to the legal environmental
regulations of the country of origin.

Printed and bound in Spain
by Litografia Rosés S.A., Barcelona

JENNA MILLS

grew up in south Louisiana, amidst romantic plantation ruins, haunting swamps and timeless legends. It's not surprising, then, that she wrote her first romance at the ripe old age of six! Three years later, this librarian's daughter turned to romantic suspense with *Jacquie and the Swamp*, a harrowing tale of a young woman on the run in the swamp and the dashing hero who helps her find her way home. Since then her stories have grown in complexity, but her affinity for adventurous women and dangerous men has remained constant. She loves writing about strong characters torn between duty and desire, conscious choice and destiny.

When not writing award-winning stories brimming with deep emotion, steamy passion and page-turning suspense, Jenna spends her time with her husband, two cats, two dogs and a menagerie of plants in their Dallas, Texas, home. Jenna loves to hear from her readers. She can be reached via e-mail at writejennamills@aol.com, or via snail mail at PO Box 768, Coppell, Texas 75019, USA.

Writing by its very nature is a solitary experience. There's always someone around to help you plot. Experts can give you advice. Research can fill in the blanks. Family and friends can offer support. But only the author can paint the story-world for readers. Only the author can write the story.

There was nothing solitary about creating THE MADONNA KEY series. Each book has a distinct author, that's true, but the gestalt of the series, the story of a diverse group of fascinating women, is the result of…well, a diverse group of fascinating women…

Evelyn Vaughn: thanks for inviting me into THE MADONNA KEY world, for your patience and wisdom and, most of all, for the gift of your friendship.

Vickie Hinze: a special thanks for welcoming me into THE MADONNA KEY world – and suggesting I kick the series off with an online prequel. Nadia and I are ubergrateful.

Lorna Tedder: a warm thanks to you, as well, for welcoming me, for the box full of books on the Mayans, and for all those questions you patiently answered.

Cindy Dees: working with you has been a joy – watching how your mind works has been incredible! If I'm in a dark alley, you're definitely someone I want by my side.

Carol Stephenson: you're simply amazing. You jumped in at the last minute and blended in seamlessly. We're all better for having worked with you!

Sharron McClellan: for always being there, and for always being so wonderfully calm, creative, flexible and funny!

Thanks also to my agent Roberta Brown for navigating the path; to my editor Wanda Ottewell for helping to create this opportunity; and to Natashya Wilson for championing this amazing, complex effort.

And as always, a special thanks to my husband and young daughter, for all the hours you let me play in other worlds!

Prologue

Long ago, when the Colosseum first rose in splendor, but before the might of the Romans reached its peak, there lived a woman who saw the dark clouds of destiny gathering on the horizon.

Desperate to prevent tragedy, she traveled to a doomed land and found a great treasure, but lost her heart. A daughter was born. A birthright buried. A legacy preserved.

With the clarity of her last breath, she left one final gift, a myth-shrouded prophecy, in the knowledge that someday, one of her descendents would save the world....

Chapter 1

It was an odd sensation, looking at the picture of a dead woman and seeing your own face staring back at you.

"Mummy pwetty, Mummy pwetty!"

Somehow I found a smile. And somehow I looked from the magazine in my numb hands to my little girl. She bounced with her own special brand of two-year-old enthusiasm beside my wrought-iron chair. Her eyes glowed with excitement. Her dark curls bobbed. She'd been the one to show me the obituary. She'd been the one to come bounding onto the veranda, babbling about her mommy's pretty picture.

The chill was immediate, despite the unseasonably warm February afternoon. After weeks of rain, the sun seemed over-bright. "Where did you get this, sweet-pie?"

Lexie's smile widened. "Nanny Olga's woom," she said, and when she moved just so, I saw the smears of pink lipstick around her little mouth and knew she'd been playing with my makeup again.

"You know you're not supposed to go in there by yourself," I said, and her expression grew perfectly solemn.

"Mommy pwetty."

Something inside me warmed at the painfully innocent words, even as the fissures of cold kept right on bleeding. "And you're a sweetheart," I said, but Lexie was already pushing her doll carriage toward the small table set for an afternoon tea party.

I watched for a long moment, as I so often did, before returning to the picture of the dead woman. I'm not sure why my hand shook. It was just a picture, of a woman I'd never met…but then, even as I slid my finger along the funky cut of her red hair, I recognized the lie for what it was.

I knew this woman, even if we'd never met.

"Where's your nanny?" I asked Lexie. "Did you find her?" Dressed in the special white dress my mother had given her for Christmas, Lexie had raced off in search of Olga close to thirty minutes before. Olga had promised fresh scones.

But I'd not seen her since shortly after lunch.

Lexie lifted her dolly from the stroller and situated her in the miniature high chair. "Nanny weeping," she said matter-of-factly, but I was on my feet in a heartbeat and heading toward the house.

Then I realized what she'd said.

Not weeping, but sleeping. Little Lexie had trouble with her *s*'s. "She was sleeping?" I clarified, and she nodded as she poured imaginary tea into two faux porcelain cups.

And something inside me twisted. For little Lexie, in her fancy dress, with a white ribbon practically glowing against her dark hair, having her tea party alone. For Olga, curled up on her bed upstairs, still lost in grief all these weeks after losing a beloved aunt.

And for the woman in the picture, the one I'd spent over fifteen years looking for, who'd lost her life far too soon.

Her name was Scarlet. Long after I'd put Lexie to bed, I sat on an old settee and skimmed my finger along the zigzag lines of the woman's red hair. Then I traced her eyes, so like my own, wide and oval and flared at the outer edges, the color of a forest on a fall day. And the cheekbones, sharp and defined. The nose, neither thin nor wide, rather like a slope.

The color on the mouth was wrong—a bright flashy pink—but the rounded bow of the top and fullness of the bottom was the exact shape I'd passed on to Lexie.

According to the obituary, Scarlet Rubashka had been thirty-two years old, just like me.

And she'd been murdered, cruelly and brutally, in broad daylight.

In Saint-Tropez.

The chill started low and stabbed through me with horrifying precision. The memory tried to form, the blur of olive trees and the desperation of running, the whir of a waiting helicopter, but as I'd trained myself to do, I blocked the image and focused on the picture. On Scarlet.

It was not the first time I'd seen her.

I've always been a dreamer. When I was little, my dreams were happy. Ordinary things. With my mother busy with her charities and my father constantly in London, I was left to dream of kittens and butterflies and tea parties. There was nothing tragic, save for when a flock of pink birdies attacked my shiny new Mary Janes.

As I grew, my dreams changed. Nadia Bishop the shy little girl grew into a young woman with a taste for adventure. I became the one in charge, on a pirate ship or a wild stallion, walking along a parapet.

Perhaps even then it was fated that I would grow up to become a spy.

But no matter how the dreams shifted, from kittens to desperate chases through a grove of olive trees, I was never alone. I had companions. Two of them—a sister who didn't exist, and a man without a face. Of course, he started out as a boy.

I was an adopted child, an only child, and these imaginary, nighttime companions were the best friends I had. I don't recall how old I was when they first appeared; it just seems they were always there. But I was a woman before the boy got a face. Standing in the dim lighting of an exhibit of Mayan artifacts in an old Portuguese abbey, I felt recognition hit like a blow to my solar plexus when I saw him. It was as if all these disparate pieces inside of me simply slid into place. The boy from my dreams stood in front of me.

And the first time he kissed me...

It had taken almost a month to unearth the lies, but by that time it was too late. I'd fallen in love.

In the three years since, I'd tried to carve him from my dreams, but he remained. Except now he had a name. And a scent. *And a child.*

The girl had remained, as well, and, like me, she matured into a woman. Sometimes we were laughing. Other times, we stood on the edge of a cliff, hugging. Sometimes I ran through the darkness looking for her. And other times I screamed.

I always awoke with my throat burning.

Seven weeks ago, I dreamed of murder. There was sunshine and anticipation, that butterfly orgy in my stomach that had erupted within me the first time Antonio touched me. Then dread. The punch of horror and the hands around my neck. Then everything faded and went black.

Now I stared at the obituary and tried to breathe. Scarlet had died in November, precisely when I'd dreamed of death. And her face was the one I'd seen in the earliest dreams I remembered.

It was the face I saw in the mirror every morning.

And the key she wore around her neck looked identical to the one sitting on my nightstand—the one I'd had when I arrived at the orphanage.

And I realized I had no choice.

Slipping from my room, I made my way toward Lexie's. I needed to see her, to hold her in my arms and bury my face in her soft curly hair. To feel her breath on my body. Were it not for her...

Were it not for her, everything would be different. I would have gone after her father with everything I had, rather than severing all ties to the alias by which he'd known me, having my files sealed, and leaving MI6 for good. For years, I'd given my life to making the world a safer place. But from the moment I'd learned I was carrying a child, I'd given mine up to keep her safe.

And that meant making sure her father never knew she existed.

But now, in the fullest sense of the word *irony,* the need to protect, the one that had driven me to drop off the face of the earth, was sending me back to the town where I'd first confronted the enormity of my mistake.

Saint-Tropez.

Because I had to know. Who was Scarlet Rubashka, and why had she been murdered? What of the key? Was it really identical to mine?

Could her life, her death, lead me to the family I'd never quit wanting, despite the lovely life my adopted parents had given me?

Throat tight, I eased open the door and felt my heart stop. For just a second. That was all it took to scan from the empty crib to the rocking chair, where Olga sat holding Lexie. Rocking. Just rocking. Quietly. Slowly. Removed somehow.

For a split second, I considered backing away.

It was an intimate moment there in the shadowy, pale pink room, a moment that encapsulated the circle of life in ways that made me achingly aware of the inescapable web of mortality. I could fight the world, fight my daughter's family, but I could not fight the cancer that had almost claimed Olga the year before—and that had claimed her beloved aunt a few weeks before Christmas.

Every moment was a gift.

I'm not sure what broke the spell, what made my Olga blink and look toward me. I was thirty-two years old, but in that moment, her warm smile made me feel like a little girl again, and I wanted nothing more than to dive into her arms like I had when I was six and accidentally dropped my Matilda doll into the Thames—or when I was thirteen and Olga came to retrieve me at school, to tell me my father had suffered a massive heart attack. That the doctors had done everything possible, but he was gone.

Then the moment broke and time surged forward, and I saw the truth: that Olga was the fragile one now, I the strong one. She'd cared for me my entire life—and now it was my turn to care for her. She'd taken her aunt's death hard. She'd lost weight…lost the vitality that had always radiated from her like summer sunshine.

This wasn't the first time I'd found her late at night in Lexie's room, quietly rocking my daughter.

Our eyes held for a long moment, then she looked down and pressed a soft kiss to Lexie's forehead. Lexie murmured something as Olga stood. I rushed forward to offer a hand, but she was on her feet before I reached her. Together, we placed my little girl into her crib. I looked at her lying there, this perfect little two-year-old doll, and couldn't resist the urge to brush the dark curls from her face. *She looks so like him.* Olga placed

Matilda 2 next to her, and we shared a brief knowing smile before turning and slipping from the nursery.

"Couldn't sleep?" I asked, after closing the door.

Olga kept her smile in place, but the sadness in her eyes deepened. "Just restless," she said, easing from her face the hair she normally wore in a long braid. Gray had begun to darken the blond strands. "And you?"

She wasn't going to like what I had to say. "I…found something." Taking her hand, I led her down the hall to my room. But before I had a chance to say a word, Olga paled. She stared at the magazine on my settee as if it were a viper poised to strike.

"*Nadia.*" The tired pleading in her voice pierced my heart. "I did not wish for you to see that."

I wanted to be angry with her. She knew about the dreams, that I'd always wondered. She knew about the letter I'd written to the orphanage, in which I'd requested information about a second infant, a sister. Who'd been abandoned with me.

She'd handed me their response one week later. "Dear Miss Bishop," they'd written, then gone on to claim they were quite sorry, but I'd been left there alone.

She knew, and yet she'd kept the magazine from me. "You should have shown me," I whispered.

"I should have burned it is what I should have done," she retorted in the brogue of her youth, and finally, finally her eyes sparked. "Just because you are too big to crawl into my lap as Lexie does, does not mean you no longer need protecting. Your mother and I thought—"

I cut her off. "I know." She and my mother wanted me to leave the past alone, just as they'd begged me not to pursue a career in intelligence. They felt it would only lead to more hurt. And while I should have been angry with her, I couldn't, not after I'd come so close to losing her the year before.

But I also knew I could not let her displeasure stop me. "You know I have to go," I said, skipping over the obvious and landing where we both knew I would. My father was gone, but we still had his Cessna. I'd already called Evan, his pilot. We would leave at sunrise. "I have to find out."

"You have to do no such thing," she said, snatching up the magazine and slapping it closed. On the cover, one of the last photographs Scarlet had taken, that of a serene-faced statue of a dark-skinned Madonna and child, made everything inside of me tighten. "Your place is here, with your daughter."

"I'll be careful." I hadn't been retired that long. I still knew how to slip in and out of shadows, how to use my 9 mm. "Two days, three max."

With an abruptness that stunned me, she took my hand. "And just what is it you hope to accomplish, Nadia?" Her own hand was thin and cool, but surprisingly strong. "No matter who this woman was, she is dead now. She cannot tell you anything. She cannot answer your questions."

Oh, but she could. "She was killed," I whispered.

"Murdered," Olga clarified. "She, this Scarlet, this woman who looks so like you. She was strangled to death in Saint-Tropez—the same place you last saw *him*."

Him. She didn't need to say the name. We both knew. *Antonio.*

Except Antonio was not really his name.

"Even more reason for me to go." Taking the magazine from her, I flipped to the picture of Scarlet above the obituary. "Look," I said, pointing. "Her necklace, the key. It is like mine."

"Nadia—leave it alone. You have Lexie to think of now."

"Don't you think I know that?" I tried not to raise my voice, but something hard and jagged broke through. "It's because of her that I have to go! That I have to know. Who killed this woman…and why."

Olga had always had beautiful eyes. Even now, when they were tired and drawn and bloodshot, and swimming with unshed tears. "And what if *he* is there? What if *he* sees you?"

I pulled back. "He isn't there," I whispered. His wife had been injured, according to a friend of mine still in the business. She was on the mend, but he would be with her. And *their* son. In Italy. Where they belonged.

"And even if he is," I said, twisting toward my nightstand and picking up the old, ornate key that dangled from a silver chain. "I do not make the same mistake twice."

Less than twenty-four hours after I first saw Scarlet's obituary, Detective Hugh Bonnet, a strikingly handsome man in his early fifties, with jet-black hair and even darker eyes, spread several photographs across his desk. "I do not know why you wish to see these," he said in near perfect English, and though I'd never met Scarlet Rubashka, my stomach pitched. She was there, captured in death in a series of eight-by-ten crime scene photos. Naked and exposed but beautiful somehow, a shattered wineglass on the patio beside her.

Like a coward, her killer had attacked her from behind. He hadn't had the guts to look her in the face while he squeezed the life from her body.

"I am afraid you have wasted your time coming here," Bonnet said. "While tragic, there is no great mystery to your cousin's death."

That's what I'd told him, that Scarlet was my cousin. Not acknowledging the resemblance between us would only have raised his suspicions.

I glanced up at his dark piercing eyes, then found myself sliding a picture of the interior of the hotel room over Scarlet's nudity. "You say she attended a yacht party the afternoon she was killed?"

"Oui." Bonnet reached for the pictures, but I picked them up first, for some ridiculous reason not wanting him to touch her.

"She'd been drinking," he said, with a stern frown. "We found evidence of cocaine and methamphetamines in her hotel room. Witnesses saw her leaving with a man."

I glanced at the picture, at the broken glass and the romantic chaise longue. "What of this man. Have you found him?"

"I am afraid not. He is said to be German, perhaps a Swede. No one knew his name."

How convenient.

"It is not something we are proud of, but sadly, we lose a few tourists every year."

And that, according to Bonnet, was that. Scarlet's death was tidy and tragic, one of those bad-for-tourism episodes to be swept under the rug, even if it meant lying. Which clearly he was. I didn't need to be a former MI6 operative to know that.

But perhaps I did need to be one to find out what he was hiding. And why. "This inventory," I said, lifting a sheet of paper. "This is all that was found in her room?"

"Oui."

I glanced at the picture of Scarlet lying so still, and felt the emptiness clear down to my soul. "What of her necklace? There should have been a key on a silver chain."

Bonnet sat back. *"Non,* no necklace."

But there had been—I'd seen it in the picture accompanying her obituary, as well as in every photo of her on her Web site. Perhaps its absence meant nothing…or perhaps it meant everything.

For the next hour, I mulled over the pieces as I walked the streets of swanky Saint Tropez, and tried not to remember. But did so, anyway.

Little about the modern version of a medieval town had

changed since the misty predawn when I'd raced through a grove of olive trees toward an awaiting helicopter. Designer boutiques, art galleries and trendy bistros still crowded the cobblestone streets. Along the harbor, pastel buildings remained in tidy little postcard-perfect rows, while nearby, local fishermen gathered in the shadow of opulent yachts to sell their catch.

The contrast between simplicity and extravagance pretty much summed up the seaside resort.

"Mon Dieu," the shopkeeper's daughter said less than two minutes into our chat. In the three years since I'd last stepped foot in Mathilde's Millinery, Giselle had transformed from a freckle-faced girl to a striking young woman worthy of any magazine cover. "The resemblance, it is *extraordinaire.*"

"She was my cousin," I explained, as I had to Bonnet.

Young Giselle pulled a bronze-and-black fedora from behind the counter and handed it to me. *"Mais oui,"* she said when I asked about the necklace. "I remember ze key. She wore it the last time she was here—she used to play with it as she spoke."

With a strained smile, I took off the pink crocheted bucket cap I'd selected that morning and replaced it with the stylish hat Scarlet had once tried on.

"She liked this one, too," Giselle said, reaching for a hot-pink turban with a rhinestone broach at the center. "She was here the day she was killed. She bought sunglasses. I thought she was acting odd, but I never imagined…"

"Never imagined what?"

Giselle frowned. "She thought she was being followed. She kept looking over her shoulder, saying something about a woman in black."

"Did you tell Bonnet this?"

"I did, but he said there was no way it was a woman who killed her."

More convinced than ever there was nothing simple about Scarlet's death, I slipped off the fedora and placed it on the counter, ran my hand over the turban. The ache was immediate. So was the rage. I'd always loved hats, the more unusual the better. Apparently she had, too.

"Did she say anything else?" Earlier, I'd stopped at an open-air café for cappuccino and gossip. The young waiter had started to tell me something about a man, but stopped abruptly. "About a man, *peut-être?*"

"Non." Giselle glanced toward the window. "Not this time. She was quieter than when we first met, said she would be in town only a few days, that she had somewhere to go…."

"Did she say where?"

"Non, she—" The words died as Giselle's eyes widened. *"Mon Dieu!"* She whispered it this time. *"C'est lui!"* It is him.

"Who?" I asked, turning.

"The man who was here with Scarlet," Giselle said eagerly. "Her lover. He's staring at you. He must think—"

I heard no more, not with that word echoing through my mind. *Lover.* I spun and strode toward the front of the boutique, leaving a trail of fallen handbags. There I shoved open the door and burst into the breezy afternoon.

The main drag bustled with activity, strolling tourists and slow-moving cars, a few bikers. "Where?" I was ready to take off running, despite my three-inch heels.

Giselle came to my side and looked to her right, where a heavily tattooed young man loitered outside a bookstore. I'd seen him on the way in, had come close to engaging him in conversation, until I'd noticed his End of Times sign. Somehow, I didn't think someone waiting to be rescued by a spaceship would provide the credible information I needed.

"I would have sworn it was him," Giselle muttered, "but I do not see him now."

"This man," I said, trying to strip the urgency from my voice. "Who is he? Does he live here?"

"Non." Giselle slid the thick, gorgeous hair from her face. "I do not know his name—Scarlet never said—only that they were mad about each other.

"He is Italian," she continued. *"Mais supposé* he has been here since she died. Some say he has been near death himself. Maurice—he owns the antique book store—has seen helicopters going to and from the man's estate."

Estate. The word threw me back for a moment, and with a clarity I didn't want, I remembered my first glimpse of the bougainvillea-shrouded villa in the hills north of Saint-Tropez. The sun had been setting and the sky was a canvas of coral and lavender, the bay aglow with the last light of the day.

Just as quickly—and far more fiercely—I shoved the memory aside. "If Scarlet's lover has an estate here, what was she doing in a hotel?"

Giselle executed one of those unmistakably French shrugs. *"Je ne sais pas.* That must not have been him, though. You know those Italians. They all look alike."

Yes, I knew those Italians.

"Giselle!" a sharp voice called from inside the shop, and simultaneously, we spun to see the infamous Maman Matilda gliding through her prized shop.

My informal interrogation had just slammed to a halt. But no matter. The girl had already provided more information than Bonnet.

Matilda's words to her daughter were sharp, and all in their native French. Which of course I understood perfectly. "How many times must I tell you not to gossip? Do you not remember what happened to Marguerite?"

"But *Maman,* I did not say anything, I swear it."

"That is what Marguerite said, too." Matilda dragged her

daughter back into the shop. "But her café burned anyway, did it not? Do you think that was a coincidence?"

Something inside me went a little colder. Trying to redeem Giselle, I followed her inside and purchased the fedora and the turban, then quickly excused myself.

A few minutes later, I stood outside the Office du Tourisme and pretended to watch the dark clouds swarming to the south. The fishing boats and yachts bobbed anxiously in the unsettled harbor, and finally it struck me that something *had* changed since my last visit to Saint-Tropez.

The ships were higher.

I blinked and narrowed my eyes, verified the oddity. The tide had been out when I'd arrived, so I hadn't noticed. But now the ships rode high against the quai—much higher than they had three years before. It was a silly thing to notice, and yet it was impossible to miss, considering the yachts now obscured the view of the old stone church I'd fallen in love with on my last visit.

Puzzled, I waited for the traffic light to turn green, then stepped into the crosswalk.

The impact came out of nowhere, a compact body thrust into mine and driving me to the cobblestones. I slammed down hard—just as a taxi sped through the red light.

The tattooed man rolled off me as I scrambled to my feet— but the cab was gone. "The end of times really is coming." A thready note of fear haunted his voice. "The time to repent is now."

Maybe. Or maybe someone was willing to kill to stop me from asking questions about Scarlet Rubashka.

It was close to midnight when I slipped my 9 mm into my satchel and made my way along the charming paths winding through the hotel gardens. Once, I would have found the olive trees beautiful. Now they scraped against memories I did not want, and for a cruel moment he was there, chasing me, shouting my alias above the drizzle.

Zoe! Zoe, come back!

The adrenaline of that long-ago moment poured through me all over again, but I kept my movements slow and deliberate. I also kept my eyes on the trees, keenly aware of the opportunity—and the danger. The garden, with its trickling fountains and strategically placed solar-powered lights, was intended for romance, but for a killer, the heavy foliage provided the perfect hiding place.

The path ended at the farthest unit on the property, a small, coral-colored building that housed only one suite. The silence was absolute, the darkness broken by a cluster of soft yellow lights twinkling from the bougainvillea. Wild roses in heavy bloom tangled along the wrought-iron railing of the patio, providing cover, but prompting me to be extra careful as I slipped overtop.

The small round table stopped me cold. This was where Scarlet had sat. This was where she'd died. I put a gloved hand to the iron and tried not to see her as she'd been in the crime scene photo, naked and sprawled in death. With a steeliness I hadn't felt in years, I turned toward the gardens and realized just how secluded the suite was.

Olive trees were everywhere. Knotted and twisted and gnarled, contorted by decades of wind lashing in from the bay. No one strolling through the gardens could see through the dense grove. And the isolation of the unit insured no one would hear her scream—if she'd even had the chance to scream.

Heart slamming, I made quick work of the lock and let myself into the suite, which had been out of service since the "incident." I didn't flip on the lights; the glow from the gardens provided all the illumination I needed.

Scarlet's suite was far more opulent than mine. The decor looked to be straight off the pages of a lifestyles-of-the-rich-and-famous magazine—the fabrics, the finest silks and brocades, the furniture big, intricately carved, clearly antique.

A king-size four-poster dominated the sleeping room, with a tapestried comforter. Two small tables flanked the bed, Tiffany lamps on each. Across the room stood a gorgeous armoire in what looked to be mahogany, while against the far wall stood a small writing desk with an oil lamp.

A quick search proved the police had at least been thorough in handling the crime scene. No trace of Scarlet remained, not a hair on the pillow, a note in the desk drawer or a pair of forgotten panties under the bed. *No key.*

In the old-world bathroom, the faint scent of something spicy and playful mingled with the harsh smell of cleaning chemicals. The dim light from the gardens showed a room of distressed tile and thick linens, with a Jacuzzi large enough for two—or more.

But other than the scent, nothing remained of Scarlet.

Swallowing against the disappointment, I stepped into the parlor. I hadn't really expected to find vital information lying out in the open—but I'd been so certain that if I stood in the room where Scarlet had stood—

The safe. I spun toward the closet and turned the knob, went down on my knees and reached for the dial.

Darkness came first. Total. Complete. Crouched low, I glanced toward the windows, where the faint light of the gardens no longer spilled in. Automatic timers, I thought to myself.

But then came the music.

Low and dramatic, classic opera drifted in from the bedroom. *Otello,* I recognized. Tragic and powerful and... Italian.

Antonio's favorite.

Not *Antonio,* I fiercely corrected. His name had not been Antonio any more than mine had been Zoe. The name had merely been a smoke screen—the only way he'd fooled me in the first place.

Unease swept through me as I reached for my satchel and grabbed my 9 mm. Quietly, I pushed to my feet—

The attack came from behind. Hands. Big and strong. Sliding around my neck.

On the plane that morning, I'd worried that motherhood had softened me. Had my time with Lexie, singing silly songs and dancing in the gardens, dulled the sharp edges that had once kept me alive?

There'd been no reason to worry.

Instinct never died.

I rammed my elbow back and drove it into what I instantly recognized as a male gut. Then, twisting hard against my attacker, I slammed my foot down on his. It took me a moment to realize he wasn't fighting me. His fingers weren't pressing against my windpipe—maybe never had been. With excruciating gentleness he turned me toward him and raised his hands to my face.

"I knew you'd come back to me," he murmured—and for a threadbare moment my whole world stopped.

Antonio.

From somewhere beyond, the music crested—and I remembered. Darkness pulsed around me, but I didn't need light to see him as he'd been the day we'd stepped off his private jet behind his Saint-Tropez estate—the same strip from which I'd made my escape less than forty-eight hours later. I could still see the glimmer in his eyes, what I now realized had been the thrill of the hunt.

Reality slammed in with the strong scent of brandy, and I again started to struggle. "Take your hands—"

"Do not make me punish you for leaving me," he said, and then his mouth was smeared against mine and I realized my mistake.

This man was not Antonio.

Repulsed, I turned from the sloppy kiss and yanked at his hands, but with the strength of a drunk, he was back for more the second I broke contact.

"…never let you leave me again," he slurred against my mouth, pulling me into his body as he did so. "Scarlet…"

Horror punched in from all directions. "No," I breathed. But the truth was impossible to dismiss. This man was drunk, and he thought I was a dead woman.

Realizing fighting him would get me nowhere, I slid my arms around his chest and pulled the gun from my satchel, felt only a brief pang of guilt as I slammed it against the back of his head.

He went down with a grunt and slumped at my feet.

The relief was immediate. So was the curiosity—and the opportunity. This man had known Scarlet. Some said he'd loved her. Others thought he'd killed her. Either way, he represented answers.

Gasping for air, I backed from him toward the bedroom, where the oil lamp I'd seen atop a desk was sure to shed some light on—

I hadn't counted on a second man.

He grabbed me the second I entered the room, his hands closing around my biceps.

But the adrenaline was flowing, and this time I attacked first. I drove into him and shoved him backward, catching him off guard and knocking him against the desk chair. He staggered back and fell—bringing me down with him.

His body broke my fall and I sprawled there, aware my advantage would last no more than a breath. I moved fast, grabbing a knife from the strap around my thigh and pressing it to his throat.

"You have exactly ten seconds to tell me who the bloody hell you are and what you're doing here," I growled. Then, for effect, I added, "And you should know I'm not afraid to use this."

He lay solid and unmoving beneath me, not fighting as I'd expected, barely breathing. Then came his voice, low and raspy—devastatingly familiar.

"*Madre della Madonna...*Zoe?"

Chapter 2

There are things you never forget. A child's laughter, a mother's scent, the lyrics to a favorite song or the last line of a heartbreaking movie.

For me, it was the birth of my daughter—and the sound of my name on the lips of the man who could dance in the shadows as easily as I could, the feel of his hard, lean body beneath mine.

Over the past three years, I'd gone to great lengths to scrape the images from my mind. In returning to Saint-Tropez, I'd known unwanted memories were bound to surface. But I'd never imagined that in less than twenty-four hours, those dark images would become reality.

Antonio.

He'd found me, just as he'd vowed to do.

"Seven seconds," I snarled above the roaring of my blood. No way would I give him the satisfaction of backing down just because his hoarse voice still twisted me up inside.

"Cristo," he swore, and I felt the force of his body gather. "What the—"

"I mean it. Not another move."

"Male detto, if he hurt you—"

"If he hurt me, what?" I challenged. "You'll punish him, too?"

He stilled. "You think I am here to punish you?"

I knew he was. No one walked away from an Adriano, after all, and that's what he was. An Adriano clear down to his well-manicured toes. Tucked securely behind a well-crafted, holier-than-thou humanitarian facade, the centuries-old Italian family took and discarded at will. Those who knew them whispered of their tragedies, unexplained accidents and sudden illnesses, a suicide here, a disappearance there.

My infiltration and subsequent escape were unprecedented. I'd one-upped the Adrianos, disappeared into the shadows and beat them at their own game. Therefore, I needed to be punished. I knew that, had always known that.

That I'd let excitement over finding my birth family lead me into their trap galled me.

Heart slamming, I refused to dwell on the feel of his body beneath mine…or the fact that the last time I'd been sprawled over him, neither of us had been wearing clothes.

Fate has a bloody grand sense of humor.

The agent I'd once been grabbed control, gloriously cold and decidedly impersonal.

"That was you in town this afternoon—watching me, waiting." It all made a sick kind of sense now. "Were you laughing the whole time? Imagining exactly what you would do to me when—"

"Cristo." With the oath his body came to life, moving beneath me, his hands reaching for my arms. "It was you he was following—that is why he came here—"

"Don't," I warned, with more pressure to his throat. I'd forgotten how good he was, how convincing his lies could be. But this time I had my eyes open and a knife in my hand, and this time I knew the truth.

Joshua Adriano could not be trusted.

Youngest son of an untouchable criminal mastermind, husband to a coldhearted gold digger and father to a doomed little boy, the man who'd once called himself Antonio had the means and the pedigree to do whatever he wanted, whenever he wanted, and stroll away with his hands squeaky clean.

Too bloody bad I refused to give him the pleasure.

"I'm wearing a wire," I hedged, and my heart pounded so fiercely I could barely hear myself speak. The Adrianos rarely traveled alone. One man was already down in the adjoining room. In all likelihood, more lay in wait. "You may have the Saint-Tropez police in your pocket, but I have friends, too. Whatever your plan is, you won't get away with it."

The Adrianos' signature opera music kept spilling in from the patio, but I heard the rasp of Joshua's breath. "Not that I do not enjoy having you on top of me, *cara,* but I grow weary of your double-talk."

If I hadn't known what a good liar he was, I might have actually believed he was frustrated.

"I am here because I am a cautious man," he offered, with a brilliant touch of weariness. "When I saw him coming here…" He paused and the tenor of his body changed. He took my forearms into his wickedly talented hands and held me firmly, the way he had the last night we'd spent together, when he'd found me walking around his house late at night. "Oh, *Dio.* Am I too late? Is that why you act like this? He hurt you just like he— "

The words died abruptly.

It was easy to see how he'd fooled so many, for so long. How he'd fooled me. Once. For three life-altering weeks.

"If I had my hands free, I'd applaud." With training and effort I kept the emotion from my voice. But it was there. God, was it there. On so many levels. "But as it is, I'm in the middle of something right now. And," I added coldly, "your ten seconds are up."

I felt the change immediately, the abrupt shift from pretend concern to deadly intent. His whole body vibrated with it, like a cobra coiling for the attack. "Go ahead then." He spoke with murderous softness, and despite the darkness concealing his slumberous green eyes, I knew they gleamed. "Cut me."

The challenge seared through me, and though I was sorely tempted, murder was not on my agenda.

Hating to have my bluff called, I started to pull away, but Joshua wouldn't let me go. "I did not think so," he murmured, and I knew the real Joshua Adriano had finally come out to play. "If you want to forget that *you* betrayed *me,* fine. We will play it your way. I will be the bad guy."

I gritted my teeth. "Let go of me."

"Why?" Very deliberately he pulled me lower against his body. "Being on top never bothered you before—but then, that was Zoe, and she did not really exist, did she? It is Nadia now. *Nadia Bishop.* Privileged daughter of the late Alistair Bishop of the House of Lords, toast of London and world-class liar."

He knew. God, he knew. I'd suspected as much, but hearing my name on his voice, my father's name—it drove home how right I'd been to have my files sealed.

"My crimes," I reminded him coldly, "are no greater than yours."

"Is that what you tell yourself?" The dangerous edge to his voice cut every bit as lethally as the knife in my hand. "Is that how you look at yourself in the mirror?"

"Don't try to make this about me," I retorted. "I'm not the

one caught in a web of lies." It was hard to know where to begin. That he was an Adriano. That he was married, a father.

That his family had been linked to the antiquities thefts they'd purported to abhor.

"Seems to me there are plenty of lies to go around," he said, his quiet voice just barely audible above the lament of the Italian tenor. "They have a way of catching up with you, do they not?" He streaked a thumb along my inner wrist. "I always knew that, with patience, one day I would find you. But *Dio,* I never imagined you would be foolish enough to come back here…"

The brief hesitation was the only warning I got.

"…unless there are so many men and so many places, the details of who, what and where all blur together after a while."

Everything inside of me went coldly still. "At least I'm not married."

"Of course," he continued, as if I hadn't just called one of his many bluffs. "I can see where it might be difficult. If it is March, which conquest does that make me? A Greek tycoon? A Russian diplomat?" Abruptly he released one of my wrists and lifted a hand to my face. "Perhaps a Spanish count?"

The insinuation that I'd become involved with other subjects of my investigations burned.

Yanking free of his grip, I stood and kept my back to the wall, the knife between us. "Are those my only choices?"

He, too, rose. "You tell me."

Adrenaline rushed through me like a strong dose of caffeine. I wanted to hate the feeling. God, I wanted to hate the feeling.

But didn't. That was the problem.

That had always, always been the problem with this man. And with myself. Danger was supposed to be frightening— not intoxicating. "It occurs to me," I said, "you've left one out."

He stepped toward me. "Just one?"

I refused to let the mockery in his voice get to me, or to acknowledge the truth of his words. Just. One.

Just. Him.

"An Italian con artist," I supplied with an overly sweet smile, though I knew he couldn't see me.

"Then what does that make you?" he demanded. Wherever the music had come from, it stopped. "Are you not the one who gave yourself to a man you wanted to destroy, all in the name of a day's work? Seems to me there is a word for those who sell themselves like that."

The jab cut deeper than it should have. "And what of the word for those who stand before God and promise to love and honor one woman, only to—"

The thud from the adjoining room, followed by a muffled curse, killed my words and had me spinning in that direction. Instinct is one of those things that never dies. If it does, an agent does, too, right along with it. I reacted as I'd been trained to do, lunging toward the room where I'd left Joshua's accomplice. Under no circumstances could I allow him to circle back and make it two against one. Joshua I could handle. I knew those odds.

It was the unknown that concerned me.

"No!" he shouted as I rounded the corner, to see the shadowy form stagger through the door and into the night.

"Stay where you are!" I commanded, but the first man kept going—and Joshua was closing in fast.

I ran into the night, where the cool breeze chased me through a maze of palm and olive trees. All the while I heard Joshua sprinting after me.

"You know not what you are doing!" he shouted, but I didn't slow. At the back of the property, I vaulted an iron fence and darted around a sprawling bougainvillea. The brush gave way to a small alley, and I ran along the edge, looking for an opening between buildings.

The sight of a shadow leaning against the wall spurred me on. The man who'd kissed me glanced up and swore viciously, then shoved away from the wall and vanished around a corner. I followed, racing between two buildings and across the main drag, which was now almost deserted. There, choices greeted me. Left, toward the office of the police. Right, toward the casino at the end of the street. Straight, toward the water's edge.

Sucking in air and ignoring the stitch in my side, I pivoted left, saw Joshua just in time. He ran toward me from the direction of the police. It figured.

"Stay away from him!" he shouted as I spun toward the right, only to find two men walking toward me from that direction, as well. Left with no choice, I dashed between the buildings and headed for the narrow beach.

The attack came from behind. Well, it wasn't an attack, not really. The second my feet hit the sand, Joshua caught up with me and grabbed my upper arm. *"Nadia..."*

I stood there and tried to breathe, stared out over the angry waters of the bay. That didn't help. The sea and I—let's just say we don't get along.

It was silly, and I knew it. A giant wave wasn't going to surge up onto the beach and swamp me. I knew that. So long as I stayed out of the water—

My friend Lex once remarked that if he hadn't known better, he would have thought I'd lived through a tsunami.

If I hadn't known better, I would have thought so, too.

Technically, it was low tide, but the large expanse of beach that should have been bared by the moon's pull had not materialized. There was only dark and moody water, the yachts crowding the marina still bobbing high against the horizon.

The yachts.

Twisting toward the quai, I realized Joshua's accomplice had likely darted onto one of the luxurious boats. The Adrianos owned one, after all. Once, Josh had talked of whisking me away for a weekend of sun, champagne and—

"I thought she was you the first time I saw her."

His voice was rough now, thick, laced with something dangerously close to regret. I didn't turn to him, though. Wasn't ready to see him. "Who?" I asked, as a cool rush of wind came in from the ocean and lifted the ends of my hair.

He stepped closer. "No more games, Nadia," he said, and I felt the warmth of his breath against the back of my neck. "We both know you are here because of Scarlet. You were in her room."

Scarlet. Just hearing her name hurt. I'd always believed I had a sister, had been looking for so long….

"I'm not the one playing games," I said, hating the dark suspicions twisting through me. I'd seen the obituary. I'd seen the Web site and talked to the police. I'd talked to Giselle and a waiter. They'd all confirmed the tragic story of Scarlet Rubashka.

And yet I'd been trained to question, and to wonder. I'd been taught that just because something seems impossible does not mean that it is.

And I had to wonder…the Adrianos, I knew too well, were capable of anything. There were those who believed they'd been experimenting with weather manipulation—for them, manufacturing a person, her life and her death, would be little more than child's play.

"There is no Scarlet," I said through a horrifically tight throat. *Deny it! Tell me I'm wrong!* The words screamed through me. So did, for one of the few times in my life, the fervent desire to be wrong. "She's no more real than Zoe or Antonio."

Joshua spun me toward him so fast I didn't have a chance to brace myself. Didn't have a chance to prepare.

He looked older. That was my first thought. Not in a bad way, but in a way that made me long to lift my hand to his tanned face and smooth away lines that had not been there before. To touch hair that had once been brown like dark roast coffee, and was now streaked by traces of gray.

I always knew I would see him again. No path led away forever, even if you wanted it to. Loose ends only dangled for so long. Eventually, everything circled back to the beginning. That was just the way of it. Some called it reckoning. Olga preferred retribution.

The farther you traveled away from something, someone, the closer you drew.

For once, I'd really wanted to be wrong.

Now the faint light of the stars played against the whipcord-lean lines of Joshua's face, revealing the gleam to his eyes. Technically green, I suppose, but they'd always reminded me of moss, dark and mysterious and disturbingly seductive. I wanted to see menace in them now. I wanted to see hate and revenge.

I didn't.

It was a glow, damn it. Warm and soft and too bloody potent.

Biting down on my lip, I kept my arms at my sides as he seemed to inspect me with equal regard. The years had been kind to me, I knew that. But I also knew there were differences. A woman didn't walk away from espionage and embrace life as a mother without the changes seeping through. The soft curves where before there'd been sharp lines. The chestnut hair, once sleek and straight, now loose and layered around my face. And my eyes. I tried to shoot the bored indifference back into them, but I doubted it was possible to fully hide the vulnerability that came from loving someone too much.

He lifted a hand as if to brush the hair from my face, but when I tensed and pulled back, he stopped. "You think I made Scarlet up to lure you out of hiding?"

The incredulity in his voice fed something deep inside. "I heard you, Joshua." Above the whir of the helicopter blades. "You told me you wouldn't let me go, that you would find me." The dark glitter in his eyes told me that he remembered every bit as well as I did.

"So here I am," I said. On the beach and in his arms—but nowhere near at his mercy. "What happens now?"

"Nothing happens." As if to prove his words, he let go of me. "You go home and forget everything you heard about Scarlet."

"You know I can find out if she's real or not," I pointed out.

He gave me one of those faint little half smiles that had once melted my heart. "Of course you can, *cara*. My family can do much, but even we cannot change history. Scarlet Rubashka was well known and well loved. But if you know what is good for you, you will forget you came here, forget you saw me—"

Giselle's earlier words cut through me. *Her lover. That rich Italian.* I'd thought of Joshua immediately, the Adriano estate, the landing strip…. "Oh, my God."

I didn't need to say more than that. Joshua's eyes went hard, and even there in the darkness, a shadow seemed to fall over him. "I did not kill her, *cara*."

The flash of relief was immediate—and stupid. He was an Adriano. Lying was what they did best. But part of me—

That part of me didn't matter.

However, every good agent knew the more you continued to accuse someone, the harder and deeper the line between you became. The truth came in the details, and the details came through pretending to believe.

So I did what I'd been trained to do. I went along with his story—and went fishing for more.

"But you know who did," I said, opening the door.

"Her death was a tragic mistake."

"Then what are you doing here tonight?"

"As I told you—I was following someone."

Convenient answer. "Who?"

"Names are not important, no?"

The door slammed so quick and so hard I almost recoiled. "You mean you're not going to tell me."

His smile caught me by surprise. It was slow, and God help me, a novice would have thought it sad. "That seems to be what we do best, yes?" The words were cutting, but his voice was not. It was hoarse, almost gentle. "Not tell each other things."

Behind me the sea roared, merging with the faint trace of opera music from aboard one of the yachts. The wind coming off the water brought sand with it, pelting my back and stinging my arms. But it was nothing compared to the sting of his words. With uncanny skill, Joshua had steered my mini-interrogation back to the past, and the lies that would always stand between us.

"What aren't you telling me now?" I asked, doing my best to yank the reins of the conversation back into my own hands.

He glanced toward the quai, let out a rough breath before returning his gaze to me. "You should not be here," he said. "You have no idea what doors you are opening."

That was true. Either Scarlet was an Adriano hoax designed to lure me into a trap, in which case it made no sense that Joshua was trying to make me leave—or she was real. And she'd been murdered. And Joshua was involved.

I didn't know which scenario horrified me more. "And I take it you do know?"

His gaze again darted toward the marina. "I know that you are putting your life in danger just by being here."

I'd never been a big fan of small, closed-in spaces. They afforded little opportunity for innovation or escape. But wide-open spaces didn't thrill me, either. They provided *too much* opportunity for innovation and escape.

The way Josh kept glancing around didn't help matters.

Standing there with the spray of the water against my back, I suddenly felt exposed and vulnerable in a way I hadn't in— well, since the last time I'd faced Joshua Adriano.

"What do you want from me?" I whispered, and felt a cruel little jolt at the way his eyes went dark.

"I want you gone." He stepped closer and took my arms, and this time I neither tensed nor tried to twist away. "I mean it, *cara*. Forget you were here, forget you saw anyone."

Forget him. He sounded almost desperate.

"I can't do that." Not if Scarlet was real. And not if an Adriano was involved in her death.

"You will if you know what is good for you."

The wind kept blowing. "This conversation is going nowhere," I stated, though in truth, I feared I'd already learned far more than Joshua had intended to reveal.

Again the regret, this time evident in the way his grip on my arms loosened. "That is how it has always been between us, yes?"

He didn't know the half of it. And God help me, I would die before I let him find out. "Nowhere," I whispered anyway.

"Go home, Nadia," he said, with that same world-weariness I'd seen in his eyes when he'd turned me to look at him. "Go back to where you came from."

Bad guy, I told myself. Evil, vile, dangerous. Clever. Cunning. Capable of anything. Everything. Among those in the intelligence community, rumors about the Adriano brothers ran rampant. The Brothers Grimm, I'd heard them called. Capable of seducing a woman straight to her death, delivering an orgasm and a final breath at the same time.

But I'd never wanted to believe that about Josh.

"You're just going to let me walk away?" I asked.

"If you promise to quit screwing with my family, *sì*."

But that was one promise I couldn't make. Not if the Adrianos were involved with Scarlet's death. "Sorry," I said, with a flippancy that hurt more than it should have. "But in my line of work it's no secret what happens when you turn your back on an Adriano."

"Then I shall turn mine on you," he said, with one last long scorched-earth look. "I will walk away, but know that I will be watching, Nadia. I will be everywhere. I will see everything, hear even your whispers. And if I find out you are coming after my family, I will make it my personal responsibility to stop you."

With that, he turned and walked off. And I stood and watched until I could no longer distinguish him from the shadows. Then I curled my hands into fists and made a promise. To myself—and to the woman I believed had been my sister.

If the Adrianos had anything to do with her murder, vengeance would be mine—not theirs.

With the sunrise, I slipped into the first open café and fired up my laptop. With a few clicks of the mouse, I sent the search engine on its way, then picked up the sturdy white mug the waiter had set down a few minutes before. I'd barely sipped the strong black coffee when my query on Scarlet Rubashka returned, and my heart kicked hard. 32,493 results. The Adrianos excelled at creating smoke screens and covering their tracks. But even they weren't *that* good.

Leaning closer, I scanned the first ten entries, one a direct link to ScarletRubashka.com. The temptation to visit her Web site again was strong, but I knew a personal Web site could easily be manufactured—or doctored.

The other links were not as simple to manipulate. Mentions of Scarlet Rubashka were scattered across Web sites maintained by prominent magazines throughout Europe. The articles confirmed Scarlet had been a freelance photographer and that several of her photographs had been nominated for major awards.

Coffee all but forgotten, I cruised the sites and read the stories, squinted at a few small grainy images of—me. Not really me, of course. The pictures were of Scarlet. And in all of them she wore the key around her neck.

A flash of light drew my attention away from my laptop and I looked up as a rumble of thunder shook the café. The sky had darkened considerably since I'd last noticed it, and with a glance at my watch I realized over an hour had flown by.

Outside, tourists and locals rushed for cover as fat raindrops splattered against the sidewalk. Three well-dressed women, American I would guess, pushed inside the café, followed by a disheveled older man whose white beard and bushy eyebrows made him look like a haggard Santa Claus.

With one last check of the approaching storm, I returned my attention to my laptop and my sister's personal Web site.

I'd taken many risks in my career. I'd flirted with danger and waltzed with evil. I'd slipped under radars and shimmied out windows. I'd photographed documents while pretending to powder my nose, and copied CD-ROMs while in search of aspirin. I was intimately familiar with the rush of each new assignment, the tingle of anticipation that came from never knowing what—or who—lurked just around the corner.

All those feelings swirled back as I again clicked on the link to ScarletRubashka.com. I'd calmly held a gun on a suspected terrorist, but there in the café, with my sister's Web site loading, my hands wanted to shake. And my throat went dry. Bloody ridiculous and I knew it, but I'd searched for my birth family for so long....

And then there she was. Scarlet Rubashka....

Against a sky of fading crimson she stands on a wall of crumbling stone. Her hair whips in the wind from the sea. Her cheeks are flushed, her blue eyes damp. "You promised," she says, fighting back tears. "You promised you would never leave me."

Naysa pulls her sister into her arms. "I know what I said, Ciara, and I am sorry. But this is something I must do."

"Then I am going with you." Ciara pulls back. "I will follow you. Together we can—"

"No." Naysa lifts a hand to smooth hair from her face. At twelve, there is much Ciara does not understand. "Your place is here, with our mother." It is Naysa the elders have chosen, Naysa being offered in sacrifice to a faraway land.

Tears spill harder from her sister's eyes. "But what if you never come back?"

Naysa wants to promise that she will return and they will be a family again. But it is a promise she cannot make.

So she pulls her sister into her arms and stands on the wall of the old ring fort, watching the sun dip into the churning sea.

A time of change is at hand, and during all times of change there must be chaos before there can be peace. Sacrifice, before there can be harmony.

Naysa has heard the whisperings from the elders' fire, stories of a great prophet, crowned in thorns and crucified many years before, when her grandmother's mother was just a girl. More and more travelers are bringing the tales to the coastline of the Gaels, rumors of a new religion trampling out the old, a growing ruthlessness among the Romans, and a

*woman arriving on the shores of Gaul, with a dark-skinned
daughter and a fantastical message of her own. A prophecy.
A calling.*

It is there Naysa must go.

*She does not want to be afraid. She knows it is an honor to
be the chosen one. Yet as she looks down at her younger sister,
something inside her starts to tear.*

*"Do not be afraid," she says, squeezing Ciara's hands. Ev-
erything will be as it is meant to be. "I have a few more days.
We will spend them together."*

Together. As sisters. Laughing and sharing, understanding.
And loving. Staring at Scarlet's Web page, I swallowed hard
as the odd, disjointed images of the two girls faded into a sea
of red. But a chill wound deep within me.

We all have memories. They are part of who we are. Sometimes they flash like a montage of weathered snapshots—a
face, a place. A feeling. Other times, they play like shadowy
film clips, the highlights and lowlights of our lives. They take
us back and carry us forward. In many ways, they conquer even
death, keeping those who make up our lives with us always.
Because they are ours. Our lives, our memories.

But sometimes I remembered other things—other people,
other places. Other feelings. From lives I had not lived. It was
like tuning into someone else's life. Except it all felt so…real.
Like a dream, but stronger. Clearer.

The first time it had happened—three years before at a field
of standing stones in Portugal *with Joshua*—I'd researched the
phenomenon. How could I tune in to someone else's
memories?

I hadn't liked the answers I'd found.

And then the memories had stopped. It had been like having
a piece of me ripped out, that's how deeply I'd felt the loss.
Like starting a book I never got to finish.

I'd told myself to be glad. Not all endings had to be neat and tidy. Some things just…stopped.

Swallowing hard, I tried not to think about the obvious: things that just stopped could also just start again. I didn't want it to be true, but the unexpected memory—of those two girls about to be ripped apart—made my heart tighten and told me that something had definitely started again.

More agitated than I wanted to be, I focused on Scarlet's blog, and the woman she'd been came to life for me. I didn't have time to read all the entries, but I skimmed her thoughts on Mercury going into retrograde, Jupiter trining Saturn, the benefits of red and green teas, and the relationship between solar flares and the earthquakes that had rocked Paris a few months before. She talked of ancient prophecies and secrets lost to time; how new beginnings could only arise from endings; of a trip to Ireland.

I couldn't help but smile as I trudged through her musings, and even though I'd never gotten into astrology, I found myself intrigued.

Blinking dry eyes, I glanced out the window, where rain slanted in almost horizontal droves, then smiled politely at the older gentleman seated near me. The shiver was automatic, as if my body knew the temperature outside had dropped with the storm. But I glanced around the crowded café anyway, made sure no Adrianos lay in wait.

With another sip of now-cold coffee, I returned to Scarlet's Web site and poked around pages listing magazines in which she'd been published and awards she'd won. Then I found the gold mine.

Row upon row of small thumbnail pictures lined up in a parade of Scarlet's life. There she was, posing like an Egyptian in front of the Great Pyramid. In Red Square, she stood soldier straight and saluted the camera. At the Berlin

Wall she had a hammer in her hand. I smiled as I dragged my finger along my touchpad, enlarging various pictures—until I came to the photo of her standing among the ruins of Pompeii. Then I went cold.

Frowning, I forced myself to move on, found myself staring at a photo of Scarlet standing beneath an unidentified waterfall, marked only with the words *Southern France*.

Then I saw the man.

Squinting, I leaned closer, at first not completely sure there was a man, standing to the side of the waterfall.

Recognition slithered in from all directions, but I refused to believe my eyes. Heart hammering harder now, faster, I slid along the thumbnails to the most recent pictures, not of Scarlet striking poses at famous sights, but beaming at the camera in the arms of a man.

"No…" Everything inside of me went painfully still as I zoomed in on a photo of Scarlet at an exhibit of black Madonnas in Paris. And again, from aboard a luxurious yacht.

I knew that man. More than knew him, I had been steadfastly avoiding him for years.

Her lover. An Italian.

Not Joshua, I realized now. But close. His brother Caleb, the most unpredictable Adriano of all.

Scarlet had been involved with an Adriano, just as I had. It had been Caleb watching me from outside the millinery, Caleb who'd kissed me in Scarlet's room—Caleb who had slid his hands around my neck.

Just as he'd slid his hands around hers?

I could only imagine what it had done to him to see me, a woman who looked so like his dead lover, alive and walking the streets of Saint-Tropez.

No wonder I'd smelled alcohol on his breath.

Caleb.

Not Joshua.

"For you, *mademoiselle*." It took a moment for the waiter's awkward English to register. Reeling, I pulled my attention from the monitor and looked at him, took the bill from his hand. Distractedly, I thought of the rudeness of hurrying me along, before realizing other patrons must need my table.

Then I glanced at the scrap of paper—and realized it wasn't a bill.

Chapter 3

Scarlet was warned—Scarlet didn't listen.
Scarlet is dead.
Now you are being warned—will **you** listen?

I surged to my feet and lunged after the waiter. "Where did this come from?"

"Ze woman over there," he said, gesturing toward a small table at the far side of the café.

A small, empty table.

"*C'est étrange,*" he muttered. "She was wearing a black hat—she was just there."

With a hard kick to my heart, I raced to the front of the café and shoved through the door, ran into the cold rain.

"Mummy come home!"

Squeezing the phone, I let my daughter's voice do what a

hot shower and thick terry-cloth robe had failed to do. Warm me. I'd spent the better part of the morning searching for the woman who'd delivered the cryptic note. But she'd vanished without a trace.

Now I took a sip of hot tea and let my little girl's sweet voice wash through me. "Soon, sweet-pie, soon."

"No, Mummy…miss you."

"I miss you, too." We'd been together nonstop since her birth. At first my refusal to leave her had been a matter of protection. I didn't trust anyone else to guard her the way I could. But with astonishing swiftness, I realized I didn't *want* to be anywhere else, didn't want to be *with* anyone else. My time with Lexie was a gift I'd never expected to receive, never even dreamed I *wanted* to receive, but having received it, I couldn't imagine life any other way.

"Mmmwwwwah," I said into the phone, hating the distorted connection. "That's a kiss. Can I have one back?"

Silence.

"Lexie?"

"She's kissing the phone," I heard Olga say, and I smiled.

"Mommy has to go now," I said as my throat tightened. "I'll call back this evening."

"I wuv Mommy," Lexie blurted, and my heart almost broke.

"I love you, too, sweet-pie."

Swallowing hard, I disconnected the call and looked at the slinky dress I'd purchased before returning to the hotel. The clerk at the boutique had looked at me, with my smeared makeup and wet hair, even wetter clothes, as if I was mad.

And who knows, maybe I was. I'd thought nothing could jolt me more than finding Scarlet's obituary. But I'd had no idea that within hours, I would run into the one man I'd prayed never to see again, that he would threaten me even as he stirred my blood. Last night, I hadn't understood Joshua's vehemence. But now I did.

The woman who might be my sister had been involved with his brother. *Caleb.*

I don't believe in coincidences any more than I believe in fairy tales. Everything happens for a reason. Sometimes the reason is obvious. Usually it isn't. Sometimes those involved made "coincidences" happen. Other times, a puppeteer lurked behind the scenes, manipulating with an express purpose in mind.

Dark suspicions twisted through me as I made final preparations for the evening ahead. Joshua and I had become lovers in a pretend world. We'd both been lying, unaware of who the other was, only of the passion that drew us together. Or so I'd thought.

Now I had to wonder.

Joshua and Caleb were brothers. Scarlet and I were sisters. The second I'd learned the man I'd been sleeping with was not an undercover Spanish agent—that he was an Adriano, youngest son of a centuries-old Italian family mired in mystery—I'd given him the slip. The dossier my superiors had e-mailed me stunned me. The Adrianos, a family renowned for its philanthropic interests, hadn't been under suspicion when I'd first arrived in Portugal. But during the course of three short weeks, information had surfaced linking the family to an appalling array of criminal activities: bribery and extortion, black market trade and antiquities theft, even murder. And MI6 feared my cover had been compromised. They'd wanted me out. Despite my insistence that I was perfectly placed to acquire inside information, they'd insisted upon extraction. I'd been angry—until I took the home pregnancy test two weeks later. Then I'd realized how fortunate I'd been.

Scarlet…had not. She'd come to Saint-Tropez to rendez-vous with Caleb, and now she was dead.

Two brothers had seduced two sisters. Scarlet and I each possessed an antique key—one of which was now missing. I'd been attacked in Scarlet's room, hands sliding around my neck....

I lifted my right hand to my chest, where the key should have dangled. Thank God I'd taken it off before leaving England.

I hated the chill that swept through me, resurrecting the irrational longing to believe Joshua was not like the rest of his family. That I'd seen a side of him he didn't trust anyone else to see. That what we'd shared had been real and powerful and—

He was married. Frowning, I looked at myself in the mirror. Joshua Adriano was married. He had a son. Even if he hadn't been an Adriano, he was so categorically off-limits it made my blood boil to realize I'd let myself become the other woman. No, I hadn't known. But that didn't change the truth.

I'd slept with another woman's husband.

And sometimes, on those dark, restless nights when I didn't fall deep enough into sleep, and allowed myself to dream, it was Joshua I'd find in the darkness. Joshua whose voice would call to me. Joshua who would reach for me, hold me—

I broke off the thought, the memory, and lifted a curling iron to my now-pink hair. Maybe Scarlet and I had both been targeted by the Adrianos. Maybe there was something in our family background, some significance to our heritage or the keys. Maybe—

The list was endless.

With a shake of my head, I lifted my chin and studied my handiwork. Once, hot pink had been my favorite alternative hair color. It never ceased to amaze me how much information could be gathered just by dying my hair. Somehow, no one considered a woman with postmodern hair a threat. Go figure.

Ready for action, I glanced one last time at the text message from earlier that day, a summons from a woman named Catrina Dauvergne. I'd left a message for her on my way to Saint-Tropez, after seeing a picture of her with Scarlet. A museum curator, she wanted me to meet with her in Paris. Anticipation quickened at the thought, but for now, I had another target in mind.

Finding him was easy enough. So was snagging his attention. All I had to do was stroll through the casino in the little bronze sheath dress I'd purchased earlier that day, apple martini in hand. The stilettos with the crystal scorpion slinking up my foot to my ankle, where a strap wrapped twice, gave me the sinuous gait of a model—or a call girl.

Either way, Caleb Adriano was sure to notice. Rumor had it he had a fondness for the former and a weakness for the latter.

A palpable silence dominated the brightly lit room as I observed well-dressed men seated around blackjack tables, smoking thin cigarettes and sipping cognac. Few women came to gamble. Generally, they simply draped themselves around the men shelling out the euros.

I spotted Caleb immediately, seated with three other men and one woman at a baccarat table. And just as I'd planned, he spotted me. I lifted my chin and flipped my hair over my shoulder as I slinked toward the roulette wheel. Adrenaline rushed, but I kept my expression mildly bored.

There was no surer lure.

Beautifully predictable, Caleb laid down his cards and stood, made his way toward me—just as I'd anticipated. It was better that way, to let him approach. To let him think he was in charge. That way he wouldn't realize that I was the one manipulating everything.

It was a game I had not played in almost three years…but one I was very, very good at.

I kept walking, pretending I didn't see him coming, all the while watching him out of the corner of my eye. He was hard to miss, a big man who looked as if he'd once belonged in the wrestling ring. But of course, he hadn't. Caleb had never been athletic like his brothers.

He'd never been a lot of things like his brothers, from what I understood.

But still. I suppose some women would find him attractive, especially in the expensively cut white tuxedo that emphasized his olive skin. Highlights lent his hair a blondness incongruous with his Italian heritage, but absolutely in keeping with his playboy reputation.

"Buona sera," he said as he strode into my line of vision, and I had no choice but to stop, standing statuesquely aloof courtesy of my four-inch heels.

The way he was looking at me made my skin crawl. It was as if he wasn't sure whether to pull me into his arms—or wrap his hands around my throat. "Can I help you?"

"You…" He stepped toward me, as if he expected me to vanish at any moment. "I certainly hope so," he said in a mildly accented voice—nothing at all like the hypnotic cadence of his brother's—and then smiled. "You remind me of someone I once knew. For a minute I thought…"

His voice trailed off, but I knew what he'd thought—exactly what I'd wanted him to think. "I've been hearing that ever since I arrived," I admitted with a baffled smile. For effect, I stripped every trace of British from my voice. "That Scarlet woman, right? The photographer? Was she a friend of yours?"

His eyes darkened. "More than a friend."

His tone sent a shiver down my back. "My condolences. I heard she—"

"Was killed," he supplied before I could finish. "And my life has not been the same since. When I saw you, I know it is crazy, but for a minute I thought there had been some kind of mistake, that somehow she had come back to me."

It was my turn to stiffen. "You're not the only one to react that way," I said, executing my plan. "From what I gather, your Scarlet seems to have had as many friends as she did enemies."

The twitch was subtle. "Why would you say that?"

I pretended to become uneasy, raising my martini to my mouth for a quick, nervous sip. "It's nothing," I said, lifting my eyes to him, then glancing away. That's when I saw the old man.

Tall and regal, with a mane of flowing gray hair, and dressed in an elegant black tuxedo, the older gentlemen stood with unnatural stillness near a potted palm. Watching. The blade of familiarity nicked hard and fast, but it took a moment for me to place him. He'd been at the café that morning—but he'd been disheveled then, almost haggard. Now—

"Are you all right?" Caleb asked.

I blinked and forced a smile. "What? Oh. That man over there…" But he wasn't anymore. A woman stood where he had, her long blond hair tapering against a black cocktail dress.

"My apologies," I said. "I thought I saw someone I knew."

"That seems to be going around." His smile was somber. "Now what was it you were saying about Scarlet's enemies?"

Maybe it was just my imagination, but Caleb seemed to vibrate with the question, as if the answer mattered a great deal.

Pretending not to notice, I ran a hand through my pink hair and let it fall against my face. "I just…well, last night I did something utterly foolish. Curiosity got the better of me and I…" Deliberately, I let the sentence dangle.

"You what?"

"Doesn't matter," I hedged, rubbing a hand along my arm. "I went somewhere I shouldn't have." The best lies stemmed from the truth, and if my suspicion was correct and Caleb was the one who'd attacked me, then he knew I'd been in Scarlet's room. I needed to give him a reason why. "Someone mistook me for her. I think they wanted to kill her again."

His eyes flared. "You…you were not hurt?"

"Just a few bruises." And the lingering revulsion from his sloppy kiss. "That is why I changed my hair, though. I hoped this way no one would mistake me for her again."

"And yet here I am," he said with a gallantry that the average woman would find endearing.

"Yes. Here you are." Right according to plan.

"And a good thing for you, too." With a possessive smile he took my hand and drew it to his mouth, brushed a kiss along my knuckles. "Pink hair won't protect you—but I will."

"I was going to ask her to marry me," Caleb revealed as we walked through the water gardens beyond the casino. "I still cannot believe she is gone."

His willingness to talk about Scarlet surprised me. But then, I reminded myself, just because he missed her didn't mean he hadn't killed her. And openly mourning her could well be part of the smoke screen he wanted the world to see.

Or…he could be innocent.

"Losing someone you love is hard." I kept my gaze trained on the brilliantly illuminated, tap-dancing fountains. Beyond, I saw the shadow of a man, and for a damning moment my pulse surged.

Then reality set in, and I recognized my watcher as the friend from my MI6 days who'd come from Barcelona for the evening to cover my back.

"Madelaine?" Caleb used the alias I'd given him. He turned to me and tucked a finger under my chin. His alcohol-saturated breath unsettled me. "You have lost someone?"

The way he was looking at me—with feral curiosity in his

glassy eyes—told me he'd heard the emotion that had slipped into my voice. "My father died several years ago—"

"No." The authority of that one word jarred me. He almost sounded angry. "Not your father. What I see in your eyes is not what a daughter feels for her father."

I tried to turn from him, but he held me steady. "There was a man," I admitted.

"And you loved him," Caleb slurred.

No. I'd hardly known him. For those short weeks we'd been great in the bedroom, but everything else had been an illusion. *So, do you think the world is going to end?* Those were the first words he'd spoken to me, there at the exhibit of Mayan artifacts, in a shadowy old abbey. At the time, the question had intrigued me.

Now, given the earthquakes in Paris and resurgent outbreak of an allegedly eradicated disease, it chilled me. "It's over now."

"Ah." The sparkling lights lent a creepy sheen to his eyes. The cognac, I told myself. He'd consumed an alarming amount, given his heritage. Not the Italian part; Italians had no qualms about liquor. But the Adriano part. The family protected their whitewashed image at all costs. Public drunkenness—and the loss of control that came with it—was an enormous taboo.

"I see," he mumbled. "It was not death that claimed this love of yours."

Considering all that he'd had to drink, his deductive reasoning remained strong. "There are many ways to die," I said. "Not all of them involve the body."

"This is true."

The night breeze blew around us, suddenly colder. The urge to stare him down was strong, but not smart. So I took a few steps toward a fountain backlit by soft pink, then wrapped my arms around my middle.

On cue, he stepped up behind me. "Madelaine?" His hands settled against my arms. "Something is wrong?"

Yes. From a purely executional standpoint, the evening was unfolding exactly as I'd planned. I'd made contact, lured him into a conversation. Bit by bit, I was learning about Scarlet.

But my technique must have been rustier than I'd realized, because the emotion seeping through me—for the woman who could be my sister and the man who was dead to me in all ways that mattered—violated every ounce of training I'd ever had.

"Not really," I said. "I was just thinking of your Scarlet, wondering what it would have been like to meet her."

"She would have loved that."

"So would I."

"She was full of life," he murmured. "Funny and exciting and curious—" Abruptly, he broke off.

"Caleb?" I asked. "Curious about what?"

"Everything," he said, drawing a swift breath. "The stars and the seas, history and archeology and art. Religions. The Mayans and the Marians."

"Marians?" I asked, turning toward him. I'd seen the word in one of her blogs, but I'd not had time to read more, only something about the coming Age of Aquarius. "What are Marians?"

The transformation was immediate. That polished, slightly tipsy facade thinned, and a hard sheen of anger poured through. "Marians are just a fairy tale," he said. "But Scarlet would not believe me. She insisted they were real, that she had descended from a band of priestesses, that she had been abandoned at birth like a changeling, sent with her precious key into hiding until the time was right."

Precious key. "A changeling? The right time for what?"

His eyes took on a strange glow. "The apocalypse, *bella,*" he said, and the acrid note in his voice made me shiver.

"Destiny. The end of an old age and the beginning of a new one."

At first, I thought the roaring came from beyond the fountains, maybe a train passing outside of town. But as I scanned the plaza, I realized it came from inside of me. My blood, and something else. Instinct, perhaps. Curiosity.

Destiny?

Then I noticed the way Caleb was watching me, and all those misshapen pieces shifted into place. He'd just told me something of importance, and was now watching for a reaction. Whatever had passed between him and Scarlet—and perhaps between me and Joshua—had something to do with what he'd just told me.

The veiled legacy of Scarlet's and my birth?

Deliberately, I let myself sway.

"Madelaine?" Caleb asked, steadying me. "What is it?"

This was the defining moment. "She was abandoned at birth?"

"Yes."

I let my eyes flare, then deliberately squeezed them shut. I held myself very still for a long moment, then opened them to Caleb's near rapturous gaze. "So was I."

Chapter 4

There were many reasons I should not have accepted Caleb's invitation to the Adriano villa, reasons my friend Nigel Fielding had pointed out while I'd slipped away to powder my nose. Nigel, still active with MI6, was one of the three agents who'd kept me informed about the Adrianos since the morning I'd fled their compound. Their secluded villa was a gated fortress, he'd reminded me. If I found trouble, no one would know.

That was true. And if I'd believed for even one second that I couldn't handle Caleb, I would never have left the casino with him. Not when I had a two-year-old daughter waiting for me in Cornwall. I've taken far fewer risks since the day I stared at the little stick of the home pregnancy test and saw two lines. At that moment, I'd switched from offense to defense.

Until now.

Now I was more sure than ever that Caleb knew about

Scarlet's key—and that her key, as well as my own, held greater significance than a mere bauble from our birth family.

So when Caleb speculated that perhaps Scarlet and I were, indeed, related, then invited me to his villa to see photos of her, how could I say no? Especially since he'd let it slip that his brother had just returned to his wife in Italy.

"I have never been a fan of coincidence," he said as he led me into the masculine library at the back of the villa. The scents of leather and patchouli came to me immediately, and with it the memory flashed. Joshua. And me. Here in this room. The soft crackle of the fireplace. The empty bottle of merlot on the floor. The sofa—

With an inaudible growl, I shoved the unwanted images back into that dark place I'd tucked them so long ago.

"Madelaine?"

My smile was practiced as I toyed with the charm dangling from my bracelet, the one that would release a colorless, odorless gas in the event that I needed to make a hasty getaway. "I'm sorry," I said. "Your home is beautiful."

"This is only a vacation home," he corrected. After shrugging out of his tuxedo jacket, he yanked at the bow tie. "Go ahead and have a seat. I'll get the pictures."

I glanced at the sofa, dark and leather and soft as butter, and wanted to throw up. "I'd rather stand."

But to further the mood, I kicked off my stilettos before wandering to the windows. The cabana lay beyond, dim lights twinkling around an elegant, vanishing horizon pool. All marble. A hot tub was tucked out of sight.

In the glass, I watched Caleb cross the beautifully preserved Persian rug to an equally well-preserved oil painting of the Virgin Mary and Child. Da Vinci, I recalled speculating, but as hard as it was to fathom, the color palette was too dark. Briskly, Caleb lifted the ornate frame to reveal a small safe.

My instincts snapped into overdrive.

The Adrianos went to great lengths to maintain their privacy and hide their secrets. True, Caleb had always been a wild card, and true, he'd been drinking, but neither of those explanations overrode my visceral reaction to the fact he was accessing a safe in my presence.

Either there was nothing of value in the safe, or for some reason he wanted me to know it was there.

"What was that you were saying about coincidences?" I asked, with no small amount of irony.

He lifted a hand to the dial and flicked several times to the right. "I do not believe in them." His diction was clear now, no longer slurred, confirming my theory that it wasn't drunkenness guiding his behavior. "You and Scarlet…it cannot be coincidence that you look so much alike and are both adopted."

I didn't think so, either.

With a soft click the safe opened. Anticipation lit within me, but when I saw Caleb glance over his shoulder, I averted my gaze to the pool. It was only when I heard rustling behind me that I resumed watching. He had his broad back to me now, his shoulders straining against a wrinkled dress shirt. In the dim lighting his gold-streaked hair looked more what I suspected was his natural color. He pulled out a portfolio and closed the safe door.

But he didn't spin the lock, and he didn't put the Madonna back on the wall.

"I met her in France," he said, striding toward a darkly polished writing desk. "At the Sorbonne. When I stepped off my jet that morning, I was thinking only of funding research into a find of religious artifacts. I had no idea the turn my life was about to take."

Talk about rehearsed. "The cache found after the earthquake?"

Caleb set the leather folder on the desk. "So shocking," he murmured. "Who would have thought…earthquakes in Paris."

Who would have thought a lot of things that had been happening lately?

"That's how the relics were found, yes?" I recalled hearing about the discovery in the catacombs beneath Paris. Some poor museum curator had fallen into a pile of decapitated skeletons when the street cracked open.

"*Sì*, that was the beginning."

Call me mad, but I didn't think he was talking about his affair with Scarlet. More curious by the moment, I turned from the window and crossed to the desk.

Caleb didn't move so much as a muscle. He just stood there, staring at the portfolio as if it were sacred.

"Caleb? Are you sure this is a good idea?"

He kept his head bowed a moment longer, then turned to look at me with the most tortured eyes I'd ever seen. There was a fire in them, a glittering sheen somewhere between horror and madness.

But the moment passed as quickly as it arrived, and before my breath could resume, he was smiling that charming, lady-killer smile again. "All is well," he murmured with a thicker Italian accent. "One learns to live with what one cannot change."

I felt another chill, this one deeper and far more slimy.

"Yes." I cringed as I rested my hand atop his. Compassion, and all that. "But we don't have to do this if the pain is too fresh."

His eyes met mine, then he lowered his gaze to the desk, where my palm covered his knuckles. I didn't recognize the murmured words in Italian, but the instant he slid his hand around mine, I braced myself for another encounter with his mouth.

The kiss was whisper soft against the back of my fingers.

"What is it they say?" The bafflement in his question almost sounded authentic. "You are tasty." When my eyes flared, he laughed softly and corrected himself. "No, not that," he amended. "Sweet," he said. "You are sweet. Just like my Scarlet."

My heart was pounding so hard I was sure he could hear it.

"When I look at you," he added—and God help me, he wouldn't release my hand, just kept holding it in his as if he never meant to let go. "It is as if she has come back to me."

I kept my smile cool and empathetic, even as my fingers itched to fiddle with the charm dangling from my bracelet.

"If me being here is too hard—" I started.

"No." He released my hand and retrieved the folder, lifted the flap and pulled out a stack of pictures. "I love sharing my Scarlet with others. It makes me feel as if she is still here."

It took effort to keep the extremely unfeminine noise locked in my throat. It was no secret among the intelligence community that Caleb Adriano did, in fact, like to share his women. With other men. And other women. And usually in the presence of a video camera. But that was another story.

"Here she is that first day," he said, pointing to a picture of Scarlet and a tall, slender woman who screamed French as only the French can. "I will never forget her surprise when I first showed her this picture, and she realized I had captured her with my camera phone within minutes of our first meeting."

Something dark and disturbing shifted through me, and for a moment I ached for Scarlet, so caught up in the throes of meeting a charming man that she'd never seen the warning signals flashing all around her. "Did someone introduce you?"

"My brother and I were in Paris on business. He saw her approaching the Sorbonne and went utterly pale."

His brother. Saw Scarlet. A woman who looked just like me. And he went pale. "Oh?" Damn my heart for clenching.

Caleb slipped the photo aside and lined up several others, three of Scarlet by herself, one of her with a cool blonde, another of her with a woman dressed in hiking clothes.

From the looks of things, Caleb had been spying on Scarlet, hiding his prurient interest behind a romantic smoke screen.

"Long story," he said as he sorted the pictures like cards. "You must know my brother to understand. He got burned once, and ever since, he has never stopped looking for the bitch."

I swallowed hard. "Isn't he married?"

"For six years."

Her name was Pauline, and she'd given him a son. "Then—"

Again Caleb laughed. "You misunderstand, *bella*. Joshua does not look for Zoe to win her back. He looks to punish her."

I'm not sure how I stood there smiling benignly, while everything inside of me went cold.

"But do not worry," Caleb was saying. "If he returns tonight, I will keep him away from you."

Joshua. Back here tonight. Before we'd left the casino, Caleb had commented that his brother had returned to Italy. "I thought—" My heart slammed hard as Caleb laid another picture on the desk, this one of Scarlet in an alley, looking intently at an older man. With flowing white hair. And a wizard's beard. Dressed in disheveled clothes.

The man from the café, the same one I'd seen at the casino.

Caleb stilled. "Madelaine? Is something wrong?"

The debate was over before it began. "That man…I saw him here in Saint-Tropez. I think he is following me."

Caleb lifted the picture, his fingers gripping the edges so tightly his knuckles turned white. *"Male detto."* Despite his accent, the words sounded harsh. "You are to stay away from him, do you hear me?"

"Is he dangerous?"

"He—" His hand closed into a fist, crumpling the photo into a tight ball. "He killed my Scarlet."

And I'd thought the room was spinning *before* his little bombshell. I'd known all along offering myself as bait would further my investigation, just as I knew to take everything he said with a grain of salt. But his accusations confirmed one thing—he knew what had happened to Scarlet.

"Are you sure?" I asked with horrified interest.

With a fierce shout, he hurled the crumpled photograph across the room. "I cannot prove it, no. The old man is crazy, out to destroy my family, that is why he killed her. Because he knew losing her would kill *me*."

Part of me kept wondering when I was going to wake up and realize this was all some crazy dream. "Why would he want to destroy your family?"

Caleb turned and strode to the window, braced a hand against the glass and stared into the night.

Not about to let the question drop, I came up behind him and laid a hand against his shoulder. "Caleb?"

He spun toward me so fast my breath caught. *"Mi displace,"* he apologized. "But I cannot do this."

Then he pushed past me and strode from the room.

Several things struck me at once. One, either Caleb Adriano was in a great deal of pain or he was an amazing thespian. And I wasn't sure which I wanted to believe more. If he was in pain, that meant he'd loved Scarlet, that she hadn't merely been a pawn in his game. And I wanted that for her. I wanted her to have known something beautiful and sparkling. She deserved it. But the coldly rational side of me countered that just because Caleb loved, didn't mean he couldn't also kill. Because he could. He was an Adriano.

Either way, I stood alone in the study, with the wall safe open. That was the second thing that struck me.

Coincidence? Only if you were gullible enough to believe the next pope would be a woman, ordained Joan the Second.

No, grief or no grief, Caleb's abrupt departure was one of those clearly calculated moves that made me want to laugh. That was the third thing that struck me. Caleb was no more taking a moment to collect himself than I was falling into his trap.

If he'd been acting before, now it was my turn. My expression troubled, I stared after him a long moment before turning to survey the room. The safe called from across the expanse, but I wandered to the bookcases. All the classics were there, Shakespeare, Joyce and Thoreau, in beautiful leather bindings, many first editions. Moving farther down, I ran my hand along the spine of a well-preserved copy of Darwin's *Origin of the Species,* only to then have my fingers come in contact with *Mein Kampf.*

The quick shiver caused me to pull my hand back.

Joshua. The ache was immediate. Apparently, more about the man who'd once melted my heart with a smile had been an illusion than even I had suspected.

Continuing, I played to the cameras I knew tracked my movements. So when I stumbled across several books glorifying witch-hunting, I kept my expression blank, despite the disturbing hum that went through me, and continued my perusal.

But inside I felt satisfaction, imagining Caleb Adriano hunched over the security monitors, watching me and realizing I wasn't taking his bait.

All Adriano compounds, even this airy Mediterranean villa, were fortresses. In addition to the standard wiring of windows and doors, lasers protected all points of entry, and at night, while the household slept—or engaged in other less public acts—motion detectors monitored every room and hallway. I'd learned that the hard way. The tightening in my chest was immediate, and though I tried not to remember, I could no more ignore the images than I could live without breathing.

Joshua. In this house. Carrying me in from the cabana. Naked. Laughing. Kissing me. Making promises there'd been no way he could keep. Of course, I hadn't realized that at the time. I'd been too drunk on the warmth sweeping through me, the sense that all the pieces of my life had suddenly fallen into place.

It galled me to realize how wrong I'd been.

Swallowing hard, I moved toward the center of the Moorish-inspired room and forced myself to sit on the sofa where Joshua and I had; what we'd done here didn't matter. I would wait for Caleb, flip through a few magazines, then stretch out and close my eyes, pretend to fall asleep. *Deeply* asleep.

If Caleb acted as I anticipated, he would carry me to a spare bedroom. Maybe with innocent intentions. Maybe not. I was prepared for either scenario. One way or the other, Caleb Adriano would sleep—naturally or with assistance—and I would have the house to myself.

Or at least the bedrooms. Security cameras monitored and recorded movement everywhere else. Courtesy of two bottles of vino, Joshua had disclosed the sex scandal that had almost rocked his family. Of course, had I realized at the time he was an Adriano, I would have known exactly what he was talking about.

Caleb. And a woman. Some said she'd been a professional thief. They'd been having sex—extremely unusual sex. Some called it rape. No one really knew. The videotape that recorded it had been shopped to the highest bidder, only to vanish without a trace—right along with the employee who'd lifted the encounter from Adriano security tapes.

Josh insisted the man went into hiding. Myself, I doubted it was that simple.

Faking a yawn, I reached for a magazine. The photograph on the cover sickened me, much as I suspected the photographer intended. A soiled white sheet lay over the body of a small child—a child who looked no bigger than my Lexie—with a tattered teddy bear sitting atop. The image was stark and brutal and horrifically real, juxtaposed against the serene beauty of a snow-covered Alpine valley.

Mysterious Pandemic, the headline read, a carefully scrubbed, clinical summation of the horror that had decimated a small Swiss village. Over one thousand people, mostly women and children, had been wiped out by a disease the medical community claimed they'd eradicated. Of course, I knew what that meant. The germ lived on, like so many others did, locked away in laboratories, where God only knew who was playing with it.

Mankind did not need God or Yahweh or Allah to deliver Armageddon. We would take care of that quite fine by ourselves.

The rage was immediate, starting low in my gut like a cold simmer and building into a rolling boil. It only took one maniac to destroy the lives of millions. That reality had driven me for so long. It still drove me, but in a far different way. It wasn't just a generic, holistic future I fought for.

But *my daughter's* future.

Disturbed by the Adriano reading material, I moved the magazine, and saw the others. Five of them stacked neatly on the coffee table, a chronicle of every oddity that had befallen Europe over the past several months—the earthquakes, the floods, the power outages, even the serial killer who had preyed on the women of Spain.

Apparently, the human fascination with tragedy and suffering had not escaped the Adrianos.

Flipping through the stack, I paused at a science journal I'd overlooked the first time. Its cover featured a brilliant sunset over the Greek Isles, with two words in bold letters: **Chain Reaction**. Intrigued, I flipped to the article and read the opening paragraph, felt everything inside of me recoil.

The dread was immediate. So was the hard kick of my heart when I realized I was no longer alone.

"Find something interesting, *bella?*"

Chapter 5

No textbook fully prepares an agent for the reality of field-work—or the body's primal response to danger. "Fight or flight" sums it up nicely in a classroom, and some of MI6's simulations do a fairly good job of making your palms sweat.

But when it comes to true, bone-deep visceral reactions, there is no substitute for reality.

As I faced Caleb Adriano, the reality of the involuntary response came back to me. I didn't want to be scared of the man. I *wasn't* scared. Between the blade strapped to my thigh and the toxin concealed in my charm, I could take care of myself.

But everything inside of me surged, anyway.

"Caleb." He still wore the wrinkled white dress shirt, but the buttons now hung open to his navel. I pretended I didn't notice. "I was getting worried about you."

The skin of his face seemed tauter, and his bottle-streaked hair was finger combed from his face. "I should not have walked out on you like that," he said in measured tones. Then he took my hand and drew it to his mouth. "Forgive me. I did not want to make a fool of myself in front of a beautiful woman."

Oh, Scarlet. My heart ached for a woman I'd never met. When turned on full wattage, the Adriano charm could blind. "I understand."

He glanced at our joined hands, where my fingers remained clenched around the magazine. "You have been to the Greek Isles?"

"Yes." Several times. Fascinated by lost civilizations, I'd even toured Santorini, the dormant volcano that had recently shown signs of life. According to the article, if Santorini were to blow again, not only would the ensuing tsunami decimate the Greek Isles, but the seismic activity beneath the ocean floor could trigger a cataclysmic chain reaction of earthquakes and volcanic eruptions.

Southern Europe would be drastically altered. Hundreds of thousands of lives could be lost or destroyed. The economic impact would be mind-boggling.

The right time for what? I'd asked only a short time before. Caleb's answer haunted me: *the apocalypse.*

With a smile I feared was strained, I pushed the hair from my face. My thoughts were ridiculous and I knew it. No matter how corrupt the Adrianos were, not even they had the power to make a volcano blow.

That power belonged to God and God alone. Didn't it?

"I especially enjoyed Santorini," I said.

Caleb stared at a picture of a man and woman embracing in the surf. Across the bay, a whitewashed village clung to the shore. "It is beautiful," he said. "My grandfather took us there when we were children. Having grown up in the shadow of Mount Vesuvius, he believed it important for us to witness both history and nature, to understand the power of each." Caleb looked up with a smile that bordered on hero worship. "He would talk of the legends of Atlantis. The lessons. That a civilization so great can just...fall."

I'd always been fascinated, as well. But Max Adriano— "Your grandfather..." Narrowing my eyes, I feigned surprise. "He's not the Adriano who was almost—"

Caleb stiffened. "I should not have brought him up."

"Of course," I said politely. But it was interesting. Clearly, he did not wish to discuss the assassination attempt that had sent his grandfather into seclusion.

Once, Maximilian Adriano had been the quiet cornerstone of the European fund-raising movement, enjoying private meetings with royalty and the Vatican, using his hawkish good looks and understated charm to work miracles. If a charity needed donations, Max Adriano was the go-to man.

Then an assassin's bullet had come dangerously close to his heart. I should know. I was the one who'd found him, lying on a cool stone floor in a pool of his own blood, mere minutes after I'd met Joshua for the first time. I was the one who'd checked for a pulse, who'd shouted for help.

But within hours, the Adriano publicity machine had been hard at work, replacing the truth of the assassination attempt with a story about a heart attack. They'd come up with eyewitness accounts, even a prognosis from a renowned cardiologist.

Maybe my suspicion that the Adrianos had created Scarlet merely to flush me out of hiding hadn't been so far-fetched, after all.

There'd been other rumors, as well: that Max had actually died on the operating table; that he'd lost his mind, a dirty secret the family Adriano tried desperately to hide; that they'd killed him themselves, to avoid the shame—*the risk*—of a man who knew too much suddenly caring too little.

"—have to call it a night." It took a moment for Caleb's words to register. Then I noticed him sliding his free hand into the front pocket of his tuxedo pants.

Immediately, I tensed. The charm dangled from my left wrist. I would need my right hand to activate it—the hand Caleb held.

"But first there's something I want you to have," he said, withdrawing a small box from his pocket.

I blinked, stared down at the box. Black. Velvet.

Something was so not right here. Caleb Adriano never called it a night—unless he had something more interesting in mind.

Maybe he was onto me, after all. "Caleb, really—"

"Please." He cut me off as he flipped open the lid.

The ornate medieval cross that doubled as a key shut me up. I felt my mouth fall open, abruptly clamped it shut.

"It belonged to Scarlet," he said as he lifted the tarnished metal chain from the box. Her key. "She wore it all the time, said it was one of her only links to her birth family."

Unfastening the clasp, he curled his hands behind my neck. "My brother gave it to me shortly after she died," he said, and I tried not to wince as he caught a few strands of my hair in the fastener. "Josh thought it would remind me of her—that, or he's even more of a son of a bitch than I thought."

Josh. I felt myself go even more still. "How did he get it?"

"I do not know. I wasn't well at the time." He lifted the bulk of my hair over the chain and slid a hand down my back, then stepped away and gazed at me with the oddest expression.

"But that is of no matter now," he murmured. "I cannot keep this, not when I know Scarlet would want you to have it."

He was giving it to me. Just like that. No questions asked, simply because I reminded him of Scarlet.

No way. It was too easy. That was another lesson I'd learned the hard way. If something seemed too easy, it was.

Glancing down at the key resting in the V of my neckline, I noticed the light glimmering against the antique silver and felt something deep inside shift. The urge to close my hand around it and hold it, protect it, was strong. But I knew better than to indicate the necklace meant anything to me.

"I cannot accept this." I reached behind my neck for the clasp.

His hands stilled mine. "Yes. You can."

"I didn't even know her."

"That is the real tragedy," he said, and almost sounded sincere. "I am quite sure her blood runs through your veins."

His phrasing sent a shiver down my spine. "Then I shall treasure it," I said, lifting my hand to finger the key. This time when I shivered, it was for a very different reason.

Olga said things and places could carry memories. That inanimate objects could absorb the essence of the person who owned them—or the residue of events that had transpired in their proximity.

Was this Scarlet I was feeling? Was the warmth trickling through me the residue of a sister I'd never known, but always longed for?

"Madelaine?" Caleb's voice was soft. "Are you okay?"

I forced my gaze to his. "Of course. Why wouldn't I be?"

"You look…" The words dangled. The speculation in his eyes gleamed. "…like you've just seen a ghost."

The blink was automatic. "No. Just feeling sad that I'll never meet your Scarlet." *My sister.*

"Ah." He tucked a strand of hair behind my ear. "I understand—"

"Cosa diavolo stai facendo?" The deadly quiet question shot in from the foyer, just ahead of Joshua. He stormed in like an avenging warrior ready to break up a mugging.

But I had no idea which one of us he was trying to protect. Me. Or his brother.

"Josh," Caleb said, in a mildly pleasant voice.

"What are you doing here?" he demanded, and I felt my heart start to hammer. Hard. One wrong word and—

"I live here." Caleb slid his hand from my face to hold my clammy hand. "I come and go as I please."

I tried to breathe, couldn't. Josh just kept staring at me— staring through me—as if I'd betrayed him by stepping foot into his home.

Of course, I had. But that was a lifetime before.

"Are you out of your mind?" he snarled. There was a wildness in his eyes, a fury I'd never seen before. And his voice. It was hard and…shaking.

"My business," Caleb said, squeezing my hand, and I said a silent prayer of gratitude that he didn't realize his brother's furious questions were aimed at me, not him. "Now please calm down before you frighten my friend."

"Your friend?" he choked out.

"My friend," Caleb said with a placid smile. "Madelaine."

Joshua's nostrils flared. *"Madelaine."*

I swallowed hard, knew I couldn't just stand there and stare at him as if he was a madman. Even if, at that moment, he rather looked like one. His shirt, a pale green raw silk, was torn, and his dark gray trousers were wrinkled. Even his hair looked as if he'd been running. He didn't look at all like…a smooth, polished, always-in-control Adriano.

"Very nice to meet you," I said with my best polite smile. To slide my hand from Caleb's, I needed to tug. Then I offered it to Josh, as any European woman would do when meeting an Italian man.

His eyes met mine. I felt the zing clear to my soul. *"Madelaine,"* he said, and my chest went tight. Because of the game, I told myself. Certainly not because his fingers closed around my palm. "The pleasure is mine."

Something inside me rebelled at the absolute mockery of his words.

"Likewise." I went to retrieve my hand, but, charming Italian that he was, he lifted it to his mouth and brushed a kiss along my knuckles. Soft. Gentle. Moist.

Bloody hell. He was enjoying the game a little too much.

But why? I couldn't help but wonder. Why was he playing? Why was he pretending he had no idea who I was?

Slowly, he lifted his eyes to mine, and God help me, the gleam there stole my breath. Because it looked like fear. Cold and lethal, the back-against-the-wall expression I'd seen too many times during my career. And in that one frozen moment, I realized just how easy it would have been to misread his intentions as protective. Rather than predatory.

"A pretty lady like you," he was saying, and I had to command myself to stay in the moment, "do you not realize how dangerous it is to go home with men you do not know?"

The thinly veiled question scored a direct hit. Caleb, after all, was not the first man I hadn't fully known whom I'd allowed to bring me into this home.

With a sharp jerk I retrieved my hand and angled my chin, crucified Josh with my eyes.

"Joshua!" Caleb scolded. "That is enough!"

"My apologies," he murmured, never looking away from me. We no longer touched, but I could still feel him. All of him. Still smell and taste and remember—

"It's okay," I said, flashing Caleb a radiant smile. "I know how it is between brothers."

Caleb laughed. "*Sì.* My baby brother has a way of wanting what everyone else has."

I braced myself for a sharp comeback, but Joshua smiled. "When a beautiful woman is involved, can you blame me?"

"No blame at all, *fratellino.*" Little brother. There was no warmth or affection in the words, just a stark reminder of family hierarchy. "But I *would* like to know what you're doing here. Pauline called. You're supposed to be returning to Naples."

Pauline. *His wife.*

"I…" Joshua's gaze raked over me, from my face down to my chest, lower to my waist and hips, down the length of leg bared by my short little dress, and instinctively I knew his late-night return was no coincidence. The cameras? I wondered. Or a more persistent surveillance system? Either way, Joshua Adriano had known I was here with his brother before he'd stepped foot into the villa. That's why he'd come.

For me.

"…had a change of plans," he explained after a brief hesitation. Then he looked at Caleb. "We need to talk." It was a command, not a question. And this time, the pronoun definitely applied to his brother. "Alone."

Caleb scowled. "I am busy."

The opening was big and beautiful and too perfect not too seize. "Actually, I am rather tired." Glancing at Caleb, I forced a smile. "It's probably best if I go."

"I will call a cab," Josh said immediately, but Caleb lifted a hand in warning.

"Alain can drive her."

Josh stepped closer, putting his body between mine and his brother's. What was he worried about? I wondered. That the chauffeur would do something other than deliver me to my hotel?

Or that I would overpower him and return to the villa in time to hear all the brothers' juicy secrets?

"A taxi is fine." Slipping my hand into my purse, I pulled out my mobile phone and a business card. "You've already been too kind." For effect, I fingered the necklace. "Much too kind."

Caleb leaned forward and pressed a kiss to my mouth. "Thank you for indulging me."

"I will walk you to the door." That was Josh. Of course. He took my hand and practically dragged me from the room.

Oddly, Caleb let him.

"Take your hands off—" I started to say, ready to fend off the attack I knew was about to begin.

"You must forgive my brother." His voice was mild, distantly polite, as if I hadn't just spoken, and we'd never met. Never been naked together. Never lov—

Well, of course. That never had happened.

"He has suffered a great loss," Joshua explained. "He is…not himself these days."

And then I remembered the cameras. From an unknown perch, the Adriano security system monitored our movements down the airy, tiled foyer. And recorded our conversation.

There were no time-outs in this game.

"There seems to be a lot of that going around," I muttered, fumbling with the small buttons on my phone.

Josh took it from me and turned it off. "There is a driver out front."

"But—"

He pulled open the door and almost pushed me outside. "Just go, *Madelaine*." The venom in his voice hurt more than it should have. "Now."

"I'd rather call my own taxi."

The answering curse was under his breath and pure Italian. "What?" he whispered against my ear. "You think I have a hit man waiting to drive you away and make sure you are never seen or heard from again?"

I jerked back from him. "Is that such an outrageous thought?"

Something hot and hard and—hurt?—flashed through his

eyes. *"Male detto."* This I recognized. Damn it. Or maybe damn me. I wasn't sure. He took my hand and escorted me to the driver's side of the taxi, jerked open the door. *"Monsieur,"* he growled, and the driver snapped to attention. "Get out of your car."

The young man's eyes widened, but he did as Josh instructed.

"Now give the *mademoiselle* your keys."

The taxi driver didn't argue, didn't protest. He handed me his keys.

"Get in," Joshua said.

I looked up at him, didn't understand. Not his actions, or the look on his face. It was raw. And intense. And so bloody desperate I wanted to lift a hand to his face and…soothe him, much as I'd wanted to do the first night we'd met, in Portugal, when he'd returned my gun to me and held out his hands, told me to shoot him if that's what I needed to do.

Instead I slid into the car, and he handed me the keys. "Go back to England," he said, and all that sugary formality was gone, leaving Joshua and me, Nadia, the woman he'd vowed to punish. "I do not want to see you near my brother again."

The hollow feeling was immediate. The sarcasm just happened. "I didn't realize you cared."

He leaned closer. His eyes glittered. "No," he said, putting his hand to my thigh. "You never did, did you?"

I sat back. Tried to breathe. "Josh—"

Looking down at my leg, he jerked the hem of my dress back to reveal the blade strapped to my thigh. Then he laughed.

Then he stepped back. "Goodbye, *Nadia.*" And slammed the door.

And I still couldn't breathe.

"I do not like this, Nadia—are you sure everything is all right?"

Exhaling roughly—because finally, two hours after leaving

Joshua, I could breathe again—I bit down on my lip and stared into the night sky. In less than an hour, I would reach Paris. In the morning, I would meet with Scarlet's friend Catrina Dauvergne.

Olga's question should have been an easy one. I'd filled her in on the basics of my trip: I was more convinced than ever that Scarlet and I were related. I'd secured her key, and thanks to my family's private plane, I was traveling away from Saint-Tropez at a rate of 190 kilometers per hour. Of course, I'd left out a few pertinent details, such as *how* I'd gotten my hands on the key and whom I'd had to go through to get it. No one had followed me to the hangar, where Miles, the man who'd once flown my father all over Europe, had waited. The soul of discretion, he hadn't asked any questions, other than where we were heading.

"Nadia?"

"I'm fine." The Cessna bumped on a wave of turbulence. "I just…saw a picture." Several pictures. And I couldn't get them out of my mind—the stark image of a dead child with her teddy bear juxtaposed against the beauty of an Alpine meadow. "You know how I get." I tried to force a smile into my voice, even though Olga knew better than to fall for the ruse.

"Ah, dear girl. You must quit torturing yourself." There was so much warmth in her voice I could feel it weaving around me like a magic spell. "Your wee one is fine. She misses you, yes, but that is only natural. Today we went for ice cream, then drove to the coast and flew a kite by the water."

I leaned my head against the window. "What flavor?"

"Mint-chocolate chip."

"Cup or cone?"

"Cone. I took pictures."

With the image of green ice cream smeared all over Lexie's

sweet face in my mind, the tight coil of anxiety loosened. "The tie-dye hoodie?"

It had been a Christmas present from my friend Lex, her godfather. Since receiving it, Lexie practically refused to wear any other outfit.

"Of course," Olga said, laughing. "With Mommy's key tucked inside."

The knee-jerk reaction was ridiculous and I knew it. "She shouldn't be wearing that." Telling myself I was overreacting, I closed a hand around the key resting against my own chest. "I—I'd hate to see it get lost."

"Nadia." Olga's voice shifted from warm grandmotherly to stern motherly. A nanny her whole life, she did both well. "It is just a silly old key." One that had actually gone missing for seven years, until, at twenty-one, I'd found it inside our heirloom Staffordshire. My mother had acted surprised, but I'd seen the look that passed between her and Olga, and to this day I couldn't shake the feeling that there was nothing accidental about the disappearance of the link to my birth family—or my mother's displeasure with the fact I'd found it.

Of course, if they'd really wanted it gone, why hide it? Why not just throw it away?

The edges of my key's twin dug into my fingers, prompting me to realize how tightly I was holding it. "Be that as it may," I said. There was no point arguing, especially in the middle of the night while hundreds of miles separated us. "I'd rather she wear the big heart that you gave her."

"I'll suggest it," Olga said. "But you know how she gets when her mind is made up."

Yes, I did. It was a trait she'd inherited from…both her parents.

Reaching into my satchel, I pulled out my wallet and opened it to a picture taken at Christmas. "Give her a hug and a kiss for me," I said, by way of goodbye. "Tell her Mommy loves her—and I'll be home tomorrow night."

"Caleb said the Marians are just a fairy tale."

At my words, Catrina Dauvergne, the undeniably glamorous museum curator whom I'd actually encountered once before, briefly, in Portugal at the same exhibit where I'd met Joshua, looked up from the lockbox in her lap. Scarlet had left it with her before leaving for Saint-Tropez. "Caleb *wishes* the Marians were just a fairy tale."

"Personally, I wish *he* was just a fairy tale." This from Eve St. Giles, whose curly dark hair I'd recognized from news reports about the Spanish flu outbreak in the small Swiss village. A world-renowned epidemiologist, she'd led the charge against the virus.

In a perfect world, the three of us would never have met. But Scarlet's friends had been waiting for me in the upper chapel of a gorgeous old Paris church, just as I'd requested.

Because we *don't* live in a perfect world. And the one link among us was dead. Catrina and Eve had been friends with the woman I believed was my sister. They'd known her and loved her, and now, with me, they mourned her.

Together, we would make sure she rested in peace.

No one had followed me from Charles de Gaulle. I felt sure of that. But my training ran too deep to not exercise extreme caution. And old churches—

Let's just say old churches and I went way back. They made a perfect covert meeting spot—hiding in public, some call it. And the eight-hundred-year-old Sainte Chappelle, situated in the shadow of Notre Dame, was no exception.

Even as we knelt behind the ornate shrine that had once contained what many believed to be the crown of thorns, few late-morning tourists paid us any attention, probably because of

Catrina, who looked utterly Parisian and completely aloof. Eve, in her wrinkled khakis and plain white shirt, looked like a tourist herself. And me, dressed in widow's weeds, I appeared to be in deep mourning. Oh, and my hair was no longer pink, but brown.

Just to be careful, however, Eve's husband, a former Swiss Guard, pretended to browse through books in the gift shop on the lower level. And at the entrance to the narrow staircase, the only access point to the upper chapel, stood a priest, of all things. Actually, from what Eve said, the man called Rhys had left the priesthood, but technically, once ordained a priest, always a priest. That much was obvious from the reverence glowing in his eyes the second we'd entered the cool darkness.

From the way he and Catrina looked at each other, it was equally obvious he did not live by a vow of celibacy. I had no doubt there was more to their story than a simple case of lust, but I didn't expect to be hearing it anytime soon. Catrina didn't strike me as the kind of woman to discuss her feelings with friends, much less strangers.

Fifteen enormous panels of stained glass surrounded us, depicting scenes from the Bible. Sunshine glinted through the colored glass, casting the chapel in a fascinating dance of shadow and light. Eve and I knelt on opposite sides of Catrina. To the few tourists filtering in before lunch, I imagined we looked to be deep in prayer. We weren't. We were sifting through the contents of a box that had belonged to Scarlet.

A lockbox opened by the key Caleb had given me.

Crouched there, with statues of the apostles looking on, I tried to take it all in—the collection of writings and research, photographs of a woman I'd never gotten the chance to know. My chest tightened at the sight of a baby picture identical to one in my possession, down to the same white baptismal dress.

The stab of longing cut off my breath. Fighting it, I pushed the photos aside and opened a binder, flipped through page after page of handwritten notes. And everywhere I looked, the word *Marian* jumped out at me. But there were other words, too: *destiny* and *prophecy, Pisces* and *Aquarius, goddess....*

"They think they can wipe us out," Eve growled, flipping through one of Scarlet's journals. "They will not rest until they succeed."

Catrina looked up, honey-gold hair falling from the loose knot at the back of her head. "Let them try."

"Because you're Marians?" I asked, intrigued. And horrified.

"Because they are cowards," Eve hissed. "And we are strong."

Catrina's eyes met mine. "If you are who we think you are, then you are Marian, as well. To the Adrianos, that puts you in a category with witches and heretics."

Instinctively, I lifted my gaze to a small panel of stained glass, where one group of men slaughtered another.

"There is no if," Eve said. "Nadia is Marian." Eve had accepted me immediately; she said she had no doubt of my identity or my relation to Scarlet.

"I suspect her notes will answer your questions," she added. "No one knows for sure where we originated, but your sister had no shortage of theories about our origins. Goddess worshippers," she speculated, "perhaps descendents of female priests who split off when the church mandated that all priests had to be men. Maybe followers of Mary Magdalene."

Catrina looked up from the binder in her hands. "Atlantis," she offered, and something inside of me just kind of stopped. Suddenly I was back in the Adriano study, staring at the research on Santorini, the doomed people of Minoa.

Lost civilizations have always fascinated me—the Atlanteans and the Lemurians, the Maya. How did advanced peoples simply vanish, with little trace of their existence left behind?

"Those who have come before us are mankind's greatest teachers," Max Adriano had said in Portugal shortly before he was shot. *"They knew the human condition for what it was, and they tried to warn us...."*

"Yes." Catrina's mouth flirted with a distant smile. "Scarlet was very much about thinking outside the box." Abruptly, she looked toward a statue of one of the apostles leaning against the ornate wall. Intricately carved in a gown of flowing white, with features worn away by time, its gender was impossible to establish. "Which is why she had to die. Because somewhere among her theories lay the truth, and that they could not abide."

In the quiet of the small chapel, her words seemed to echo. But no one else seemed to hear—or care. And so I asked the question. "The truth about what?"

Catrina's eyes met mine. "The apocalypse."

Chapter 6

I stared at the final picture in stained glass, the one that depicted the end of times. "That's what Caleb said...."

Had it really been less than twelve hours ago?

A very French sound broke from Catrina's throat. "Rest assured, he is up to something," she sniffed. "Him, or that brother of his."

"Joshua?"

"The charmer," she said derisively. "Or as some say... *snake* charmer."

I wanted to attribute the iciness crystallizing through me to the chilly marble floor. But I knew better. Only one man had ever turned me from cold to hot, back to cold again, with little more than a smile. And a lie. "You know Joshua?"

Her mouth twisted. "Not as well as he hoped, but yes, I know him," she confirmed. "And you?"

The truth burned. "I know Joshua," I said, looking away from her—and straight at the depiction of Cain killing Abel.

"That's not just a casual 'know,' is it?" Eve asked, and when I forced myself to look away from the slain brother, I saw worry in her eyes.

"No," I admitted.

"Do not be a fool," Catrina said, and though the words were sharp, her voice held the same worry as Eve's eyes. "No matter how charming Joshua is, you must remember he is an Adriano. Never forget that. They are dangerous, every last one of them."

Eve lifted a hand to her arm. "Catrina, Max said—"

"I care not what Max has said," she snapped. "Is he not also an Adriano? He cannot be trusted."

"Max?" The reference surprised me. "Joshua's grandfather? I thought he was in seclusion at some private hospital."

"That is what the family wants you to think." Catrina drew more notebooks from Scarlet's box. "In truth, he has been chasing Marians around Europe, talking in riddles about countdowns and sacrifice and—"

"Redemption." Eve's eyes glowed. "That's what he said to me. A chance to earn forgiveness against a legacy of sin and betrayal."

"Since when does someone get redeemed by wiping out innocent women and children?" Catrina asked.

"Not him. His son and grandsons. They see it as purification, a way to cleanse the world for what's to come."

"It is the God complex, yes?" Against the notebooks, Catrina's fingers went white. "Certainly you have heard of Sodom and Gomorrah? Noah and his ark? When the world becomes dirty and bleak and overrun with sinners—"

"God wipes the slate clean and starts over," I finished.

"*God* being the operative word," she said. "Not *man*."

Eve reached for both of us, gestured with her eyes for us to be quiet. Glancing toward the staircase, I saw the single man enter, saw his long dark trench coat, and felt instinctively for the gun that was no longer in my satchel, courtesy of the metal detectors at the entrance to the church. Everything inside of me tightened, until a young girl in a soft pink dress bounded up behind him and grabbed for his hand.

We all let out a collective breath, despite the fact the Adrianos had left Catrina alone for months. "The Adrianos believe they *are* God's instruments," she said.

"But we're talking about mere men here," I pointed out, not taking my eyes off the man and little girl. Because of caution, I told myself. Not because the sight of father and daughter fascinated me…even as it destroyed. "Mortals, not supernatural beings. An outbreak, I can understand." Actually, I was stunned that that kind of thing didn't happen more often. "There are germs in quarantine all over the world. It's not a stretch to imagine a madman getting his hands on enough tubes to wipe out the world.

"But earthquakes?" I asked, watching the man lift the girl in his arms so that she could touch the stained glass. Their jawlines, their eyes, were identical. "Volcanoes? Man can't just—"

"Yes, he can." Eve's rock-solid voice came like a slap, and had me swinging toward her. "It is called the butterfly effect," she said. "All it takes is something as simple as the flapping of a butterfly's wings to produce the most miniscule change in the atmosphere. Over a period of time, because of that butterfly, the atmosphere diverges from what it would have done had the butterfly not existed. So, in a month's time, a tornado that would have devastated the Indonesian coast doesn't happen. Or maybe one that wasn't going to happen, does." With a dry smile, she bit down on her lip. "Ian Stewart," she explained, citing the reference. "*Does God Play Dice? The Mathematics of Chaos*—standard reading for any good scientist."

I let out a slow breath. Retired-spies-turned-stay-at-home-moms tended to read more about big red dogs, lost teddy bears and rascally dinosaurs, but I had managed enough popular fiction to know about the chaos theory.

One small change in the natural order, and all bets are off.

"Take the Parisian earthquakes," she said. "That one change in the earth's core can launch into motion an endless number of changes, some big, some small."

Like the ripples from a pebble being dropped into a pond.

"The unseen consequences are endless." She sounded every bit the scientist she was. "By manipulating the earth's magnetic field, the Adrianos have launched an exercise in cause and effect."

I rocked back. "Manipulating the earth's magnetic field?" It sounded like science fiction, particularly odd words in such a reverent place of worship. And yet, I knew it was possible. I'd heard the whisperings within MI6. I knew of the experiments.

"Ley lines," she was saying, reaching for the several sheets of parchment she'd unrolled a few minutes before. She laid them out on the cool marble floor, revealing what looked to be a map of Europe with a net grid over it. "That's what these are. Running through them is energy."

I'd heard the concept. My father had fancied himself an antiquarian. As a girl, I hadn't been all that interested in his theories, but later, as I'd gotten older, I'd become fascinated with his assertion that ancient peoples built their holy places in alignments not understood by modern man. Stone circles, megaliths, holy wells, burial sites, even castles…he maintained they were all situated according to straight-line alignments.

"Wasn't there something about astronomical connections?" I asked, unable to remember exactly what he'd told me.

Eve's expression softened. "That's what Scarlet thought."

Catrina dragged her finger along a line cutting straight through France. "You may think of it as chi," she said, as if granting permission. "A life force running through the earth and keeping the planet in harmony."

"Until maniacs like the Adrianos manipulate it," Eve interjected.

Catrina tapped her finger against southern France. "It makes one wonder, does it not? Are natural disasters truly natural? Or are they the result of someone playing with ley lines?"

I stared at the intersecting lines, those that ran through France and those that ran through Italy. It was impossible to tell exact locales, but I could not look at the thick line streaking along the Italian coast without thinking of the Adriano palazzo in Naples, and the dormant volcano that lorded over the quiet countryside.

It was a lot to take in. While with MI6, I'd heard rumors of the British government experimenting with techniques to better regulate crops. Weather manipulation had been mentioned, but I'd dismissed the concept as fantasy. That was God's realm.

"That is how everything fits together," Catrina said, but I did not look up from the map of Europe. "The Marians discovered a way to control the energy running through the earth's ley lines."

"It was a mosaic." Eve put her hand next to mine, circling her index finger around southern France. "More beautiful than words can describe," she said, and suddenly her voice sounded singsong and faraway. "Comprised of tiles from all over the world. Seashells and metals, volcanic rock. Gemstones.

"Because in all things, there must be balance," she continued. "Where there is evil, there must be good. That's how the mosaic worked, as a filter to cancel out attempts to manipulate the earth's energy for evil."

My breath caught. "Yin-yang."

"Exactement." This, naturally, from Catrina.

I looked up. "Where is this mosaic now?"

"They were peaceful women," Eve said. She'd started to rock. "Healers. For centuries they shared their wisdom and their skills, their hope, their humanity."

Inside me, something shifted. Maybe a memory. Maybe the echoes of a childhood story. I wasn't sure, just felt it slide through me like a spool of thread unraveling in the wind.

"Then darkness came," Eve said, as if she herself had been there, "and blood ran in the fields. To stay alive, they moved their worship to a temple underground, where they'd already built the mosaic across a powerful ley line." Her eyes hardened. "Until they were betrayed by one of their own."

I leaned back against the shrine and drew my knees to my chest, much as I'd done as a child listening to bedtime stories.

"They knew they were beaten, but they couldn't let their enemies get their hands on the Lady. They would use her for evil, whereas she'd been designed for good."

"The lady?"

"The mosaic." Eve closed her eyes, opened them a moment later to reveal a light so pure it made me want to look away. "The Blessed Mother. Hope in her eyes and a sword at her hip."

Everything flashed. Glowed. "And a child," I said. Cherub-like. Innocent. "A jug at her feet." Beautiful.

It was Catrina's turn to stare. "You have seen the mosaic?"

I blinked, tried to orient myself. "No." But the image had been so vivid. So...sacred. "Just a guess," I said. "My mother collects religious art." But nothing like I'd just described. "I must have gotten Eve's description confused with something I've seen before."

"I never saw a child," Eve whispered. "Maybe she was already gone."

She never saw—now that was odd. "Already gone?"

"The priestesses fled," she said. "Taking tiles of the mosaic with them. They were to hide until it was once again safe…"

"But safety never came." Catrina's voice was soft. "Time passes. Memories fade. What was once of great value slips from the lexicon. Buried and forgotten." She paused. "Lost."

Until now.

"That is what I found in the catacombs." Slowly Catrina's eyes met mine. "It is how I met the Adrianos. They were to fund my research, but I suspect they really wanted the tiles I'd found."

Eve reached for a bright pink folder and flipped it open, allowing several pages to slip to the floor. "Your sister believed the time for the Marians had returned. That her key was somehow linked to the search for the tiles."

The key identical to mine, one of the few belongings surrendered with two baby girls whose parents didn't want them. The key the Adrianos had stolen from Scarlet—after killing her. The key that had opened her box.

Throat tight, I looked at the photographs and notebooks, the scraps of paper, drawings and brochures—and saw the map.

It was of Ireland. That was nothing unusual. There were other European maps in the box, of France and Italy and the Greek Islands. Like the others, various regions on the map had been highlighted, with small notes jotted in the margins.

But the circle was different, a red swirl drawn around the northern coast. There was a name, and a date, like an appointment. Except Scarlet had been murdered two days before the date scrawled in the margin.

And I knew where I had to go. What I had to do. Who I had to find.

The veiled legacy of the Marians, the power of the mosaic and the threat of apocalypse, the mystery of my birth: these were not separate threads. Whoever I was and why Scarlet had been killed were linked directly to the Marians—and the Adrianos.

And maybe, just maybe, to a woman in Ireland named Deidre.

Lexie cried. I tried to explain why Mommy couldn't come home, but being two, she didn't understand. She only knew that instead of walking through the door, I'd called. And broken her heart.

Twelve hours after I'd tried desperately to soothe her, the memory of her disappointment still wound around my throat and squeezed. I'd wanted to go home. I'd wanted to read Lexie her favorite story and tuck her in bed, kiss her soft innocent face and promise her I'd be there if she needed me during the night.

But I couldn't return to life as it had been before, not after all I'd learned about the Adrianos and the Marians. About Scarlet—and her planned trip to Ireland. Time was winding down. I could feel that in my bones. Scarlet had known it, too—Scarlet, whose murderer still walked free. Dark clouds that had nothing to do with the storms plaguing Europe gathered on the horizon.

The Adrianos had to be stopped.

So many thoughts and questions accompanied me to Ireland. From her notes, I knew Scarlet had been piecing information together for a long time. Not the apocalyptic angle, but the Marian one. And she'd discovered something in Ireland that had excited her. Not our birth mother, as I'd tried not to let myself hope as I'd followed Scarlet's notes from Belfast to the northern coast. Scarlet had been scheduled to meet with a woman young enough to be my sister, who claimed she had something very important to show me—something her own grandmother had showed her mere days before she'd passed away at the age of ninety-nine.

"She waited as long as she could," Deidre said. "She had a keen desire to meet ye in the flesh."

The words sent a shiver down my spine.

And so it was that, in the misty light of dawn, the ruins of a sixteenth-century castle came into view, perched on a remote cliff a few kilometers away. Separating Deidre and me from it were the angry, boiling waters of the Atlantic.

"Nadia?" Deidre asked. We'd left her cottage under the cover of darkness. "Are ye all right? Ye look peeked."

I was. So long as I didn't look down. "Right as rain," I said from my perch just inside a high cave. Offshore, whitecaps churned. Closer, wave after wave rushed forward like zealots on a suicide mission, shattering against the limestone cliffs and spewing seawater like frigid shrapnel.

Fate really did have a wicked sense of humor.

The pelting rains had diminished, but the wind whipped harder, shriller. Wailing, the locals called it, and I tended to agree.

Pushing the hair from my eyes, I looked toward the mist-shrouded ruins of the castle. The Normans had chosen a brilliant site to establish their fortress, bordered by water on all sides but one. To breach the castle, an enemy had to travel the narrow road leading to the gates, or approach from the cliffs below.

We'd chosen the cliffs. What we lost in comfort and ease we made up for in caution. According to Deidre, men in a black Saab had been spotted outside the castle shortly before Scarlet's death. For the past few weeks, they'd been gone. Until yesterday. Yesterday the dark car had returned, and with it the two men in sunglasses, watching.

The timing was too perfect to be a coincidence. The Adrianos had given me the key, and now they waited for me to fulfill Scarlet's quest.

There was only one problem—at least, a problem for them. Scarlet had been an innocent in the ways of deception and trickery. I was not. I was trained. I knew how to handle men like Caleb and Joshua. I knew how to come out on top.

"Here," Deidre said, inching toward me along the side of the cave. Scarlet had mentioned her trip to Ireland in a blog, but not Deidre. The Adrianos knew nothing of the woman Scarlet had planned to meet—of the secret her grandmother had passed on to her, and her alone. If they had, Caleb would not have needed me to do his dirty work. He would have done it himself—and Deidre would have paid a steep price.

"You said you have a little one," she said, holding out her hand to me and revealing three small, crystalline stones. "Granny gave me a handful when I was just a wee thing," she explained with a soft, reminiscent smile. "Said to keep them with me, that they'd keep me safe."

I took them from her, felt the rip of emotion clear down to my toes. "They're lovely, thank you."

Rocks, that's all they were. Pebbles. Shards of granite left from an ancient volcano. And yet, in cradling the small crystals, it was as if I cradled Lexie.

Being unable to return to her, hearing the disappointment in her voice, had bruised my heart in ways I'd never known possible. But no matter how badly I wanted to see her little face or giggle with her during a sloppy kiss war, my trip to Ireland was not merely an assignment handed to me by some anonymous bureaucrat.

It was personal, fueled by a legacy as much Lexie's as my own.

"Come on." Briskly, I shoved the crystals into the front compartment of my backpack. "It's time to move out."

Eyes round, Deidre nodded and started toward me. "Aye."

With one last glance around the cave, we ventured into the

gray light. The silvery sunrise, such that it was, had revealed a narrow trail winding along the cliffs.

On second thought, maybe it was better not looking too far ahead.

"I'm guessing we have about an hour," I said as Deidre moved to stand beside me. The castle would open to the public then, and our window of opportunity would vanish.

She raised a hand to shield her eyes, and gazed toward Dunluce's turreted gatehouse, standing against the gray sky like an abandoned soldier. "Then we must hurry," she said, and took off down the craggy path. I followed.

The trail wound alongside a red sandstone cliff, made all the more treacherous by the torrential rains. Rocks that had been formed millennia ago crumbled from high above and rained down on us, making each step a delicate balancing act. One misstep would be the last.

"This next part is tricky," Deidre called over her shoulder. Glancing toward the sea, she shoved the damp hair from her face. "Last summer a poor lad from Boston lost his footing and…"

Her words trickled off, but as I followed her gaze over the ledge to the rocks below, I knew what fate had met the boy from across the pond.

Deidre went first, rounding the corner and disappearing from my line of vision.

Taking baby steps, I eased down the steep decline. From below I heard the roar of the surf, but I refused to look, not while perched on the ledge with pebbles slipping beneath my feet. My throat closed up anyway, and my heart pounded hard. It wasn't that I had an aversion to water. I didn't. I swam regularly.

But the ocean…

"Are you sure you didn't almost drown as a child?" my friend Lex had asked long ago on a joint family vacation.

The vast expanse of sky and rock and ocean had closed in on me like a tight little box. "I'm sure," I'd said, fighting to breathe.

"Then it must have been in a past life," he'd teased, then dived beneath the surface. I'd stood there, horribly still, waiting for him to come back up. Because if he hadn't, I would have had to go in after him. I. Would. Have. Had. To.

Shoving aside the memory, I watched Deidre press her slight body to the cliff as she navigated a hairpin curve, then vanished.

Her scream sliced through me.

"Deidre!" Scrambling over the sliding rocks, I edged around the corner—

A significant portion of the ledge was just…gone. The thin sliver that remained couldn't have been wider than a footprint.

"Deidre!" Dropping to my knees, I crawled to the edge and looked down—straight down.

Below, water swirled like acid in a vat.

Two massive basalt boulders stood guard at the mouth of the inlet, shielding it from the violence of the sea. Rather than boil, the water simmered. The good news was that we'd been making our way downhill for the past ten minutes. Only twenty-five meters or so separated the ledge from the water— for cliff divers, that was nothing. For me…

"Deidre!" She was wearing a dark blue top and jeans, hardly colors that would stand out against the rocks or the gray water. I searched anyway, looking for movement, something that didn't belong.

I'd seen men and women jump from perches much higher than where I crouched. I'd seen them dive. In the right place, such as the Pacific Coast at Acapulco, the sport wasn't even considered all that dangerous.

Once, I would have taken the chance. But that was before.

Before Lexie. Then, I'd been an adrenaline junkie, thriving on the thrill of risks. Now every decision I made, every step I took, served one purpose and one purpose only: securing the most brilliant future possible for my little girl. I'd face down the devil himself before I left her without a mother.

I would not dive off a cliff with no knowledge of what dangers hid beneath the water.

"I'm coming!" Scrambling from the edge, I inched along the strip where she'd fallen, then ran down the last of the steep path. The roar of the sea grew with each step I took, rising to an all-out battle cry as I reached the slabs of rock that rimmed the inlet like the sides of a giant bowl. I blinked in the mist and squinted against the salty spray, searching for any trace of life.

Then I saw it, movement near one of the boulders. "Deidre!" Lifting a hand to shield my eyes, I ran to the edge of a jagged slab of rock…and saw red.

Relief flashed so sharply I couldn't breathe.

She clung to one of the boulders, red hair screaming like a beacon against the black rock. She lifted an arm and gestured wildly, and though a good twenty meters separated us, I saw her mouth moving.

But I heard only the low keening of the wind.

Twisting back toward the cliff, where the water slammed against the steep rock face, I tracked the narrow path as it descended yet again, this time vanishing beneath the surface. The high tide, which had saved Deidre from crashing into the rocks, had washed out the land bridge.

There was only one way to the other side—through the sea.

The breath jammed in my throat, a purely visceral reaction that no amount of meditation or yoga could conquer. My muscles tensed. The forsaken caw of a gull barely registered as I turned to see Deidre gesture toward the opposite side of the cove.

Following the movement of her arm, I found a steep path winding from the misshapen slabs of granite toward Dunluce.

There really *was* only one way. One choice. My future depended on it. So did Deidre's life. I needed to get to the other side so I'd be close enough to toss her the rope in my backpack. Anchored with it, she could pull herself ashore.

The fact I could hardly breathe didn't enter the equation. During my time with MI6, I'd trained relentlessly and ruthlessly, determined to overcome the claustrophobia that struck when I neared an ocean. I'd competed in a triathlon, just to prove I could.

I'd thrown up afterward, but I'd done it.

Now, jaw clenched, I toed off my shoes and shoved them into my backpack, then tightened the straps over my shoulders. "I'm coming!" I lifted my arms and prepared to jump.

"Not another step, Zoe."

The quiet voice stopped me, for all of a fractured heartbeat. Then instinct took over and I spun.

He stood in the mouth of a narrow cave, tall, dark, as unyielding as the ancient rock that surrounded him. "Joshua."

Shock robbed me of breath. After the past forty-eight hours, I don't know why I was surprised. I'd seen Joshua Adriano many ways, after all. In a tuxedo. In silk shirts and casual trousers. In biking gear. Naked.

But I'd never seen him like this, in a black T-shirt and torn cargo pants, a wet field jacket in a camouflage pattern, mud-caked hiking boots. An MK-49 in his hand. Pointed at me.

He looked…so un-Adriano-like, more reminiscent of a mercenary than a playboy jet-setter who'd once been heralded one of Europe's most eligible bachelors.

The dark hair falling across his forehead accentuated the glitter in his eyes and the dark stubble on his jaw. If I didn't know better, I'd think he hadn't shaved in days. And the scrape—it was long and jagged and red, streaking down from his ear to his chin.

Kind of made a girl wonder just what he was up to—and what Scarlet had been so close to finding.

"Do not look so surprised, Nadia. I warned you I would know every breath you take."

The words brought another shiver. He *had* warned me. But ridiculously, even after everything I'd learned, I'd remained under the delusion that the man who'd once made love to me with exquisite tenderness wouldn't actually hurt me. I'd allowed myself to hope....

Seeing him with a gun in his hand pretty much took care of that foolishness.

"You said if I got too close to the truth about Scarlet, you'd stop me." The words scraped on the way out. So did the memory of how he'd looked at me, the desperate glint in his eyes. "Well, here I am," I said, watching the way his finger curved around the trigger. "Too bloody close."

For emphasis, I lifted my hands. "Go ahead. Make your family proud. Shoot me."

The planes of his face went tight. "*Male detto,* this is not a game, *cara*—you are walking into a trap! Scarlet was killed—"

Scarlet was warned—Scarlet didn't listen. Scarlet is dead.

"Not going to work," I said, sickened. Slapping the increasingly damp hair from my face, I scanned the rocks for another trap, the bodyguards and their assault weapons that followed this man everywhere.

But saw only the sheer limestone cliff walling us in. "Your vague threats don't scare me," I told Josh, formulating my plan.

"I know that," he said, stepping from the shadows. "But they should." His gun never wavered. "Do you not understand? If you do not stop—"

"If I do not stop, what?" I inched backward. "You will kill me, too?"

Something dark and indefinable glinted in his eyes. "Trust me, *cara*." His voice was deceptively quiet. "Of the many ways I would like to see you, dead is not one of them."

The wince was automatic. So was the way my throat closed up. Because of the voice. Once, I would have found the hoarse rasp sexy. Once, I had. Now I could do nothing but narrow my eyes against the spray of the sea and search for a glimmer of the man I'd known, and thought I'd loved.

I saw only a stranger.

"Then it looks like you have a problem," I stated.

"You are the one with the problem," he retorted. "The only way to Dunluce is through the water."

And clearly, he didn't think I would take the plunge. His bad. My advantage.

Hair slapping my face, I kept my chin at an angle and turned to survey the inlet. Some rocks I could see. Others I could not. Those were the ones that worried me. That and the feel of all that cold water closing over me—

I blocked the thoughts before they paralyzed me. It was a task, that was all. I was a good swimmer, in the Olympic-size pool at the training facility. I had only to steer myself, allowing for the tide pushing me out to sea. If everything went right, I'd reach the opposite shore, and the castle. I would find what Deidre's family had been hiding and protecting, what Scarlet had given her life for. If I didn't—

The Adrianos would win.

Decision made, I pivoted toward the edge.

"*Cara,* no!" Josh was on me before my heart could beat, his hand curled around my upper arm. "You cannot—"

"I have to!" I shouted above the wind. "She'll die."

His eyes went wild. "Then let me!" He tossed the gun to

the ground and kicked it away, shrugged out of the jacket. "Give me the key. I am a strong swimmer. I can—"

"No!" To this day I'm not sure what I was denying—his request for Scarlet's key, or the fact that he knew me so well.

"*Male detto,* I am not trying to hurt you!" On the edge of a slab of rock that jutted out over the water like a primitive diving board, he yanked at the laces of his shoes. "This is not the time to pretend," he was saying. "Not with me, *cara.* I was there when you had the dream, remember? I was right next to you."

The words, the melting intimacy, stopped me cold.

"I held you," he said, shucking off a shoe, "and you…you clung to me. You cried. You asked me to hold you."

The memory lacerated.

His other shoe off, he straightened to pierce me with his gaze. "Do you remember what I told you?"

Yes. I did. I also knew it was a lie.

"I promised that I would keep you safe—"

I didn't need to hear more. Couldn't let myself listen. Knew better than to make the same mistake twice.

Twisting from him, I did the only thing I could.

I jumped.

The normally gentle inlet is awash with violence. The wind drives the sea through the giant boulders at the mouth of the cove, whipping the trapped water into a frenzy. Salt water sprays into her eyes and her nose, her mouth.

I fought the images as strongly as I fought the water, but like a horrific memory that won't go away, the struggle kept playing like a faded movie in my mind….

"Ciara!" Squinting, Naysa uses her arms to stay afloat as she searches for her beloved little sister. Ciara doesn't swim the sea every day like she does, only when she begs.

"Ciara!" she cries again. Waves surge, gather and surge again. Try to take her, as well.

"This way!" A voice pierces the violence, and she twists toward it, sees a young man running toward the water. "Get out of there!"

Not until she finds her sister. "Ciara!" Another wall of water crashes over her, and this time she doesn't fight, just rides it. And when she breaks the surface and gasps for air, she sees frantic movement against one of the boulders.

"Zoe!"

It was more a roar than a shout, and it had me twisting toward the shore in time to see Joshua dive after me.

Her sister clings to the rock. Her mouth moves, but Naysa can hear no words. "I'm coming," she vows, and starts swimming.

"No!" the boy shouts. "You must not!"

But she must. He doesn't understand. He doesn't love.

She swims harder, bobbing in the waves, sputtering against the water.

I turned and swam harder against the frigid tide. Faster. Josh was a strong swimmer, but so was I. Just because I despised the ocean didn't mean I couldn't hold my own.

"Look out!"

It is the only warning she gets. Twisting, she sees the rogue wave too late. It slams down, shoves her under. There is no time to draw breath. The water holds her down until her lungs scream and light explodes behind her eyes.

Abruptly, the assault ends. She breaks the surface to see the boy swimming toward her through the boiling water. Choking on it, she twists toward her sister.

But Ciara is gone.

Chapter 7

The waves rocked me. The urge to fight them was strong, but I knew doing so would waste energy. So long as I ended up on the other side of the cave, it didn't matter how I got there.

With a quick breath, I glanced behind me to see Josh's long, powerful body cutting through the vicious waves.

Choking on salty water, I twisted to check on Deidre, only to feel my heart stop. The big black boulder was empty.

Fighting the churning water, I twisted in time to see a flailing arm vanish beneath the surface.

Deidre.

With a renewed surge of adrenaline, I battled toward her. "Coming!" I shouted, even though, below the water, there was no way she could hear my promise.

I could hear Joshua's voice shouting my name. But I did not turn around. Instead, I swam with a strength born of desperation, tilting my face every two strokes for breath.

Deidre's head surfaced. Her arms waved wildly. "Can't fi—"

A wave slapped her down before she could finish.

I was close now. With another volley of waves closing in, I said a quick prayer and dived into their fury. Chaos consumed me, churning sand and violent riptides. I didn't fight them, but used their force to propel me toward Deidre.

The need for oxygen burned through every cell in my body. My lungs tightened and my blood screamed. I wanted to shoot to the surface and gasp, but doing so would consume precious time.

Colors exploded behind my eyes. Dizziness swept through me. Still I swam, forcing myself to stay in the watery grave.

Watery. *Grave.*

The realization squeezed my heart, bringing with it the sound of Lexie's sweet voice as she whispered three little words into my ear. *I wuv you.*

Groping, I brushed something slick and closed my hand around Deidre's wrist. I held on and pulled myself closer, until I could slip my arm around her chest.

Then I scissor-kicked.

A swell crested over us as we broke the surface. Sucking in air and coughing on water, we rode the force and let it carry us to the rocks at the far side of the cove.

Over the violence came Josh's voice, no longer deadly quiet, but desperate. He shouted my name, cursing and pleading. It was impossible not to twist back.

Near the spot where I'd gone down, he dived into the churning waves.

"Thy kingdom come," Deidre gasped, and when I turned back I saw what she did—the shore. We reached for the small boulders and grabbed, pulling ourselves to safety.

Frigid wind lashed our wet bodies. *"Saol fada chugat,"* Deidre gasped. Her voice held gratitude. Then desperation. "We must hurry."

That was true. And yet…something held me back.

"Josh…" No matter what had gone down between us, the thought of him drowning in the cold furious frenzy…

He surfaced near the shore, throwing his head back and gasping for breath.

Who was I kidding? He wasn't going to die here in this cove. He was an Adriano, and Adrianos didn't die natural deaths.

"Can you run?" I asked Deidre.

She nodded. "With God's speed," she said, and I noticed the color returning to her cheeks.

I reached for her hand. "Then let's go."

Together, drenched and shivering, we took off toward the path. The urge to glance back like Lot's wife and make sure Josh pulled himself to shore burned through me, but I refused to allow myself. There was no time for looking back.

The path wound upward, snaking along a ledge as narrow as the one from which Deidre had fallen.

"Almost there," she shouted above the wind.

The castle loomed in the distance, larger now, more forlorn.

"Nadia!" shouted Josh from behind me. "…trap!"

The threat slammed into my back like a bullet. No bloody kidding I'd walked into a trap.

But I was going to walk right out of it, too. Dunluce Castle's secrets, her truths, were going to be mine.

The Adrianos could flat go to hell.

Deidre stopped abruptly. "Here we are!"

I skidded to a halt and stared over her shoulder, to where a deep ravine cut between the cliff where we were and the one on which the castle stood.

"Nadia!" Josh called again, and this time I allowed myself to look, allowed myself to absorb the sight of him running toward me. Even soaking wet, with his clothes and hair plastered to his body, he still had that aura swirling around him, the one I'd first noticed in a field of standing stones in Portugal, that dangerous combination of quiet intensity and deadly ferocity.

I backed up and turned toward the gorge, assessing whether a running start would give me the propulsion needed to reach the other side.

The chances were slim. The gorge had to be at least seven meters across.

That's when I saw the plank in Deidre's hands. She squatted at the edge, angling it toward the other side.

Driven by pure undiluted adrenaline, I joined my hands with hers and together we positioned the board over the chasm.

"You go first." Under no circumstances would I risk her falling into the Adrianos' hands.

"I canna let—"

"You can! Now go! Hurry!"

She did. I watched her start across the haphazard bridge, and prayed the piece of wood was sturdier than it looked.

The second she reached the other side, I started after her. The wind rushed harder up the ravine, with no land mass to break it, forcing me to spread my arms for balance.

"Stop being a fool!" Josh called to me, but I kept right on going. I'd been a fool, all right. Once. Maybe twice.

But not this time.

With a quick leap I reached the far side and dropped to my knees, grabbed the plank and yanked it toward me.

A low, masculine roar echoed between the cliffs.

I glanced up and saw him standing on the other side, winded and glaring at me like a man who'd just found his lover in the hands of his enemy.

Funny that it would come to the two of us, cold and shivering, standing on opposite sides of a deep ravine.

"Run!" I called to Deidre, and she did.

I should have, too. That was the smart thing to do. The logical thing. But when it came to Joshua Adriano, logic had never been my strong suit.

"Dolce Madre di Dio!" His hoarse voice joined with the wind, but still sounded dangerously quiet. "Zoe—"

I corrected him through clenched teeth. "Zoe doesn't exist anymore."

"You are playing with fire," he shouted, his hair blowing into his face. "I cannot let you—"

"You cannot stop me," I yelled back. Then, turning from him, I scooped up my backpack and ran for the castle.

He called after me, tried to stop me with threats and promises, but I never looked back.

God willing, this time I never would.

Places carry memories, every bit as powerful as those that live within us all.

No one had lived in the castle for centuries, and yet it was far from deserted. Legacies lived on, immortalized through invisible photographs that greeted me everywhere I turned. To the naked eye, the closed mind, there was only gray. And yet beyond the cool, damp stone glimmered the past—tattered remnants of love and hate, honor and betrayal, of births and deaths and bloodshed.

Of secrets.

They all lived within the walls of the old castle, trapped. Waiting.

The thought, the possibility, tickled deep. I've always been fascinated by the past. History brims with legends about amazing men who changed the world. But the more I studied, the more I discovered an army of equally amazing women who'd lived and breathed and bled right alongside the men, only to be delegated to the shadows of time. Their stories are everywhere—their raw courage and fierce passion, their driving convictions. But they, unlike their male counterparts, didn't change the world. They *created* it.

Motherhood is a sacred thing.

"Nadia, I am thinking—"

Deidre's voice ripped through the fog and sent my heart into overdrive.

"—you're looking a little pale. Are ye all right?"

I spun toward her and brought a hand to my chest. "W-what?"

She frowned. "You've barely had a chance to catch your breath. Mayhap we should rest a bit."

The thought appealed. We had, after all, just hiked miles along the cliffs, swum the frigid inlet, outrun an Adriano, then scaled the rock face of the castle. We seriously needed to get warm.

"There's no time." The castle would open to the public soon, giving the men in the black Saab free access. Quickly, I studied the room, zooming in on an empty fireplace on the far wall, tall enough and wide enough for the two of us to stand within its mouth without touching the sides.

At the hearth, I sank down to my knees and ran my hand inside, working my fingers across the stones, not sure what I was searching for until I felt the rift in the smooth surface.

Leaning into the fireplace cavity, I shone my penlight on the spot my fingers caressed.

An image stared back at me, crudely carved, of a woman cradling an infant.

Deidre moved closer. "What is it?"

I rocked back on my heels. Memories, I thought again. Yes,

they lived in this room that had once been the hub of the castle. But as I studied the childish drawing, I couldn't help but wonder if memories could live in the blood, as well.

If my ancestors had once loved and laughed within these cold stone walls.

If a little girl had once crawled inside the cold fireplace to carve a picture that would withstand fire and neglect and abandonment, to be discovered centuries later…

"Just a drawing," I said. But within me roared a great protest.

I ignored it, turned toward the door. "Come on," I urged. "We do not have much more time." My watch showed it was nearing 10:00 a.m. Soon, the gates would open and tourists would overrun the grounds.

Once that happened, our exploration would have to wait.

The sensation of being watched crawled over me the second we left the privacy of the great room. Spinning, I used the penlight attached to my keychain to illuminate the corridor. Saw no one. But still I could not relax. I knew they were there.

Adrianos, after all, tended to travel in packs. One had already been spotted. Others no doubt lay in wait.

"This way," Deidre whispered, leading me down a musty corridor. The stone path dead-ended at a spiral staircase, leaving us two choices. "Not much farther," she said, taking my hand as we hurried up the narrow steps. Behind us, voices grew louder. Guides, maybe.

Adrianos, more likely.

The stairs ended abruptly at a pile of rubble.

And the voices grew closer.

"Deidre…"

"I am hurrying," she promised, and I could feel her moving her hands frantically against the stone wall. "The last time I was here I had a flashlight…"

And then I got it, realized what she was doing. I lifted my hands to the cool rock and used my palms to feel through the darkness. The stone here was old but not quite smooth. Spared from the assault of wind and rain, the rock maintained more of its original facade. Rough edges and sharp valleys greeted my fingers, but we kept exploring, exerting more pressure all the time.

"This way!" a male voice called from the bottom of the stairs.

We skimmed the rock urgently, until finally my hand slipped into an indentation and my fingers found a lever. I nudged it, and with a small rumble, the wall pushed open.

Through the darkness I grabbed Deidre's hand and pulled her forward, dragged us both into the small dark room. Just as quickly, I released the lever and the door closed.

Less than a minute later, furious masculine voices drifted from the other side. "She is not here!"

Holding myself still, I waited until I was sure they were gone, then flicked on my penlight and glanced around the small, unremarkable room, buried so deep within the castle. "This is what you wanted to show me?" I asked, trying to understand.

"Aye," Deidre said.

"But…" There was nothing here. "Did your grandmother say why? What is supposed to be here?"

The glow in Deidre's eyes dimmed. "No," she whispered. And I tried not to think it, not to think that we were too late, that someone had been here before me and taken what Scarlet had wanted so desperately to find.

Heart sinking, I leaned against the wall and pulled my knees to my chest. My mind refused to slow, though. It raced with possibility. With nightfall we could continue our exploration— or I could admit that I'd smashed into a dead end, and call the whole thing off.

That would have been the smart thing to do. Abort this mission, slip past the thugs outside and return to Cornwall. Abandon my obsession with my birth family and pretend I'd never heard word one about Marians and ley lines and a powerful mosaic. And my sister. Scarlet. Forget about her dreams—and her murder.

But I couldn't do that. Not when I could feel the truth pulsating within me like a fierce, primal hum to my blood.

In the darkness, Deidre took my hand. "We're safe here. The bad man, he willna find us."

"I know." Shivering, I directed my light around the cramped space. Then I crawled to my left and laid a hand against the cold stone. "What do you think this room was used for? Did your grandmum tell you?"

"Hiding," Deidre answered simply.

The word seemed to echo through the silence. "Hiding what?"

"Treasure," she said in that lilting way of the Irish. "Weapons." With a faint smile, she brushed the hair from her face. "People."

Hugging my knees, I watched the beam of light play across the wall, the red color it revealed, like many of the sandstone cliffs lining White Rock Beach. "People?"

"There are many stories," she said. "Many rumors and legends—a Viking maiden fleeing her husband, the daughter of the English king in love with a local lad, a giant's only child…a pregnant Gypsy escaping Hitler's wrath."

I smiled. The Irish had a way with lore.

"For a long time me *máthair críona* said it wasn't true," Deidre said. "But then I got older and she became increasingly frail."

Studying the light on the rock, I found myself leaning closer.

"Nan was a nurse in the Second World War," Deidre said. "And while she hated to speak of the atrocities she'd witnessed, as her mind slipped she would sometimes talk to me of people and places she had never before mentioned, of a woman she'd befriended named Nanette and—"

My breath caught. Because right there on the wall, exposed by the beam of my penlight, was the crude carving of a stick figure, identical to the one in the fireplace: a woman holding a baby.

"Look!" On my knees, I lifted my hand and traced the outlines of the woman and child, cataloging every fissure and jagged edge—

The small compartment should not have surprised me.

Almost blindly, I felt the shape of an especially small rock at odds with the rest of the stone. Driven by instinct, a memory that certainly was not mine, I took hold of the edges and pulled, revealing a small chamber within the sandstone.

Behind me, Deidre invoked the Blessed Mother.

Bracing myself, I lifted my light to the dark crevice. At first I thought it was empty, a fluke of fate and time. But then I saw the small leather wallet stashed toward the back.

My hands wanted to shake, but I did not let them. With a calm that was as irrational as it was ominous, I withdrew the pouch and unfastened it, found a sheet of yellowed paper inside. The jolt came immediately. I eased the paper toward me and, in the glow of my flashlight, unfolded the tattered edges.

Handwriting. That was my first observation. A beautiful, flowing script, in a language I did not recognize.

Deidre hovered over my shoulder. *"Dia linn,"* she whispered. Oh, God. And her voice, soft and raw, faraway, more that of a lost child than a woman, had me twisting toward her. She knelt there, staring wide-eyed at the writing, her expression as stunned as her voice.

"Deidre?"

Slowly, she reached for the letter. "Nana," she whispered, tracing her fingers lovingly over the elegant handwriting. It was a long moment before she lifted her eyes to mine. "Gaelic," she said. "My grandmother wrote it."

The revelation pulsed through me. "Your grandmother—I don't understand." That was what I'd come here to find? A letter from Deidre's grandmother?

"'The legends are true,'" Deidre whispered, and it took a second to realize she was reading. "'All of them. About the prophecy and the secret, the lady and the treasure hidden from those who want only to destroy. All my life I have heard the tales, but I thought they were fables, magical stories grandmothers tell their little ones. I did not learn the truth until it was too late.'"

Everything inside of me stilled. "A prophecy and a secret?" I managed to ask. "Do you know what legend she's talking about?" The Irish had one for almost everything.

"She does not say," Deidre answered, scanning the letter. "She just… 'My dearest daughter,' she says," and oddly, Deidre's voice no longer sounded like her own, but distant and lost, sad. "'I am so sorry. What I wouldna give to see your beautiful face and touch your hand. But that can never be.'"

Daughter…

"'I have made a terrible mistake,'" Deidre continued, "'one I will regret until my dying breath. I pray you will never know what it is to be hunted and persecuted, first by the followers of a genocidal dictator, then by a man I thought I loved.'"

Shivering, I wrapped my arms around my middle, but the gesture did nothing to ease the sense of loss. For a second, I'd let myself believe this note had been written for me, that the blood of the woman who'd left it ran through my veins.

Then a different thought struck, and I looked at Deidre,

crouched there in the shadows of the small room. Could her grandmother…

"'He was handsome and charming, not in a dashing way, but in the way of a poet. Mayhap it was the despair I sometimes heard in his voice, or the lost look in his beautiful gray eyes, but he swept me off my feet before I knew what was happening.'"

I closed my eyes, let the picture form.

"'I knew it was wrong, though,'" Deidre continued. "'And dangerous. My family had fled famine in Ireland only to be forced into hiding in Poland. Hitler had as little use for Gypsies as he did for Jews or cripples or lepers. But…'" Deidre hesitated while her words echoed through time and space. "'But one young officer promised he would take care of me. Take care of us. He promised he would get us all to safety.'"

"My God," I whispered. "Did she ever talk about this?" I asked. "Do you know the soldier's name?"

Deidre's eyes met mine, and in them I saw a solemnity I did not understand. "My grandmother did not write this letter," she said. "The handwriting is hers, but the words are not."

I stilled. "What?"

"Her family never left Ireland. They lived here, always. She was a grown woman when she became a nurse in the war… after my da enlisted. We were never Gypsies."

Which meant… My mind spun back to Deidre's mention of a Gypsy woman who'd sought refuge in Northern Ireland after fleeting Hitler's forces, a woman named Nanette. Whom her grandmother had befriended. Her grandmother had been a nurse, a woman trained to help and to heal. She'd been the one to tell Deidre of the secret room, who'd instructed her to bring me here, should a woman ever show up on her doorstep. With a key that matched an old sketch—a sketch identical to the key that had been left with me at the orphanage. And identical to the one Scarlet had worn, which the Adrianos had given me....

My conviction that I was exactly where I needed to be solidified, along with the bone-deep knowledge that Caleb had sent me here to see what I would find.

Scraping back my hair, I swallowed hard and concentrated on Deidre. "What else does she say?"

Deidre frowned. "'But then Tobar came for me,'" she read. "'Tobar, whom I'd known my entire life. Who'd been born a mere two days before me, who'd pulled my hair as a little boy, given me my first kiss, taken my heart as a young man. Tobar, who'd gone off to fight the Nazis, but had never come home. Tobar, who'd been believed dead.

"'Despite the dangers, my joy was absolute, as if a day had never passed since we'd parted. All the love came pouring back, and as we reunited in the way only lovers can, I knew there was no room in my heart for any man other than Tobar.'"

Deidre spoke of a time over half a century in the past, of lovers I'd never met, and yet my body tensed with dread.

"'This is how he found us, wrapped in each other's arms. I'd never seen him in such a rage. I'd never thought him capable of it. I remember screaming, insisting he didna understand, and he did stop, briefly. And I knew hope. But then he turned and walked away.

"'We fled, thought we were safe, but the next day I found Tobar dead, murdered in his sleep, his throat slit from ear to ear.'"

Deidre glanced up. Horror drenched her eyes.

"Is there more?"

She nodded. "'He was the first. By the end of that day three aunts, four uncles, a sister and seven cousins also lay dead.'"

The chill came so fast and sharp I doubled over, as if someone had buried a knife in my gut.

"'My parents had warned me,'" Deidre continued, her voice breaking. "'That the charm and charisma, the wounded act, were a mask to conceal the heartless monster he really was. But I didna believe them. Not until it was too late. One by one, he hunted down my entire family. And executed them. Aunts, uncles, cousins. My sisters. My parents. Everyone except me. I went to him once, to sacrifice myself, to save the few remaining, but he told me I was to be last. I was to live long enough to see the consequences of betraying an Adriano.'"

Everything inside me went horribly, brutally still. I sat there in the cool damp darkness of that forgotten stone room, in a silence so thick I could hear the wall breathing. It certainly wasn't my own breath whispering around me. Or Deidre's. She sat with her head bowed as if in prayer.

An Adriano.

Dear sweet merciful God. Whoever had authored this letter had made the mistake of loving an Adriano—and paid a price more heinous than I could imagine.

"Can you go on?" I asked.

"'Now I am here,'" Deidre read aloud. "'Safe for the moment, thanks to a kindness I can never repay. But I fear he will find me, even here. There is no one left. No one who shares my blood, no one to help me destroy the monster who took everything from me. No one but you, little one. No one but you who are not yet born.'"

I shifted my hands to my now flat belly, just as I'd done when I'd carried Lexie.

"'I will survive.'" Tears thickened Deidre's normally lyrical voice. "'I will do whatever it takes. I will not let this darkness defeat me. I will not let my family's legacy die with me. I will find a way to live long enough to bring you into this world, and see to it that you are safe. Because without you, there is nothing.'"

Deidre's voice trailed off, but when I glanced up, I saw that she continued to read the letter, only now in silence.

"Please," I whispered, and her eyes met mine.

"'I feel you kick and my heart soars,'" she said, not even looking at the paper. "'There is so much you need to know, truths and destinies I must impart to you.'" She glanced back down, read on. "'It will be up to you, my precious one, up to you to preserve a legacy more breathtaking than most can imagine. A legacy the cowards who record history have tried for centuries to erase, but one that endures, now and forever, expanding, growing, thriving in the shadows.'"

I sat a little straighter.

"'If you are here, it is because the time is right and you are ready. The prize you seek, the key to the puzzle that drives you, is near.'" Deidre gasped. "'But not in the castle,'" she revealed, "'which has stood only a few short centuries. Go to the place where the past is buried, my daughter. That is where you will find the answers you seek, the secret our family had guarded for generations. But be careful. Be ever vigilant. And remember, trust is not a gift to be lightly given.'"

Old places have always fascinated me. Maybe it's part of being a Brit, that deep and abiding sense of history, the innate respect for and curiosity about those who came before. Those who shaped the world in which I live, and turned me into the woman I am.

Being adopted only fuels the fire.

Give me an old castle or an abandoned church and I can lose myself for days. But my nights…my nights have always been reserved for cemeteries. Somehow, they just seem different after the sun goes down. Exploring by day seems like cheating. The spirits, the souls, prefer the cover of darkness.

To get a feel for them, so do I.

St. Cuthbert's Church was like many others I've explored across Scotland and Wales. A stone's throw from Dunluce, the forlorn structure alluded to in the letter occupied the site of the old medieval church. The roof had long since been lost to time, leaving only the four walls standing against the glittering stars. Ivy crept everywhere.

But it was the rambling, overgrown field of tombstones that stole my breath.

"No one's been buried here for a century," Deidre explained.

An hour after leaving Dunluce, well into the dark of night, with no trace of the Adrianos' men, I pushed open the silly excuse for a gate and walked into the realm of the spirits. Weathered crosses jutted up from graves overgrown by tangles of grass and thistle and clover. After so many years at the mercy of the elements, the majority of the tombstones couldn't even be read.

"Marco?" Going down on one knee, I traced my fingers along the cold rock. "Spanish?"

Deidre crouched beside me and joined the beam of her flashlight with that of my penlight. "Probably one of the sailors from the galleon that perished offshore." She brushed back a clump of weeds. "Few bodies were recovered—locals say when the wind blows, you can hear those lost crying out, begging to be found."

Ignoring the shiver down my spine, I moved through the knee-high grass, inspecting each tombstone.

The woman named Nanette had promised answers in her letter. I would find them here, where the past was buried. I had only to look in the right place.

There. Everything inside of me slowed as I stared down at the weed-covered tombstones, one large, one small. Almost trancelike, I went to my knees and touched my fingers to the distinct, crudely fashioned image of a mother cradling a child.

"Over here," I called softly to Deidre, then turned my attention to the other tombstone. Time had worn down much of the engraving, leaving but one word still legible. *Natalia.*

NA-talia.

NA-nette. NA-dia.

My blood sang and my heart soared. Natalia. I rolled the name around in my mind, my heart, and knew I'd found someone else whose blood flowed through my veins.

Deidre gasped. "'Tis just a baby."

"It's a sign," I corrected, fumbling for my backpack. I didn't have a trowel, but I did have a knife. It would do.

"You canna—" Deidre exclaimed, when I started to cut into the moist earth. But she stopped just as quickly. Clearly, she knew I not only could excavate the grave, but would.

It was slow going. Knives were designed to slice, not dig. Fortunately, the storms that had assaulted Ireland for the past several weeks had made the ground damp and pliable, allowing me to make better headway than I would have if the dirt had been hard and packed.

"Keep your eyes peeled," I instructed. "If a shadow so much as moves, let me know."

"Aye," Deidre said, but her disapproval of what I was doing leaked through the single word.

It didn't matter. She was a sweet girl, but this was my legacy. My birthright. A secret, a promise, that my grandmother—if that's who Nanette was—had tried desperately to protect.

I'm not sure how much time passed. Five minutes. Fifteen. Maybe thirty. Perspiration gathered on my brow and my breathing turned shallow. My arm muscles cried out at the abuse. But I kept driving my knife into the ground and twisting, bringing up clumps of earth, until finally I hit something solid.

Chapter 8

"Oh, dear Mary and Jesus in heaven," Deidre muttered, when I'd cleared the last clump of dirt. It was another several minutes before I freed the crate and heaved it up from its muddy grave.

The beauty of it staggered me. Here at the northern tip of Ireland, far removed from the lights of big cities, the glimmer of the stars illuminated the dirty carved chest. I didn't want to call it a coffin. I didn't want it to be a coffin. If it was a coffin, that meant—

I shoved the thought aside, not willing to go down that path. The remains of a child did not lie inside the metal box. That was just part of the illusion, the deception, the centuries-old protective mechanism that guarded whatever lay inside. Nanette said her family—*our family*—had guarded it for years.

"This is it," I murmured, wedging the tip of my knife under one of the rusty hinges.

Deidre gasped as the clasp popped free.

The apprehension surprised me. Here I was, at a moment I'd craved my entire life, and my hands wanted to shake. Refusing to let them, I went about dismantling the other hinge.

For a long moment after that, I didn't move. I just knelt there in front of the box, with the stars at my back and the knife in my hand, staring at the beautiful floral carving. Someone had taken great care in crafting this. The need to discover what lay inside hummed through me, louder by the second, and yet I did not want to remove the lid. To do so felt like a desecration of the worst kind.

But I had no choice.

Bracing myself, praying I wasn't about intrude upon a child's eternal rest, I took the lid in my hands and lifted.

Deidre crossed herself.

The truth went through me like a surge of electricity. Unsteady, I reached out and grabbed the edge of the trunk, stared.

The chest was empty.

All that hope I'd been holding on to deflated, like a balloon rapidly losing air, leaving nothing but cold, hard reality. The secrets I'd come for did not hide inside the trunk.

But then I noticed the satchel. Dark brown and tucked in a corner, it blended with the interior of the muniment chest.

Reaching inside, I let my hands settle around the centuries-old leather. Then I withdrew the satchel and opened it, found several sheets of vellum.

"'Tis a map," Deidre whispered.

Several maps, actually. I spread them on the ground and shone my penlight on the intricate series of drawings.

They all looked alike. That was my first thought early the next morning as we approached the Giant's Causeway, the area Nanette had so painstakingly mapped. I'd thought her drawings to be an exaggeration, but now I saw that she'd been accurate. And saw why she'd been compelled to create submaps to lead us through the maze. Quite literally, thousands of dark, basaltic columns crowded the beach like a junkyard of ancient stone.

"'Twas built by the giant Finn," Deidre explained. "He lived most happy and content, obeyed no law and paid no rent."

Focused on the enormity of the task that lay before us, I flashed her a tight smile.

"But then he fell in love with a lady giant on a nearby island, so he built this highway to bring her across the water."

I love the Irish. I love their culture and their heritage, their legends, their lore. But at that particular moment, I didn't find the giant Finn's odd romance the least bit amusing.

The hour swept toward dawn as we traversed the geological fluke, the result of a volcanic eruption in the distant past. Countless millennia had passed since the cooling lava fractured into countless hexagonal columns, and yet an energy remained, a low, droning hum, much like I'd experienced at Stonehenge. It all gets back to memories, I suppose—and beneath a lightening sky, with the sea surging up against it, Giant's Causeway teemed with them.

I would have preferred stillness. And quiet. That way it would have been easier to detect intruders.

Crouching before one of the proud hexagons, I used my penlight to compare the monolith to the image meticulously drawn on the vellum. Same rounded top. Same gouge two-thirds of the way up. Same crevice running down the left side.

Same crude etching of a mother and a child.

The whole place buzzed as I skimmed my fingers along the surprisingly smooth surface. I hesitated, glancing around, half expecting to find a swarm of bees, but seeing only Deidre's pale face as she crouched beside me.

Thunder rumbled offshore as I turned my attention to the

rocky beach and dug through it with my knife. Clouds skittered over the fading stars, bringing a mist. I worked on, not about to sacrifice even a second to Mother Nature.

Somewhere in the distance, another sound caught my attention. This time I stopped digging, stopped everything, even breathing. And listened for the crunch of rocks.

"He's here," I whispered. I felt him.

In the fading moonlight, Deidre paled. "The bad man?"

The description, accurate though it was, brought a quick slice of pain. "We must hurry."

Earlier, the maze of rock formations had overwhelmed me. Now, they lent security. Yes, Joshua was here, but "here" wasn't exactly an empty street or a well-manicured valley. Here was a windswept beach crowded with thousands of basalt monoliths. Here was sheltered by darkness. Here our voices were muffled by the surf and the roar of the wind.

To find us, Joshua had a lot of territory to cover.

I dug faster. Small jagged stones and pebbles stabbed into my hands, but I kept going, knowing—feeling—that we were getting close.

The front of the column yielded nothing. Neither did the side. But the back... After several minutes of thrusting against the pile of small rocks, my blade ran into something solid. And for the second time that night, I unearthed a trunk.

The chant soothes her. It's familiar, sacred. Like liquid oxygen, it flows through her blood and nourishes her body. Her heart sings with it, even as it weeps.

Closing her eyes, she listens to the ocean wind swirl through the monoliths that surround her.

This is a holy place, the land of her ancestors. Legend attributes the black rocks to a giant. But those more in tune with nature and the universe understand the truth, that the columns are here to serve them. Feed them. Sustain them.

"Da dhuit." The words, not from the disjointed memory but from Deidre, made me aware of the mist shifting into a steady rain. Breathing hard, I glanced skyward and opened my mouth, accepted the offering of water. It had been awhile.

It is here they come to celebrate, here they come to mourn. Here they gather beneath a gray sky to welcome the young, unite lovers and say goodbye to the departed.

She wants this day to be a nightmare, a dark dream from which she can awaken and resume her life. But as she opens her eyes and sees the women in white dancing before the fire, she knows the truth.

Ciara is never coming back.

Swallowing, I raked the damp hair off my forehead and focused on the box, far smaller and less ornate than the one from the cemetery. Older, too.

This, I thought. This, I knew. The secret Scarlet had searched for, the destiny Nanette had promised, the birthright the Adrianos wanted to steal, lay within the small chest. I had only to pry it open—

"Excellent work, *bella.*"

The pleased voice stopped me cold.

"Impeccabile."

Something dark and primitive flashed through me. Jaw clenched, I jerked Deidre behind me and twisted toward the voice, wished looks really could kill.

Because our new intruder would most surely be a dead man.

He stood beside one of the larger columns, tall, his expensively cut coat hanging elegantly against his bullish frame, a glow in his eyes and a semiautomatic in his hands.

"Caleb." The name ground out of me like a curse.

"I knew I could count on you," he said, clearly pleased with himself. "Less than two days after giving you the key, and here we are. It was exceedingly kind of you to lead the way."

He'd followed me. The realization sank through me like a dead weight. I'd taken extreme precautions, but he'd found me anyway. And now all pretenses were gone, the nicey-nice game we'd played in Saint-Tropez no longer necessary. I'd gotten what I wanted from Caleb—and somehow, despite my precautions, he'd tracked me to Ireland. The key, I wondered….

Regardless, he thought he was about to get what he wanted from me.

It would be an understatement to say I had other ideas. "Why didn't you just follow *her?*" I scanned the hulking rocks surrounding us. "Scarlet. She would have led you here, if she'd been allowed to live."

His eyes flared with something curiously close to pain. "Do not talk to me of Scarlet."

"Why not?" I flung the taunt at him. "She's the reason we're both here, isn't she?"

Rain plastered his hair to his face, stripping away that urbane look he so prized. Unlike Josh, who wore the unpolished look irritatingly well, Caleb just looked…common. "What is in that box belongs to me."

And the second he got his hands on it, I was of no more use.

Behind me Deidre shifted, and I could only pray she wasn't doing something foolish. "Really?" My 9 mm, damn it. I'd set it down to dig. All I had to do was get my hand on it…. "I suppose that's why Scarlet didn't tell you she was coming here?"

"The gun is just beyond your right hand," Caleb said, closing the distance between us to less than three meters. "But I would not go for it, if I were you."

My fingers inches from their target, I froze.

"Now be a good little Marian and hand over the box."
Marian.

"Le do thoil." I recognized Deidre's Gaelic word for devil.

Through the damp hair falling into my eyes, I glared up at him. "Over my dead body."

He shrugged. "If that is the price, so be it."

"I get her first." The second voice was neither low, nor amused. And Joshua stepped from behind another rock and moved to stand beside his brother. He still wore the heavy camouflage jacket, still wore the torn cargo pants—still looked like a mercenary.

And my breath, damn it, still caught.

Like his brother, he held a gun in his hand, pointed directly at my chest.

Nothing subtle in that irony.

The sea is greedy. It asks for neither permission nor forgiveness, just takes and returns at random. That is the cycle of all things.

At least, that's what the young man who appeared out of nowhere to pull her from the churning water says. She can still hear the rough edge to his breathing as he dragged her onto the shore and begged her to live. Still see the violence in his eyes. Still feel the desperation of his breath, his touch.

"Zoe." The raw edge to Joshua's voice overrode the odd memory playing at the back of my mind. He was one of those men who prided himself on staying in control. The more intense a situation, the more steely he became. His eyes betrayed no emotion. His voice never broke. He possessed that rare ability to discuss life and death like the weather on a bland summer day.

Not now. Not here on this predawn, windswept beach with my destiny square and center in the crosshairs.

"I warned you not to come here," he said in a voice so low and hoarse I would have sworn he'd spent the night making love to a bottle of cheap whiskey—or hiking down a cold, windswept cliff. "Now it is time to learn about consequences."

"It is time." At the words, Naysa turns to see her mother emerge from behind one of the monoliths. Nara is a slight woman, worn down by time and tragedy, small of frame but big of spirit, and Naysa's heart aches. No parent should bury a child. It's not the natural order. *"You cannot put off your destiny."*

"Do not ask me to leave," Naysa cries. *"My place—"*

"No." Nara squeezes her daughter's hands. *"No matter how much either of us may wish it so, your destiny lies elsewhere."*

The look in her mother's eyes, an eerie combination of devastation and pride, twists Naysa up inside.

"I know you are scared," Nara says, *"but the time has come. You are a woman now, and you are ready."*

Chapter 9

In my mind I saw the mother and the daughter. With my eyes, I saw the semiautomatic in Joshua's hand.

"Stand up," he ordered.

Everything around me blurred. Slowly, as if in an alternate reality, I shifted my legs and stood, all the while gazing at Josh.

The wind whipped at Caleb's coat. "This is none of your concern, *fratellino*," he snarled. "I told you not to follow me."

"I did not follow *you*," Josh said, speaking to his brother but looking at me. It was just a look. There was no physical contact. But my whole body responded, as if he'd put his hands—normally elegant and well-manicured, but now dirty and blood streaked—on me. "I followed *her*."

Caleb shot his brother a glance. "Her?"

"You still do not know who this is, do you?" Joshua asked, and everything inside of me froze. Of course Caleb knew. Joshua was his brother. He would have told him everything—

and yet the icy look in Caleb's eyes told me he had no idea what his brother was talking about.

"Just imagine my surprise," Josh continued, his gaze practically drilling into me. "When I stumbled across none other than my favorite love-them-and-leave-them spy in Saint-Tropez of all places—at our villa."

Betrayal cut to the quick. He might as well have just signed my death warrant.

Caleb's face went tight. "Madelaine is the MI6 agent who snowed you?"

Josh flinched. "Her name is Zoe."

He was hanging me out to dry—why lie about my name?

Caleb, eyes hard and glittering, turned to look at me. "This is why you lost control when I kissed her."

Josh showed no reaction to the taunt. "She is mine," he said, walking toward me through the emerging light. "You had no right to touch her."

My mind raced. My body prepared. Something else… something I refused to name…shook. Do something, I commanded myself. But my gun lay on the ground. True, I had my arms and my legs and could certainly take out two men, but not two men with guns. Not quite yet, anyway.

So I stood there with my back to one of the monoliths and watched Joshua close in on me.

"For almost three years I have waited for this moment. I looked for you," he said, and abruptly I realized he no longer spoke to his brother. "And waited. And imagined." The wind whipped his hair, blowing dark strands against his forehead. "Because I knew the moment would come."

My heart kicked hard. Because I'd known it, too. But God, I'd never imagined the final hand would play out like this.

"And then I see you in Saint-Tropez, with my brother. Do

you know how much restraint it took to pretend you were a stranger? That you were not the woman who—"

I angled my chin. There was no Caleb now, only Josh. He stood between me and his brother, right there in front of me, almost close enough for me to unarm. Almost. "The woman who what?" I demanded.

"The woman whom I wanted to find alone," he said, "without witnesses to what I had planned."

Deidre gasped, but I could no more have looked to reassure her than I could have pulled in a full breath. "You have witnesses now," I pointed out. Just as he'd had witnesses in Saint-Tropez.

He lifted a hand to my face. "I no longer care."

"*Cristo,* Josh, do it and get it over with!" Caleb shouted. "The sun is rising."

Josh kept his hand to my face, his thumb playing across my lower lip. And looking at me. God, how he was looking at me…

It was all I could do to breathe.

"You should never have come here," he whispered.

My options were finite. There were two of them, one of me, and Deidre. They had guns. Deidre and I did not. To get out of this alive—

I had but one choice.

My eyes met his. I felt the steel move through me, felt my body tense and ready. "No," I whispered, so softly only he could hear. "You are the one who should have stayed away." Then, with a hard smile, I lunged.

The force of my body ramming into his drove him backward. "You idiot!" Caleb roared as his brother slammed into him, knocking him down and pinning him against the rocks. Momentum on my side, I went for Josh's gun, tried to jerk it from his hand

The single gunshot stopped me cold.

For one brutal fraction of one horrible second, I hung there frozen. Unable to move. Think. Breathe. I waited for the burn of pain. None came. Rain-slicked hair falling into them, Josh's eyes met mine. In them I saw sorrow. And—*God help me*—pain.

His mouth worked. Little sound came forth. I would have sworn he said…*go*.

Three seconds. That's all that could have passed. No more. But in them I lived and died. Loved. And wept.

Joshua.

I knew I had to run. Protect whatever lay in the small chest. Get away from the Adrianos before Caleb found his footing and came after me. Already he struggled against the weight of his brother sandwiching him against stone. But my body didn't seem to work. Everything felt thick and cold and useless.

"Hurry!" From behind me Deidre pressed my 9 mm into my hand and dragged me toward one of the large monoliths, the chest tucked beneath her other arm. I knew better than to look back, but couldn't stop myself from twisting around to see Josh slumped against a struggling Caleb at the base of the big megalith.

Not moving.

Horror sliced deep. *No!* I wanted to shout. But I had to run. The sun was rising, bathing the sky in a pinkish wash. Caleb would be on his feet soon. And he would come after us. No matter how badly wounded Josh was.

"This way!" Deidre urged, leading me in a quick zigzag among the rocks. Rain stung my eyes and my ankle twisted beneath me, but I neither slowed nor cried out.

But as we fled through the tight maze from ancient times, I couldn't get one thought from my mind.

Too easy. It had been too bloody easy. Joshua Adriano was not a huge man, but he was a strong one. A well-conditioned athlete. I'm not saying that he could take me without a fight—

but there should have *been* a fight. Not him standing so close, paying more attention to his fingers against my mouth than the gun dangling from his other hand. It was almost as if—

Almost as if he'd been inviting me to take him down.

All her life she's been told the story: in a faraway land, there awaits a sacred place. A temple of love and learning, of peace and hope. A refuge blind to all but that which is in the heart. A sanctuary that will draw its strength from all corners of this land, the mountains and the valleys, the deserts and the prairies and the oceans.

Naysa cannot stop the tears. The elders consider her a woman, but inside she feels like a child. Her heart still needs her mother. "I don't want to leave you...." Because if she does she will never return—and they both know it.

"I will always be with you," her mother promises, pressing a cloth bundle into her hands. "In your heart, where it matters."

Naysa knows what she is saying.

Goodbye.

"You will not get away!" The desperate voice echoed not from the past, but through the stones. It was impossible to discern how close or how far Caleb was. Whether he was left or right, in front or behind us.

The big stones all looked the same. Beneath our feet, smaller stones shifted. It was like racing through a maze. At last we broke from the forest of standing stones and ran toward the cove where we'd stashed my rental less than two hours before.

"A chest?"

Sitting cross-legged on a bed inside a hotel near the Belfast airport, I turned the box over in my hands. "Yes," I told Catrina. After taking Deidre to a friend's house in a neighboring town, where she'd promised she would be safe, I'd driven several hours to Belfast. As soon as it could be arranged, the Cessna would take me to London. "With two locks."

"I am assuming Scarlet's key fits?"

"Both locks." Anticipation had quickened through me as I'd made that discovery. Just as quickly, it had turned to disappointment. "But both locks must be opened simultaneously." Therefore requiring two keys, turned at the same time.

Through the phone line, I heard Catrina relaying the information to others. "The second key, it is the one in your possession, yes?"

"In England."

"You must hurry," Catrina said. "We spotted armed men hiking through the area near the temple today. *Certainement* they are on the Adriano payroll."

My breath caught. "Did they see you?"

"No." In the background, another woman spoke. "And you?" Catrina asked. "You are safe?"

The image formed before I could stop it, of Josh slumped against his brother. The look of surprise on his face. The way his mouth had moved… *Go.*

I opened my eyes to the steady rain falling beyond the window. I'd taken a shower so hot my skin turned red. I'd wrapped myself in every towel I could find. I'd put on all my clothes and turned on the heater. But the fissures of cold just kept right on bleeding, seeping deeper into my bones. And every time I closed my eyes, I saw Joshua….

So I tried not to close them.

"You are safe now," he'd once told me, in a small stone room beneath an abbey in Portugal. *"No one is going to hurt you."*

Then, my heart had swelled. Now it clenched, and wept. Joshua was an Adriano, that was true. But for three incredible weeks he'd been Antonio, a man with no links to a family teetering on the verge of insanity, no wife, no child. He'd just been…mine. And I'd wanted him with everything I was.

Now I repeated the words he'd once said to me, and worked hard to keep my voice from breaking. "I am safe," I told Catrina. "But there was a shooting—Joshua Adriano went down."

"Joshua?" Catrina said his name sharply. "Is he dead?"

Through the phone line I heard the murmurs of the other women. I focused on that, on the rain, on the rumble of a jet roaring into the sky, anything other than my last sight of Joshua, the horror in his eyes.

The thought of him dead… "I don't know," I said honestly.

Catrina murmured something under her breath. Then, "The Adrianos, they do not seem to die of natural causes."

If that was supposed to make me feel better, it didn't. I'd heard the rumor, though. It ran like a bad joke through the intelligence community. I'm sure somewhere, there was some Adriano who had passed from heart disease or kidney failure, but no one I knew could name anyone.

"I left him with Caleb."

"That is no guarantee," Catrina said matter-of-factly.

The cold seeped deeper. I reached for the bedspread to wrap around me, looked at its threadbare tapestry and thought better of the action.

My throat burned. So did my eyes. Blinking against the sting, I glanced at the small photograph I'd set on the nightstand. Lexie was an innocent in all this, and yet her future most surely hung in the balance. If I really had descended from this line of Marian priestesses, then so had she.

And if I was being hunted because of the blood that flowed through my veins, if Scarlet had died because of it, Lexie might be in danger, as well.

Her father's family would not care whose intense, soulful eyes she had.

"He said he was trying to warn me." I couldn't get the words out of my mind. Or the look in his eyes. The way he'd touched me in those tenuous moments before I made my move. "And at the Causeway, he almost seemed…"

"Almost seemed what?"

I reached a finger toward the picture and skimmed it along the curve of Lexie's face, so like his. "Nothing. Just my imagination."

"You must guard against that," Catrina advised. "Adrianos have survived on charm for centuries."

"I know." And I did.

"Call us when you have the box open."

"I will."

"And Nadia?" Catrina's voice thickened on my name. It almost felt as if she was reaching across the miles to take my hand and squeeze. "Be careful."

The whisper of warmth surprised me. "You, too." I'd known the woman less than forty-eight hours. She wasn't even all that nice. *Brusque* was a better word. But in those last seconds before we said goodbye, I knew I could count on her with my life.

The afternoon passed. I talked with Lexie and tried not to think of the father she might never know. She was having a tea party with her Boyds Bears and wanted my opinion on which flavor of tea to serve—Earl Grey or English Breakfast. I suggested the Earl Grey. She chose the breakfast.

Evening brought conversations with my mother on holiday in Hong Kong and Olga, and my good friend Lex. He was an ocean away, but I didn't know who else to call. And I couldn't just sit there in the quiet hotel room with the walls pushing in and the silence screaming at me.

Not when my mind saw only the mysterious beach of standing stones and a body slumped against a massive rock.

As a girl, I was quite sure I would marry Alexander Rothschild Stuart III, the only child of one of my mother's dearest friends. That's what my mother always said, anyway, and given my friend's lineage—he can trace himself back to Mary Queen of Scots—can you blame her? Bloodline matters a great deal to Eleanor Bishop, which is rather ironic considering she shares not one ounce with her only child. And Lex and I had shared several rather important firsts. All things considered, it really wasn't surprising that for many years I thought myself in love with him.

That silliness passed, thank goodness, but the bond between us remains. It's a good thing, too, because I had a huge favor to ask. One I wasn't sure his new wife would appreciate.

With the darkness my eyes grew heavy. Flights out of Belfast had been grounded due to a freak lightning storm. The power in my hotel room flickered, but never went out for longer than fifteen minutes. My pilot hoped to fly out with the sunrise. I didn't really want to sleep. But my body had other ideas. It had been over forty-eight hours. And not even a pot of cheap coffee seemed to cancel out the fatigue.

Bedside lamp on, I said good night to Lexie's picture and slipped between the sheets. My 9 mm lay under my pillow. I had the old box in my hand.

I drifted. The lethargy came first, followed by the molasses-like paralysis. The room spun slowly, like it used to when I went to bed after one too many glasses of wine. I fought the sensation, but my arms and legs were too heavy to move.

I slept. At least it might have been sleep. Wherever I went, Joshua was there waiting. Smiling. Laughing.

Falling.

I awoke with a start, my heart pounding as I stared through

the semidarkness. I felt like I'd been running with a wet rag over my nose and mouth.

I lay there and listened. Rain pelted the window. Every now and then, thunder rattled the windows. From the next room, I heard someone coughing. Closer, I heard someone breathing.

Slowly I slid my hand under the pillow and curled my fingers around my 9 mm.

The urge to twist toward the door was strong. But my patience was stronger. As long as my visitor thought I slept, I had the element of surprise. And as long as I had the element of surprise, I was in control.

I very much liked being in control.

Time dragged. Each tick of the bedside clock taunted me, but I did not let myself move. Barely let myself breathe.

Against the wall, shadows shifted. I saw his image appear before I heard the creak of his ankle. He moved slowly. Quietly. I'm not sure what sense had alerted me to his presence. Leftover training, perhaps. The will to live is a hard thing to snuff out.

He was tall. And lean. Ridiculously patient.

Joshua.

Everything inside of me surged violently. Then I saw the beard and realized my mistake.

Heart pounding, I rolled from the bed and lunged across the room, grabbed him by the arm and twisted it behind his back, shoved the old man against the wall. "Hello, Max."

Chapter 10

Perhaps I should have been surprised. I wasn't. Where one Adriano walked, others tended to follow. They were rather like a pack of elegant wolves that way.

"I did not mean to wake you," Joshua's grandfather said, and the quiet words, spoken in an obscenely genteel voice for a man who killed with neither conscience nor remorse, made part of me want to laugh.

The rest of me wanted to drive the man who'd been watching me in Saint-Tropez to his knees.

How very typical for an Adriano to greet me in the stillness of my hotel room like an old friend, rather than the man who'd massacred my family.

"Of course not," I said, taking his left wrist and pressing his palm to the wall. Eve believed the Adriano patriarch was merely a shadow of his former self, a haunted soul in search of redemption. Perhaps it was possible. But redemption came with a price. As did sin.

"After all, it's infinitely easier to slit someone's throat while they are asleep," I added, still raw from the horror of my grandmother's letter.

A broken sound rasped from Max's throat. "I did not follow you here to kill you, either."

"Oh?" I wedged my foot between his dirty boots and nudged them shoulder-width apart. He made no move to fight me. A less seasoned agent might have mistaken his stillness for complacency. "Then to what do I owe the pleasure?"

"I am here to help you."

The dampness of his clothes oozed into the T-shirt I'd been sleeping in. "Were those the last words Scarlet heard?" I knew better than to let emotion seep in, but the question tore out of me, anyway. "And what about Tobar? Nanette?"

I had no proof—her letter ended with her pregnant and in hiding—but somehow I knew she had not enjoyed a happy ending. If she had, my life would have been infinitely different.

It was nearly impossible to reconcile this shell of a man, with his sunken eyes and scraggly silver hair, with the elegant but reclusive Adriano patriarch I'd once found bleeding on the floor of an old abbey.

The last time I'd seen this man, he'd been in a tuxedo. His silver hair had been queued behind his neck. Now that hair was wet and tangled, and his shoulders sagged. "You have learned much since I last saw you."

Jaw clenched, I was grateful for the bedside lamp that allowed me to see his hands, one splayed against the wall, the other wedged behind his back. Once, they'd been elegant.

Now they looked parchment thin, knobby and bruised with bulging veins, spotted by age and scarred by violence, drenched in a lifetime of blood that could not be seen. Only remembered.

And avenged.

"Why should I trust a man who once pledged his allegiance to Hitler?" I was willing to bet the copy of *Mein Kampf* I'd seen in Saint-Tropez had a personal inscription. "Who thinks nothing of killing anyone who got in his way, even children and pregnant women? Who presents a benevolent front to the world, when it was your experiments that exposed them to diseases eradicated decades before?" I stopped and drew a shaky breath, felt the burn clear down to my lungs.

Max did not move.

"The man who," I added, refusing to allow myself to tremble, "according to your *own* grandson, murdered my sister."

Now Max did. It was subtle, but his whole body seemed to wince. *"Scarlet."* Her name was barely more than a rasp. "Yes, I suppose Caleb would say that."

Caleb. Interesting that he did not assume I meant Joshua. "You don't deny it?"

"With my dying breath."

The irony was not lost on me. "Never mind the fact you've already had one of those," I muttered.

But he ignored my sarcasm. "I cared a great deal for your sister," he said, and if I'd not known exactly who it was I held pressed to the wall, I would have mistaken the thickness in his voice for fondness. "She was…a magnificent light in my otherwise darkened existence, a chance for a lost old man to see a future that could have been, but never was."

Everything inside of me stilled. "You're talking about our grandmother," I realized.

With the hoarse words, he twisted around and pierced me with his fathomless gray eyes. In them, even through the shadows, I would have sworn I saw every death on his soul. "I am."

It was hardly the time for me to relax. I knew that. But the virulent hatred that had driven me to ram him against the wall morphed into something thick and swirling that I hardly recognized. I didn't release him. But my grip on his wrist loosened, allowing his blood to once again flow.

"I need you to listen very carefully," he said, making no move to shake the hair from his gaunt face. "No matter what you have heard or what you think, you must listen." He glanced toward the desk. "Would it be easier if you tied me up?"

I blinked. "What?"

"There are things I need you to hear. Perhaps it would be easier for us both if you restrained me."

I'd never had a perp offer to be restrained before. But the dampness of his clothes had already soaked into mine. That's why I shivered, I told myself. With him tied to the chair, I could keep my distance. Quit touching him.

I very much wanted to quit touching him.

Heart slamming, I lifted his right hand to the wall and pressed it there, then ran my palms along his rain-soaked coat. Despite finding no weapons, I retrieved my 9 mm. "Move to the chair. Slowly."

He obeyed, giving me the distinct impression that slowly was the only way he *could* move.

"Pull it from the desk," I instructed.

And again he obeyed.

Once he sat, I yanked the lamp cord from the wall and carried it toward Max, pulled his hands behind the chair and used the cord to secure them there.

"Now talk," I said.

He looked up at me through long scraggly hair. "When a man finds himself standing at the end of his life and must account for the devastation caused by his sins, he has but two choices. He can accept the punishment fate has in store for him…or he can fight death to undo the damage." Something dark and damaged glittered in his eyes. "An awakened conscience, I have discovered, neither allows rest nor permits light at the end of the tunnel."

I steeled myself against the words, but could do nothing about the way he looked sitting there. This once powerful man, who'd rubbed elbows with world leaders while plotting their downfalls, was now dressed in rags, tied to a chair, wet and cold and…broken.

It was the only word that fit.

And it made him infinitely more dangerous.

"That is why I am here," he was saying. "Time is running out. My family must be stopped—they will not rest until they secure what you unearthed this morning."

"Your family does not scare me."

"They should." This time the rasp to Max's voice was sharper. "Caleb and his father do not see things clearly. Simon's mind does not work right."

"Funny. That's what Caleb said about you."

"Because I scare him—and you do, too. It is easier for him to think I am insane than to think that I am right and he is wrong. I have the power to stop him. My son knows I have seen the error of my ways and am trying to stop him before he—" The words broke off abruptly.

"Before he what?"

Max looked toward the window. Rain no longer fell in thick sheets; it had abated to the incessant drizzle that had plagued me the prior morning. A tapestry of droplets dripped against the glass, illuminated by a streetlamp in the parking lot.

A long moment passed before he returned his attention to me. And when he did, the holocaust in his eyes chilled me. "Before Simon can no longer *be* stopped."

The insanity of it all weighed down on me. Just four days

ago, I'd served tea to my daughter and her three favorite bears. We'd all dressed for the occasion. Now, I stood with a gun on Joshua Adriano's grandfather in a hotel room in Belfast, talking about redemption and—apocalypse.

That was the word Caleb had used. Apocalypse.

Questions jammed through me. So did incredulity. There had to be some other endgame. Nothing would be served by ending the world. That couldn't be what the Adriano family— *Joshua's family*—wanted. There had to be something else, something born out of the darkness and the chaos.

"Everything that's happening—the earthquakes and the disease, the storms and the volcanoes—"

"A prelude," Max confirmed, and I blinked, reminding myself to focus on his words and not the horrible image of Joshua sprawled at the base of a hulking monolith....

"For centuries, my family has existed in the shadows," Max said, sitting there in absolute stillness, his eyes never leaving mine, "quietly working in the background, studying and learning, preparing for our ascension."

"Your *ascension?*" I breathed.

He glanced around the room, as if looking for something. "You have no idea of the role you play in all of this, my dear. Neither did Scarlet, though she was getting close."

Her notes. Her journals. I had them all.

"But I do," Max said. "I have spent over half my life looking for first your mother, then later, you and your sister." His mouth curved into a dark parody of a smile. "Your parents hid you quite well. There were times I actually believed the two of you really were dead."

The room tilted. *"Dead?"*

"You and Scarlet," he said sadly. "According to the authorities, you died when you were fourteen months old."

All my life. All my life I'd hungered for information about

my birth family. Who they were. Where we'd lived. Why they'd given me away.

Now this man, this man who by all accounts I should despise, talked of my past with a familiarity that robbed me of breath.

The world thought I was dead.

Had my parents thought so, too? Is that why they'd never come looking for me? "We were kidnapped—"

"No," Max said, shaking his head. "Everything you wish to know about your past—everything Scarlet wished to know—is in that file." He glanced toward the door to the hotel room, where a large envelope lay. "I promised your sister that if she came to Ireland, I would tell her everything I knew." His voice lowered. "But she never made it."

I stared at the envelope. "You were the one who told her about Dunluce."

"And Deidre, yes. Her grandmother…" He hesitated. "Let us simply say I have watched her grandmother for a long time."

I tried not to think it, not to imagine it. Deidre's grandmother and mine. Up against this man. He knew of the secret between the two women, but without Scarlet, without me, he'd been powerless.

"You knew about her key," I breathed. Whereas Caleb clearly had not known about Dunluce, or he would not have needed me to lead the way.

He would have kept the key, come here himself.

"And yours," Max said. "Yes. That is why you are so important. The box cannot be opened without the original keys."

I knew it! "I'm sure a hammer—"

"Only if you wish to destroy its contents, and that is one wish I do not have."

The mystery of it all kick-started my heart—and my imagination. "What's in the box?"

"That, I do not know," Max said. "I can only tell you what my grandfather told me, his oldest grandson—what his grandfather told him. What I told Aaron, *my* oldest grandson, the week before he died."

In a hunting accident, if I recalled correctly. With Caleb.

Through the shadows, Max's eyes seemed to glow. "There will come a day when the world is ready for change. When great powers fall and despair rises, when the very future hangs in the balance. And when this day arrives, he with the key will win."

The enormity of it all awed me. "Or she," I corrected.

"It was the Adriano goal to make sure it was a he."

"An *Adriano* he."

"Yes."

"But my grandmother got her hands on the key," I murmured, realizing the truth. Had it been in her—*in our*—family all along? "That's why she had to die."

All color—not that there was much—leached from Max's lean face, casting his cheekbones in sharp relief. "I do not wish to speak of your grandmother."

Every man has an Achilles' heel, I'd once heard. You had only to find it. "She loved you," I pressed. If he truly wanted to be redeemed, it was more than just the future he had to protect. It was the past he had to face. "Not in the way she loved Tobar, but she did love you."

His shoulders sagged. "I know."

"Did you love her?"

His eyes closed. And his head fell, as if in silent, reverent, damning prayer.

The truth rocked me. I'm not sure where it came from, the knowledge that this man had already faced the sins of his past, but it was there, sucking the oxygen from the room like a dark swirling vortex. "Oh, my God. It's true, isn't it? About when you died on the operating table." Eve had mentioned something about a near-death experience. "My grandmother was there, wasn't she? Waiting for you."

Damning him.

Slowly, his eyes opened, exposing me not to the soullessness of a man without conscience—as I'd so wanted him to be—but the agony of a man who could not wash the blood from his hands. "I am an old man, Nadia Bishop. I stand at the end of my life. It is too late for me. You, however. You and the others, you have the chance—*the key*—your grandmother sacrificed everything to protect."

Long after I allowed Max to slip into the darkness beyond my hotel room, I sat on the bed with the contents of the envelope spread on the sheets. With the night pushing toward dawn, the rain had stopped and the temperature had dropped.

I barely noticed.

There were newspaper articles. Several of them. Obituaries. And pictures.

It was summer. June. A family of four had gone for a drive along the eastern coast of Scotland. It was a stunning day, a picturesque road. No one knows why the man—Gunther, his name was—lost control. He skidded, the brakes did not stop the car, and the vehicle plunged over a cliff to the rocks below.

The car was found first. Gunther's broken body was still inside. The bodies of his wife and infant daughters were thrown clear and washed out to sea, never recovered.

My throat closed up on me, and there in the shadowy light of predawn, I started to rock. Gunther. And Natasha. Those were their names. My mother and father. The newspaper talked of the tragic loss of their toddler girls, Nadia and Natalia.

Somewhere along the line, someone had changed Scarlet's name.

Natasha. Nadia. And Natalia. Further back—Nanette.

The thought struck me that I'd named my own daughter incorrectly. I'd actually thought about Natalie, but my adoptive mother had strongly discouraged me, and the need to hide Lexie's parentage had made Alexandria the perfect choice, even if it has caused my friend Lex Stuart a fair amount of grief.

Shaking inside, I picked up an old black-and-white photograph of two little dark-haired infants dressed in adorable frilly dresses, and saw my own tilted eyes staring back at me.

And I knew. Finally, at last, I had the answers I'd been seeking. I knew why Scarlet and I had been abandoned to an orphanage. We had not died, as the newspaper article and obituaries stated. Against all odds we'd survived, finding our way, somehow, to the loving arms of our adoptive families.

An odd sense of homecoming collided with a piercing sense of loss. Because there was something else that I realized in that hotel room. All my life I'd wondered what would make a man and woman give away their children. Now I knew. It wasn't choice.

It was death.

The keys fit. Turned in unison, the keys Scarlet and I had treasured all our lives freed the lock on the old metal box.

After half a day of travel, including a stop at MI6 headquarters in case anyone had managed to follow me, where my former superior had insisted upon a helicopter to ferry me back to Cornwall, I knelt on the rug in my bedroom and spread the contents of the box before me. No one had followed me. I'd gone to great lengths to ensure that. Still, I kept my 9 mm at my side.

Broken. That was my first thought. Then…beautiful. Glassy, almost. Amber. The misshapen tiles glowed against the white sheet like puzzle pieces waiting to be fit together. I almost didn't want to touch them.

"They're smooth," I told Catrina, who'd been waiting on the phone as I emptied the box. Energy hummed through my blood the second I touched the first tile. "Almost like glass."

"Excellent," Catrina breathed. "Most excellent."

I moved a few of the broken fragments together until I found how they fit. "An eye," I said. Wise. Serene. "And a mouth." Again, serene. Gentle. But fierce somehow. Protective.

"The face." Awe danced through Catrina's voice, and I could hear Eve, or maybe one of the other women, whisper something to her. "Is there anything else?" she asked.

Excitement eddied through me. An ancestor of mine had hidden these tiles. There they'd stayed for centuries, buried. Waiting. Scarlet had been so close….

My throat closed up at the thought of my sister and the remarkable legacy we shared. At first, there was a stab of grief for all that she'd never had the chance to know. But then I realized that she *did* know, and that even though Olga and Lexie had yet to return from their afternoon outing, I did not kneel there in my bedroom alone.

"Definitely a face," I confirmed, as a few more tiles fit together, forming the smooth, elegant line of a nose.

"You must bring them to us immediately," Catrina purred.

I planned to. But first, I had something else to tell her. "There's more," I said, shifting my attention to the scroll that had fallen from the box along with the tiles. I picked it up and removed the beautiful thread binding it, unrolled the movie-poster-size vellum.

And forgot to breathe.

There she was. The Lady. The Blessed Mother. Exactly as Eve had described her, serenity in her eyes and a sword at her hip.

Torn.

Desecrated.

But still beautiful.

The sense of loss was acute. Part of the lady had been ripped away, stealing the child from her arms.

"Nadia?" Catrina's voice was sharp.

But I could not speak. The detail was exquisite, not just a drawing or a portrait, but a representation with the painstaking detail of a stained glass window.

Trancelike, I turned to the glowing tiles scattered on the white sheet, and selected one. Part of the eye, so peaceful and quiescent and blessed. I brought the glassy tile to the vellum and compared it to the Lady's eye.

The fit was perfect.

"A blueprint." The realization roared through me with a rush of adrenaline, and I felt the energy of all those who had loved and lost and hoped before me at work in my body, urging me on.

"A blueprint?" Catrina questioned. "Of what?"

"*The Lady.*" Vibrating from the inside out, I retrieved another tile, this one part of her mouth, and placed it over the vellum. Then another. And another.

"It's like a…" The realization struck me, threw me back to the Belfast hotel room, where Max had spoken of the prophecy handed down from Adriano grandfather to grandson: *There will come a day when the world is ready for change. When great powers fall and despair rises, when the very future hangs in the balance. And when this day arrives…*

"He with the key shall win," I whispered. "My God. Not a key," I told Catrina. "Not in the sense we thought. But a key like you would find with a map. A legend."

"What are you saying? This blueprint? It is for the Lady?"

"Yes." I slid another tile into place. "How she once was."

Catrina relayed the information to those gathered at her farmhouse in southern France.

"Nadia, this is Tru." The new voice was urgent. Excited. We had not yet met, but I was familiar with the geologist who had located the area where, centuries before, the main Marian temple had flourished in southern France. "Are you sure?"

"Yes." I was. "But she is torn. Only half of her is here." The half Eve had described.

"The Adrianos—" The name sounded every bit of a curse. "Probably."

"Bring her anyway. As quickly as possible. We've been assembling the tiles as best we can, but with this—"

"I'll be there in the morning." But first, I had some documenting to do—and precautions to take. With mystical powers similar to the legendary Ark of the Covenant involved, I could not allow the key to the mosaic to fall into the wrong hands.

After mapping out details with Catrina, I retrieved my digital camera and began photographing the Madonna Key. It was a leftover habit from my time with MI6. Hope for the best, plan for the worst. I captured the blueprint in copious detail, then uploaded the images to a secure Web site, where Tru would be able to access them prior to my arrival.

"Mommy home! Mommy home!"

Nearly done, I looked up to see Lexie racing into my bedroom. My heart swelled at the sight of her little toddler legs moving as fast as they could, her dark pigtails bobbing as she ran.

"Lexie!" I went down on my knees, welcomed her into my arms. She hit me with the force of an eager two-year-old, bounding into my lap and throwing her little arms around my neck. "Mommy home."

"Mommy home," I repeated. Shooting a quick smile at Olga, who stood in the doorway, I pulled back from Lexie and grinned. "Give Mommy a kiss?"

She looked at my mouth, then presented me with her cheek. I laughed out loud.

Not sure why I wanted to cry, I kissed her all over, tickling as I did so, until she was on her back and I was crouched over her. Giggling, she squirmed playfully, then tried to wiggle away. "Pwetty."

That stopped me. I looked up to find her reaching for one of the tiles. "Yes, pretty," I agreed. "But not for play."

"I will take her," Olga said in her accented voice.

I glanced up to tell her that wasn't necessary, but stilled when I saw the way she frowned at the tiles. It was the same way she might look at a spider crawling alongside her charge.

I'd known this woman all my life. Loved her. Trusted her. But in that one frozen moment, everything fractured, and doubt slipped in.

Then I blinked and the scene crystallized, revealing not Olga looking in horror at the tiles, but a nanny concerned her charge was flirting with trouble.

"Remember what I have told you about Mommy's pretties?" she asked with a perfect combination of patience and reprimand. "Look, but do not touch."

I rocked back and watched them, the tenderness as Olga brushed a curl from Lexie's face and my little girl beamed a smile at her, and realized just how tired I really was. It was the only way to explain the ridiculous thoughts that had paraded through me like some kind of toxic residue.

That lingered even now…

Olga and my mother were distant cousins. She'd been a companion to us all, splitting her time between our home and that of a spinster aunt in ill health. Usually she'd visited Lucinda once a month. Sometimes more often.

As a child I never understood why she was so religious about her visits, because she always came home sad. At the time, I hadn't understood that sometimes we do things not because they make us happy, but because doing so is right.

Olga did not work for the Adrianos. Logically, I knew that. If she had, Max would have approached me long ago, when I was just a babe, long before an assassin nearly ended his life and allegedly changed his heart. And he would have killed me. My key would have been his.

"Nadia?" Her long graying hair pulled into a loose ponytail, Olga stepped closer. "Are you okay?"

I willed the cold fist around my heart to release. "I'm fine. Just…tired."

She sent me a sharp, concerned glance. "You do not look well," she said, lifting Lexie to spin her like an airplane. "Perhaps you should let me take our girl, so you can have a nap."

The sharp visceral reaction drove home the truth. Watching them, feeling my heart swell, I realized why I had doubted Olga, for even one shameful moment. Everyone had an Achilles' heel, after all. Lexie was mine.

"Last one to the kitchen doesn't get cookies," I said, surging to my feet and racing toward the door, trying not to think about how I would find the strength to do what must be done.

"Down!" Lexie called, and Olga must have obeyed, because my daughter raced beside me. I pretended to trip, let her breeze past me.

Anything, I told myself. Anything for my child.

Twilight falling around me, I watched the small helicopter lift like a giant insect toward the hazy sky. Everything inside me hurt, as if I'd just ripped out a vital organ without the luxury of anesthesia, and the rest of me was trying to figure out how to cauterize the wound.

"I do not understand," Olga said. She stood beside me in

the gardens. Hurt thickened her voice. "Why are you sending Alexandria away?"

I swiped at the tears, but more came. In my mind, I could see Lexie's face pressed to the window, her little hand waving bye-bye as my mother ferried her away.

This must have been how Jochebed had felt, I thought inanely, placing her infant among the reeds of the Nile.

But Lexie was not an infant anymore. She was a little girl. And instead of the reeds, I was sending her to her godfather in New York, who I knew would protect her with his very life. Lex was like that. He couldn't have loved her more had she been his own.

"Because I must," I answered vaguely. In less than an hour I would leave for France. I didn't know how long I would be there. And while I'd gone to great lengths to make sure the Adrianos never found my Cornwall home, their reach was far. And now that I had half of the Madonna Key, their desperation was rising.

"I could have gone with her—" Olga stared.

"No." The force of the word shamed me. So did the lingering unease from that brief, fractured moment in my bedroom. "It is safer for us all this way."

"Safer?" Olga took my arm. "Safer from whom? What is going on, Nadia? Has something happened? Have the Adrianos—"

I jerked back with more force than I'd ever displayed to this woman, and stared at her as if I'd never seen her before.

I'd never mentioned the name Adriano to anyone in my family. Not my mother. Not Olga.

Her eyes darkened. "Nadia?"

"I have to go," I said, not trusting myself to say anything further. To do anything. To so much as think. "You may go, as well," I said, turning back toward the house. Somehow, I didn't run.

But I wanted to.

The sea gods are angry. The men readying the seafaring vessel are angry. Storms have delayed their trip by a week. Rumor has it the ship that left the week before has been lost. Several oarsmen have fled. The captain promises the weather will soon permit travel, but standing onshore, hands clutching a fur tight around her as protection from the cruel wind, Naysa sees only the endless dark gray of sea and sky.

The thought of spending weeks in one of the small, crescent-shaped boats terrifies her. She has not been in the water in the five weeks since Ciara—

And yet she must.

"Soon it will rain," a rough voice says behind her, and though everything inside her tenses, she does not turn to look, does not want to see the gleam in the oarsman's eyes. "Come with me," he says, "and I will keep you dry."

Her hand tightens around the pouch given to her by her mother. "That is not necessary."

He presses in behind her, bringing with him the scent of ale, and sandwiching her against a wooden post. "A pretty little thing like you," he says, sliding a hand around her waist, "all alone…"

He does not finish his sentence, but she knows what he means. What he wants. "I am quite well," she begins, but he grows rougher this time, uses his strength to turn her around and hold her against the filth of his body.

"Well, I am not," he snarls, and the rancidness of his breath makes her stomach convulse.

"Nadia!"

I spun around and found her hurrying toward me, a slender woman in her late fifties with time-streaked hair blowing in the wind, and desperation in her eyes, and I felt something inside of me twist. "I'm sorry!" I almost cried, then turned again and hurried for the door, pulled it open and rushed inside.

His hands are all over her, big and strong, violating her even through her clothes. "But I am going to—"

She does not give him a chance to finish. He is big and she is slight, but she is strong, and he is foolish. She stomps down on his foot and rams her knee into his groin, twists away as he lunges for her.

But the second attack does not come. His eyes fly wide as he slumps to the ground, revealing the man standing behind him, holding an oar.

But he is no man. He is just a boy. Eighteen, maybe. His face is still soft, marred not by wind or time. His body is thin, not yet full in the way of a man. But in the green of his distinctive eyes glows the same intensity as the last time she saw him, when he'd dragged her from the boiling inlet, when she'd thrashed in his arms, too lost in grief to even ask his name.

Muttering harshly in a language she does not understand, he steps toward her and opens his arms, and she realizes how easy it would be to drown in the compassion in his eyes.

Stepping toward him is the most natural thing in the world. "Who are you?" she whispers against his chest.

Gently, his arms close around her and he tangles a hand in her hair. "I am Joakim," he says, and for the moment, it is enough.

I didn't stop at the base of the curved staircase, not until I reached my room and pulled the door shut behind me, leaned against the thick wood and tried to breathe.

That's when I saw him.

Chapter 11

He turned from the heavily curtained window, but made no move toward me. He just stood there, all tall and disheveled, no longer dressed in torn and damp clothes, but olive cargo pants and a dark gray collarless shirt. On most men, the outfit would not have caused me to look twice.

But Joshua Adriano wore rugged just as well as he wore everything else—and nothing at all. With a style and confidence that made everything inside of me clench.

Alive. The thought streaked through me with reckless disregard for logic and caution. Josh was alive, not dead on the beach or in some anonymous morgue along the Irish coast. He did look worse for wear, though, the jagged cut on his face now drawn together by dark stitches, his eyes shadowed, but burning somehow. There was a stillness to him, a coiled energy that sent my heart slamming into my ribs.

The sight of him—God, the sight of him standing there in

the hazy light of my bedroom, where I'd imagined him so many times, where I'd awoken from dreams with the remembered feel of his touch burning against my damp skin—almost made me forget everything I knew about this man.

Almost.

"Lock the door," he said in that dangerously quiet voice of his, the one that made my blood hum rather than roar.

My eyes met his, and something inside me stirred. But I did not do as he instructed. I dashed toward my nightstand and yanked open the bottom drawer.

"*Cara,*" Josh said, and from his voice I could tell he was moving toward me. "Surely you realize that is a risk I could not take."

I twisted around to see my 9 mm dangling from his hand.

He removed the clip and tossed it on the bed. "But nor I am here to hurt you."

Something inside me shifted. The words—God, the words were not fair. They whispered within me, taunting with a temptation I had taught myself not to feel.

"That's not what you said yesterday," I reminded him, unable to forget the way he'd looked at me in the cold drizzle, with heat in his eyes and a gun in his hand.

He kept right on coming, crossing the floor where I had sat with the tiles and the mosaic blueprint not an hour before.

"I never said I wanted to hurt you," he pointed out. "Merely that I wanted you alone, without witnesses."

My mouth went dry. I took an instinctive step back, but my legs bumped against the mattress.

"*Nadia.*"

I could have shoved past him if I wanted to. The blood pooling in various parts of my body would not have stopped me.

But in that moment, I did not want to.

"Did you really think I wanted you alone to hurt you?"

The question whispered through me, bringing with it the scent of sandalwood that had haunted me for years, prompting me to spin around in a crowded room, looking, searching....

"Did it never occur to you?" he asked, his fingers skimming my cheekbone. "That I meant only to do this?"

I had no time to prepare. But that was a lie. I knew what Joshua meant before he so much as breathed. I could have moved. I could have turned away. I could have stomped on his foot and sent him to his knees, if I'd wanted to.

But again, in that moment, I very much did not want to.

I wanted— Damn it, despite everything—the blood that ran through his veins, and his family's legacy, the lies that stood between us and the one that would forever bind us—I wanted him. His mouth. On mine. Hard. Without mercy or reprieve or regret.

Just like before.

The bed is soft. The sheets are softer. And they are clean. She is clean. All the dirt and grime and stench is gone, replaced by lavender and well-kept fur.

It should all be a dream. But it's not. She is in the land of the Gauls, at a stronghold a day's travel south of the port of her arrival. Joakim did not lie. He'd protected her and brought her here, for a meal and a bath.

And so much more.

The contentment is almost more than she can bear. So is the knowledge that she is no longer a girl. She is a woman now. Snuggled up against him, with her head on his chest and her fingers toying with the trail of hair beneath his navel, her legs tangled with his, she can only think of destiny.

"Joshua," I whispered, because no, it *had* never occurred to me that he'd wanted the same thing. He was an Adriano. I was an intelligence agent. There'd been no way I could have trusted anything he said, not after all the lies.

Now I felt myself pushing up toward him, felt my arms reaching for him. Everything else fell away. Everything. There was only Antonio and Zoe, and a need that had simmered for three years.

The feel of his mouth against mine, moving hesitantly at first, gently, almost reverently, blanked my mind. I sagged against the warmth of his body and played my fingers along the whiskers at his jaw. Normally he was a man who shaved twice a day, but clearly he had not taken a razor to his face since Saint-Tropez.

He held me to him, running a hand down the small of my back while the other threaded up into my hair. The sensation was immediate, that of being safe and protected and—home.

That should have made me pull back. It didn't. His kiss was too dark and desperate, so mind-bogglingly needy that I wasn't sure how I stayed standing there.

I'd kissed with hunger before—this man, that very first time, after a thrilling game of cat and mouse, when neither of us had known who the other really was.

And I'd kissed with desperation—again, Joshua, that last kiss on the very last night, when he'd found me by the windows and urged me back to bed. I'd known the helicopter was coming. I'd realized everything had been a lie, that Antonio did not exist, and the second he realized Zoe did not exist, either, that she was in fact one of the MI6 agents working to solve a series of antiquities thefts—thefts his family had perpetrated— I would not have been allowed to leave the villa alive.

At least, that's what I'd thought as I'd kissed him that last time. But now I had to wonder.

And now…now the combination of hunger and desperation rocked me. Drove me. All I could think was Joshua. Finally. *Joshua.*

"You are so beautiful," he whispers, and the heavy accent of his voice does wicked, wicked things to her body. She starts to want again. To dream. Lifting her face to his, she drags him down for another kiss, and soon he is over her and inside her, filling her, and everything is right.

He is Roman. A poet. Disenchanted with the increasing aggression of his land, he fled life as a slave and has been searching for something more. Something else. You, he whispered last night. He has been searching for her.

The night stretches on, and her body burns. She'd heard stories about coupling from an older cousin, but nothing had prepared her. There'd been a moment of pain, yes, but Joakim had been gentle, and then there'd only been pleasure.

Slowly she drifts and the dreams take over.

When his hands found my face and he pulled back, something dark and punishing tore through me. But then I lifted my eyes to his, and felt the intensity clear down to my soul.

Stripped bare. I'd seen a tree like that once, the bark stripped away, leaving the big redwood standing so strong and yet so vulnerable. I'd never imagined Joshua Adriano could look the exact same way.

He stood tall and unmoving, body to body, breath to breath, his hands cradling my face as if he never meant to let go.

It was the look in his eyes that gave him away.

I'd seen struggles before. I'd seen hand-to-hand combat. Ambushes. Executions. Man against man. Man against nature.

This was different. This was worse. This was man versus… self. Versus heritage. Legacy. The struggle raged in the impossibly dark olive of Joshua's eyes, a silent holocaust that bloody well broke my heart.

No matter what Joshua the man wanted, Joshua the Adriano could not be pushed aside.

She wakes with the sun and stretches, feels the cool silk

sheets slide against her naked body. Feels soreness in places she's never been sore before. Opening her eyes, she reaches for Joakim. Finds only emptiness.

Confused, she sits up and clutches the sheet to her chest, looks around the room. "Joakim?"

But he is gone. His clothes are no longer on the floor beside the bed. Hers are—but the pouch is gone.

"This," I whispered, skimming my thumb along his lower lip, "is not why you came here."

His head lowered, almost as if in prayer. "No."

"You came for the box."

"Yes."

The word, the truth it revealed, hung between us like a grenade ready to blow. But the explosion didn't come. From either of us. There was only an odd, quiet acceptance.

Perhaps I should have ripped myself away from him. Or perhaps I should have taken him down. He'd just confessed to following me to steal something I would never surrender. In that moment I could have done, either. He made no move to stop me.

"How did you find me?" I asked instead. After what had just passed between us, it seemed a rather inane question, but I'd gone to great lengths to vanish, flying from Belfast to London, where I took the tube to MI6 headquarters. From there, my superiors had agreed the safest route home was via helicopter.

"How does not matter." The words were hoarse.

"It does to me." No one had followed. I knew that. Which left very few possibilities. Either he'd tracked me somehow—or someone had led him to me….

Olga.

He lifted his head, met my eyes. "You are safe. That is all you need to know. Caleb did not follow me."

Safe. The word slammed into me, jarring me out of the haze and into reality. I stood in my bedroom with Joshua Adriano. *Adriano!* Less than a foot away, on my nightstand, stood a black-and-white photograph of my daughter—

—a daughter not yet born when Joshua and I became lovers.

The intimacy shattered, leaving the truth of who and what we were spilling through me. We weren't lovers anymore. We weren't allies. We weren't even friends.

With a jerky movement, I twisted from him and bumped into the nightstand, flung out my arm to knock the picture over. He reached for me, but I yanked back.

"What?" I snapped, with a vehemence that surprised me. "He sent you to do his dirty work, thinking you could seduce me into compliance?"

He stilled. "My father did not send me."

"But you are here for the box," I reminded him.

"Nadia, please. I know you do not trust me, but you must listen—"

"Why? So you can ply me with more lies?"

His expression went dark. "Think what you will of me, but were it not for me, you would not be standing here right now. Caleb would not have hesitated to shoot you in cold blood."

"And you would have—" I started, but stopped abruptly, realizing that he had. Joshua *had* hesitated. More than hesitated, he'd all but gift-wrapped the opportunity to lunge at him.

"That is right." He stepped closer. "I see it in your eyes. Had I not come between you and Caleb, he would have killed you."

The truth surged through me, bringing with it a reality that stunned me. "You could have been killed."

"I could have," Josh conceded. "But I was not."

I stared at him, no longer knew who I saw. "Caleb—"

"Thinks I am an idiot and a bad shot," he finished for her. "But he still has no idea where my true allegiance lies."

"Your true allegiance?" Somehow, I managed to say the words.

"I am standing here, am I not?" He took another step closer. "*With* you. Not against you."

Lies came in all shapes, sizes, forms and textures, I knew that. I also knew how to recognize them—a twitch of the eye, a hand to the nose, a subtle shift from foot to foot.

"You have stepped into a giant chess game, *cara,* with life or death consequences beyond anything you have ever imagined. I cannot stand by and let you end up among the casualties."

The words, or maybe it was his quiet voice, did wicked things to my defenses. I looked at him and tried to see the dangerous man I knew him to be. Simon's son. Caleb's brother.

But I saw only the man I'd once fallen for, so hard and fast and completely that I'd almost lost myself in the process. The man whose daughter I'd just sent to New York.

"I can help," he said. "All you have to do is trust me."

He made it sound so easy. Trust him—just as Scarlet had trusted Caleb. "You should go, Joshua." I glanced at the clock, saw I had only a few minutes before I needed to leave. "Stop Caleb, if that's your true intent. But you cannot stop me."

He moved so fast I didn't have time to blink. Almost by magic a gun appeared in his hand.

Not by magic, I realized. From just beneath an old quilt folded atop the chest at the foot of the bed.

An Adriano down to his toes, he'd come prepared.

"Do not force my hand," he said. The words were of steel.

But so was I. "And if I do?"

"Have a seat, *cara.* You are not going anywhere." With the handgun, he gestured toward a wing chair on the far side of the room. "I would rather you hate me than end up dead."

Some women may have found the words foolishly

romantic. Bloody hell, once even I would have. But I had a plane to catch and a legacy to restore. I could not simply turn it over to Joshua, just as I could not let him—or the low thrumming of my heart—interfere with what had to be done.

"Then you'd better not pull that trigger," I advised, backing toward the door.

He tracked me with the gun. "Nadia, do not—"

"Because you're wrong, Joshua. This is not a big chess game. My grandmother and sister were not simple pawns. They were people. Living, breathing, *good* people."

Something dark flashed through his gaze. "Your grandmother?"

Five more steps and I'd be at the door. Downstairs, my suitcase and satchel awaited. "He killed her." My voice broke on the words. "Your sainted grandfather, the almighty benefactor Maximilian Adriano, executed my grandmother in cold blood, just like your brother executed my sister."

"Who told you this?"

My eyes met his. "He did." I saw the words slam into him, saw him reel in much the same way a man recoils from being sucker-punched in the gut.

On Joshua, it was not a sight I enjoyed.

"My grandparents, my parents, my sister…they're all dead, everyone in my family—" with the exception of my daughter "—all dead because of yours." I picked up my jacket from a chair near the door. Joshua hadn't moved. I wasn't sure he'd breathed. His stillness was almost…unnatural. "So do not tell me you're protecting me by holding me prisoner in my own home."

The light in his eyes went dark.

"Because if you do not let me walk out this door, you are not helping me—you are helping the brother you claim to hate." I should have turned around right then and left. Slammed the door, locked it.

But I stood there one heartbeat longer, my eyes locked on to Joshua's. Or maybe it was his gaze holding mine. I don't know. I only know that despite the two meters separating us, he'd never touched me more intimately. More passionately. Not even when we'd made love.

Slowly, he lowered his gun.

Only then did I turn and walk down the wide hallway, lined by portraits of the family who had taken me in and given me sanctuary, but whose blood did not run through my veins.

"Nadia?"

I glanced down the curved staircase to see Olga hurrying toward me. The shock in her voice was evident, as if it were somehow an odd sight to see me coming downstairs.

"Are you all right, darling? You look pale—"

"He's in my bedroom," I said, brushing past her. The disappointment cut like a knife. *Olga. God, Olga.*

Ignoring the sting, I picked up my suitcase and satchel, opened the door and walked to the top of the circular drive, got into my Astra and drove into the night.

Only one route led to and from my country estate. I sped along and tried to focus on the curving road, the rugged shoreline to my left and the desolate moor to my right. But through the darkness, it was the look in Joshua's eyes I saw, the stark combination of sadness and regret.

I suspected it was a look I would never forget.

The lights almost blinded me. They cut through my windshield and spilled in from the rearview mirror. Noise then, loud, the sound of a speedway on a hot summer afternoon.

Cars.

Coming toward me.

Racing behind me.

Pulling alongside me.

Slamming on my brakes, I swerved—there was nowhere to go.

The impact of steel against rock blasted me.

An air bag exploding against me was the last thing I felt.

The sound of my scream the last I heard.

Darkness, the last I saw.

Lexie...the last I thought.

Chapter 12

"Nadia? Can you hear me?"

The soft voice carried through a tunnel of time and space. Recognition hovered just out of reach, much like the arms of a parent teaching a child to swim. Close, but not close enough. *"S-Scarlet?"*

A flash of red against a field of green. A woman going down on one knee. Opening her arms. A small girl rushing in...

With a cruel jolt, I opened my eyes and arched up for a breath, squinted against the glare of sunlight.

"Easy," the dark-haired woman said. Leaning over me, she put a hand to my face while watching me through the most amazingly compassionate eyes I'd ever seen. "Take it slowly."

Her hands. They were soft. In them she held a cool damp rag, which she used to gently stroke my face.

It was only then that I realized how hot I was. How fast my heart was beating. How it hurt just to move.

Everything shifted, and the room started to spin. Disoriented, I looked around for something I recognized. To ground me. The picture of Lexie next to my bed. The heavily curtained windows—

I saw only a sparsely furnished room, walls of weathered white and an unadorned window.

"Breathe," the woman whispered, pressing the rag to my brow.

And I did. Or at least tried. But my throat was too tight.

"You're safe now."

Now. The word cut through the fog and I could see the bright lights again, cutting through the darkness. Nowhere to turn. No time to react. The screech of tires and squeal of brakes.

The collision.

I surged up and winced, felt more than heard the guttural sound that ripped from my throat.

Hands then. The woman's, soft and capable. On my body, easing me back. "Oh, sweetie, you mustn't—"

"Eve!" A different voice, heavily accented. Alarmed. "What is happening...." The honey-haired woman rushed into the bright room, then froze. Our eyes met. Hers widened. *"Nadia."* My name was barely more than a whisper. "Thank God."

For a moment I just stared at her, taking in the wisps of hair falling from a ponytail, her white peasant blouse and the faded blue jeans, knowing instinctively that she was not a ponytail and blue jeans kind of woman.

"Catrina." My voice rasped her name.

"I see you have decided to join us, after all."

"Here," the first woman said, propping a pillow behind me. I glanced over to find her handing me a glass of water.

Eve. The epidemiologist I'd met a few days before in Paris. "You gave us quite a scare," she said.

Awareness came swiftly then. Scarlet's friends. At Catrina's farmhouse in southern France. I'd been en route to bring them the blueprint—

The ambush.

The stark certainty that I was dying.

I brought the glass to my mouth and sipped, savored the feel of cool water sliding down my throat. "How did I get here?"

Catrina and Eve exchanged a sharp glance. "You do not remember?" Catrina asked, crossing to the narrow bed.

I started to shake my head, but stopped as other sensations washed over me. There was something there, hiding amid the fog. Running. Shouting. Gunshots. Hands. Warmth.

Safety.

Catrina leaned over me and lifted a palm as if to smooth the hair from my face, but jerked back at the last moment. "Joshua Adriano brought you here."

The denial was immediate. "No." Joshua had not been there. He couldn't have been there.

But he had. I'd left him at the house, with Olga. He could have been as close as two minutes behind me on the road, arriving just after the accident, to claim what he'd come for.

The Madonna Key.

I sagged against the pillows and tried to breathe, but pain splintered in from all directions. Some of it physical. Most of it not.

Joshua—God, Joshua. For a daft moment there in my bedroom, when our eyes had met, I'd actually believed he was different, that despite the fact he carried his family's name and blood, he did not carry their ruthlessness. That he had a conscience.

"I…" Catrina hesitated. "I've never seen Joshua like that."

Everything inside of me stilled. I looked at the hair falling against Catrina's face, at the dark curls framing Eve's, and knew I had to ask them. Had to know. Every detail. I would immerse myself in them, use them to destroy the draw that refused to die. "Like how?"

The women exchanged another quick glance. "It is hard to say," Catrina said slowly, translating her thoughts carefully. "He has always been so composed—"

"Tortured." This from Eve. She put the rag back to my face and blotted beneath my eyes. "Joshua Adriano was tortured."

"Yes." Catrina slid a few scraggling locks behind her ears. "That is the word. *Tortured.*"

Running. Shouting. Gunfire.

Warmth. Safety.

Joshua.

The images swirled through me, merging and taunting, tempting.

"He said you were ambushed." Eve returned the rag to a tray on a small wooden table. "Six or seven cars. That he came across the accident just as men in black hoods were pouring gasoline onto your car."

The hiss. The smoke. The blast of heat.

"I do not know how he got you out of there before the car blew," Catrina said. "But he brought you to a private airstrip and got you out of the country."

I shifted beneath the thin white sheet, resisting the urge to draw it higher.

"He called me from the air, said he had a doctor on board looking you over, that he was bringing you here to me. Told me to have medical treatment waiting."

"I went with Rhys to a small airfield about fifteen minutes from here," Eve added. "I…" It was her turn to falter. "I thought I was going to have to pry you out of his arms."

Never let you go.

He'd held me. Joshua had. He'd pulled me from the burning

car and carried me to safety. He'd brought me here, to these amazing women. And in the process, he'd held me and cradled me, run his hands along my body and spoken to me in whispers only my heart had understood.

I, in turn, had insisted he was a coldblooded murderer.

"Where is he now?" I asked, opening my eyes to the bright light slanting through the blinds. Even before Catrina spoke, I knew what she would say.

"Gone."

I absorbed the finality of the word. "And my tiles?"

Her expression turned more grim. "They are gone, as well."

"Stolen?"

Shame floods her. It has taken her weeks to complete her journey to the land of the Gauls, where a beautiful temple flourishes in the shadow of the mountains. The land—she has never seen such unspeakable beauty. Big, bright yellow flowers dot the countryside. Fruit grows freely. And the sky, it is the deepest of blues, with only the softest lazy clouds.

She looks at her feet. She has failed. Others have arrived, carrying with them bundles of rock and stone. Only Naysa came empty-handed.

"I was foolish," she says, fighting the dizziness that has swamped her since awaking to find Joakim gone. "I was careless."

The elder priestess, dark-skinned, in a robe of white, smiles softly. "You made a mistake, dear one. That is all."

"I lost the rock."

"There will be other rock," she says, lifting a hand to ease the windblown hair from Naysa's face. "But there is only one you. You must not be so hard on yourself."

The image of her mother flashes so fast and so hard that Naysa feels herself sway. "I cannot stay here," she says. Not among these amazing women whom she failed. "I do not belong."

The elder cradles Naysa's face, slides a finger to wipe the tears from beneath her eyes. "Everything is as it should be. You are exactly where you belong—you and your unborn babe."

The unsettling sense of déjà vu whispered through me, unraveling the threads I'd ruthlessly tied together. Joshua was an Adriano. I'd been attacked. My tiles were gone, and so was he.

It didn't take a highly trained agent to see the link.

Two and two were bloody well adding to four. True, Josh had saved my life, but that did not mean he was on my side. Just because Joshua Adriano didn't want me dead didn't mean he'd turned on his family.

The agent I'd once been knew that.

But the woman I'd become—the woman who'd seen the torment in his eyes, who'd felt his touch even when he stood across the room, who remembered the way he'd carried me from the burning car, held me on the plane; the woman who'd given birth to his daughter—that woman was having an increasingly difficult time believing Josh was the monster I'd once thought him to be.

"I'm going after him." With those words, I stood, wincing at the sharp twinges that shot up my legs.

Eve rushed over to steady me. "You can't."

"I have to." I was fine. Eve had said as much. Just banged up. Cracked ribs. Nothing I hadn't dealt with before.

And even if I hadn't been fine, I had to go. Doing so was the only way to get back what belonged to me. Finding the truth about Joshua had nothing to do with my decision. Nor did the odd, visceral feeling that he…needed me.

Eve released my arms and stepped back. "Toward what end?" she asked. "You think if you ask nicely enough he'll simply give you back the diagram of the mosaic?"

I blinked. "The diagram?"

"Caleb will never let that out of his possession," Catrina said from the doorway. "It is part of his endgame."

Dizziness swept closer. "Endgame?"

She looked down at two silvery stones in her hand. "He with the key wins," she muttered, and my heart kicked.

"Max—"

"—taught his grandson well," Catrina said. "Without the key, the Lady will never be whole again."

I could see her in my mind's eye, the intricate collection of colors and shapes to create her serene expression, and the babe in her arms, the sword on her hip and the jug at her feet. "We need to find the other half."

"It has already been found," Catrina said. "Long ago—"

"—by the Adrianos," Eve finished for her.

"Now that Tru has seen the pictures you e-mailed, she believes the tiles can be recreated."

"But without the other half, that leaves us with only a partial mosaic," Eve said. "The design is far too intricate to reconstruct without a key."

"Whereas the Adrianos now have both pieces…"

For a moment I just stood there. The gravity of all they were saying pushed down on me, but for the first time since I'd opened my eyes to the bright light of the farmhouse, I smiled.

Ignoring the pain in my side, I limped over to a small wooden chair, where my jacket lay in a heap. "No," I said, reaching into an interior pocket and pulling out the plastic bag I'd placed there before leaving Cornwall. "They don't."

I'd been ambushed, my tiles stolen, but I had not dropped the most critical ball entrusted to me. I had the vellum.

The game was still on.

"…gave me wings," Lexie said excitedly. "Like the cap'in."

I drew a deep, slightly smoke-tinged breath and let the

sound of my daughter's voice wash through me. She was safe. She'd made it out of the country undetected and unfollowed.

"Miss you," she said. Then, *"Mwah!"*

Even though it was a recorded message, I returned the kiss.

"Everything is fine here," her godfather, Lex added. In the background, I could hear Lexie chanting "baby-baby" and wondered how her first experience being around a real infant was going. She was wonderful with her dolls, feeding and bathing and dressing them, even putting them down for nighty-night.

"You just take care of yourself, *Brigid.*" The endearment made me smile. Lex had referred to me as a warrior goddess since we were kids. "And I'll take care of our girl."

Throat tight, I saved the message and limped out of the small room. Soot stained the narrow hallway, courtesy, Eve had explained, of a fire set by none other than Joshua's wife a few weeks before. It was nothing short of a miracle the farmhouse hadn't gone up in flames.

"Nadia!" At the sound of Olga's alarmed voice, I went very still. "Nadia, you must call me immediately."

I'd never heard her sound like that, so alarmed and…desperate.

"They say there is no way you could have survived," she said, more rapidly than I'd ever heard her talk. Her voice was thick. Broken. "That the fire, it was too intense, but I know that cannot be true, you are somewhere, you are safe, I know it."

She thought I was dead. The realization rocked me.

"Please *leanb mo croide,*" she said, crying incoherently. I could hardly make out her words, "You must call me."

The message faded into silence. For a long moment I stood there breathing deeply, staring down the staircase. Then, slowly, I hit Replay and listened again to Olga's frantic words. The message had been sent almost twelve hours before. I should call her, I knew. I should tell her I was safe.

But something held me back.

The next three messages were hang-ups, containing nothing but the sound of breathing.

The final message was from a man. "Not all things are as they seem, Nadia," he said, and the sound of his voice, brittle and wise and sad, stirred something inside me. It was Max, but I could not place the memory that hovered just out of reach. His hands. Reaching for me. "Sometimes illusion is your friend, sometimes your enemy. The key is knowing the difference."

The key.

I started downstairs, trying not to think about the pain streaking through my rib cage. Eve said nothing was broken, but that the car's air bag had likely caused deep bruising.

"Keep the faith," Max went on. "The hour is always darkest in those final moments before dawn. No setback lasts forever, *leanb mo croide*. The sun always finds a way to rise."

Leanb mo croide.

The warmth made no sense. The phrase should have sent a chill oozing through me—they were, after all, the same words Olga had used, both on the phone and throughout my childhood. Once, I'd asked her what they meant. She'd smiled and talked of the old language, said they simply meant that she loved me.

I did not think that Max Adriano loved me.

But it was blimey well warmth that I felt radiating from my chest as I saved the message and walked into the small room beneath the house.

And it was most certainly warmth when I saw the women gathered around the table—Catrina and Eve and a heavily pregnant Interpol agent named Ana, plus a tall woman with a light strapped around her head. The way she studied the tiles, much like an eager child might study the pieces of a puzzle, told me she was Tru.

I looked at the tiles, the photographs I'd e-mailed blown up and taped to the sides of a large box. Someone had jotted notes in the margins. On the table, the Lady was taking form.

I'd seen mosaics before. I'd always admired the painstaking detail required to shape so many disparate shapes and colors and textures into something beautiful and cohesive.

"There're so many," I whispered, moving closer. In my mind, I'd pictured the Lady smaller, more like the mosaic of the Last Supper that hung in the Adrianos' villa. That, I could have smuggled out by myself.

Not this.

Life-size, I realized. Tru had strung together enough of the stones and seashells and metals to illustrate that when all the pieces fit together, the Lady would be a life-size replica of a woman who remained shrouded in mystery even after the passing of thousands of years.

It was an amazing legacy for a woman of simple origins.

"The Adrianos have been collecting these for centuries," Catrina said, looking up from the table. With that effortless manner that was all hers, she brushed hair from her face and resecured it in a baroque clip. "Sometimes violently. Always discretely. Stealing what they could and securing them beneath their fortress, all the while hiding behind the carefully cultivated image of unassuming benefactor."

"Aligning themselves with whoever is in power," Ana added. "That's how they didn't get caught."

The shimmering array of tiles called to me. I stepped toward them and put out my hand, ran my fingers along what had to be a priceless collection of crystals and semiprecious stones. Some I recognized, like lapis and agate and amethyst.

Others, like a crescent so blue it reminded me of the sea, I'd never seen before. "These came from the Adrianos?" I asked.

"They came from our ancestors," Catrina corrected. "The Adrianos merely imprisoned them."

"Until we liberated them." This from Tru, with a pleased girl-next-door smile.

I couldn't help but return it. "Brilliant." And it was.

Gathered around the table, they told me of a woman named Aubrey, a thief who'd once worked for the Adrianos. She'd turned against them, aligning herself with Max to clean out the Adriano vault shortly before Scarlet died. According to Catrina, Scarlet had been at the Adriano compound when the theft occurred.

"Aubrey tried to warn her," Catrina added. "But Scarlet was too good, too enamored with Caleb, to believe he would hurt her."

I wasn't sure which was worse. Being too in love to accept the dark possibilities, or being too jaded to allow one's self to believe in the possibility of being so in love.

But I did know, I realized, glancing at a rustic old bookcase. On it sat a picture of a smiling Scarlet and an urn that looked like a perfume bottle. I was alive. My sister was not.

Emotion stabbed into my throat, the sense of loss for something I'd never known, but always treasured. Fighting the cold swirl inside me, I picked up the blue stone.

The shimmer of warmth was immediate.

"Larimar," Tru said. "Extremely rare."

I closed my fingers around the smooth edges, as if I could somehow hold on to the warmth. "I've never seen it before."

"There's no reason you should have," Tru said. "Unless you lived in Atlantis."

That got me. My heart kicked as I glanced up and found her eyes glowing. "Atlantis?"

"Or the Dominican Republic," she amended, "which, according to numerous prophets, is all that remains of Atlantis."

I opened my hand and looked at the swirling blue stone in the shape of a crescent, and saw the vast, restless sea. "But that's impossible," I breathed. "The mosaic is almost two thousand years old. There's no way the priestesses could have traveled to the Dominican Republic, and even if they had…"

I let the thought dangle—and remembered the peculiar map of western Europe found among the relics of the Maya.

"That's where it gets interesting." Eve moved to my side and picked up what looked like a silver rock. "Iron," she said. "With properties found only in meteorites."

Catrina selected another tile, this one jagged with glimmering specks of gold. "And this one? No one knows."

"Space dust is my best guess," Tru said. "But I can find nothing like it documented anywhere. In some ways it's like glass, with tremendous cutting abilities. But it's also soft, almost shifting."

I looked down at the amazing collection of rocks and stones, glass and seashells, that had once formed the Lady.

And would soon form her again.

The enormity of it stole my breath. Two thousand years before, women very much like Catrina and Eve—*and Scarlet*—had not only assembled these tiles into a mosaic of great beauty and even greater power, but they'd gathered the tiles. It should not have been possible. These women who lived so long ago should not have had access to gemstones found only in the Dominican Republic—or Atlantis—or on other continents not yet discovered.

How had they found the substances? How had they traveled around the world? How had they returned to France?

But then, there are many mysteries of the ancient world that defy all logic—the pyramids of Egypt, Stonehenge in England, the Dragon Castles of Greece and Cuzco in Peru, even the Giant's Causeway in Ireland.

Just because something seems impossible does not make it so.

Chapter 13

"There was an explosion west of here a few months back," Catrina said as we made our way through the damp, rocky fields of Minervois. We'd left the farmhouse thirty minutes before with Eve, en route to a hot spring. She insisted it would help ease my sore muscles.

Considering where I was headed with the sunrise, I was quite interested in healing. With each chilly breath I took, my ribs reminded me they were bruised. My whole body ached. But it was more of a dull pain, nothing sharp or debilitating—nothing that would keep me away from the Adriano compound in Naples—or Joshua.

He'd said he wanted to help. I would give him his chance.

A north wind whipped through the valley, as if some higher power was trying to push us back. In the distance, the ancient walled city of Minerve loomed like the sole survivor of another time, perched defiantly on a desolate outcropping.

Below, the Cesse and Briant Rivers merged to create an unforgiving gorge.

Our destination, according to Eve, lay not too far beyond.

"What kind of explosion?" I asked Catrina. Every time I so much as looked at her, something inside of me lightened. She had such an air of nonchalant sophistication to her, the way she walked, the way she talked. It would be easy to see her strolling among the trendy Parisian boutiques.

But now she hiked through the remains of a vineyard. After years of decline, only a few grapevines remained, thin and struggling and unlikely to produce fruit. Catrina, with her hair in a ponytail and a backpack slung over her shoulders, hacked her way through them with uncanny grace. In place of her tailored clothes, a bulky field jacket dwarfed her, making her willowy body look petite and delicate, despite the khakis, denim button-down shirt and work boots.

I was quite certain those among the Paris elite would never have guessed Catrina Dauvergne even owned work boots.

"That is the question." She swiped at a tangle of vines. "By all appearances, the building was merely a barn behind a winery."

"A winery owned by the Adrianos," Eve interjected, shoving the dark curls from her face.

I almost stopped. Almost.

"And the barn turned out to be a biochemical lab," she added, and in that instant, I knew. I remembered. The outbreak in the small Swiss village…

"I was there," Eve said, frowning. "No matter what kind of spin the family put on it, I know what I saw—who I saw."

"My God," I whispered, and once again marveled at the family's ability to deflect blame. "How could no one have noticed what was really going on?"

"It is simple, really," Catrina, standing ankle-deep in mud

several steps ahead, said. "For years there have been strange goings-on in this region of France, ever since that book about the Holy Grail was published."

Ah, yes. I knew the book well. And the controversy.

"The area has been flooded with those who do not belong," she added, trudging forward heedless of the sucking mud. The Languedoc region was known for its extreme weather and high amounts of rain. But even the oldest villagers could not recall such a rainy winter. The rivers swelled, running viciously down from the mountain. "So-called pilgrims in search of what is true and what is urban legend.

"How did the priest Saunier of Rennes le Château get his wealth?" she mused. "Is it possible he indeed found the genealogy of Jesus, proving that he had, indeed, married Mary Magdalene? Did he use this to blackmail the Vatican?"

My pulse quickened. I glanced around the countryside, the ancient Marian temple abandoned somewhere below, Minerve perched against a leaden sky, stone farmhouses scattered on the brown hillsides, and felt the stirring deep inside. Time marched on, but here in this quiet land, there were no cars or highways, no convenience stores or shopping centers. Only the whisper of the wind and the rush of water, the song of birds.

It was like walking back in time.

"According to some," Catrina said, stopping to study the thigh-high grass around us, "there never was a lab. Its existence was simply a cover to divert attention from the truth."

Eve stumbled. "What truth?"

"The Holy Grail," Catrina said simply, and this time it was I who almost tripped.

"Excuse me?"

Her eyes were narrow, intense. Hair blowing into her face, she stared toward the west. "*Certainement,* it is just rumor," she said. "But Rhys believes it is possible. There are caves throughout this region. In all these foothills and mountains. Some are tourist destinations." Rennes le Château, with its infamous network of mystical caverns, was only an hour and a half away by car. "Others are too treacherous to allow the public inside. They all hold secrets."

Spatters of moisture drifted against my face. "Rhys thinks the lab was a cover for a cave?"

"That's ridiculous," Eve practically snarled. She owned a chateau near the lab. "I was there. I saw it."

But Catrina went on. "Perhaps. But Rhys has spent years in search of the Holy Grail. That is how we met," she said, brushing the damp hair from her face and refastening her ponytail. "The Grail, the Ark of the Covenant, King Solomon's treasure…they are rumored to be hidden in this area."

Courtesy of the priest, Saunier, I'd heard. "The explosion? Rhys thinks it's connected?"

"Peut-être," Catrina said, with one of her trademark shrugs. "Perhaps not. It does make one wonder, though, does it not? Rhys drove over a few weeks ago and spoke with an old farmer who once saw a little girl playing on a rocky ledge. He tried to follow her, was concerned she would be hurt. But he never found her…until a week or so later when he saw her in the same area. This happened again and again."

Chills shot down my spine, despite the warmth of my jacket.

"He thought perhaps she was a ghost. His wife thought she was a figment of his addled mind. For a long time, he did not see her at all. And then he spotted her again, shortly before the explosion."

The path grew steeper. I placed my foot carefully on the loose stones and stepped upward. "This girl? She was in the area at the time of the explosion?"

A choked sound broke from Eve. I twisted toward her

against the backdrop of rock and gray sky, looking at Catrina with the oddest expression. "Eve?" I asked. "What's wrong?"

She shook her head. "Rumors," she said softly. "Stories and urban legends. I was there. The lab was real—surely Rhys knows better than to believe everything he hears."

"Of course he does," Catrina said, toeing the mud off her field boots. "But he also knows not to merely discount something because it seems implausible."

"What if there is no Grail?" Eve asked. "What if it is all a hoax? A centuries-old parable designed to test man's faith?"

Catrina straightened. "There is always that possibility."

The wind rushed around a rock formation and slammed into us, making me glad I'd secured my hair in tight French braids.

"In medical science," Eve stated, "we start out trying to pinpoint a disease or find a cure, and while that is important, I have found that the search is every bit as critical. Along the way, we discover so much that would have remained a mystery." There was a glow in her eyes now, a passion that revealed just how deeply she loved her work. "Take something like penicillin. An accident," she said, and finally a smile touched her lips. "An accident that has saved countless lives."

"Rhys knows that." Catrina sounded a tad defensive. Lovers or not? I couldn't tell the exact parameters of their relationship, but the bond between them ran deep. "He once said that in searching for the Grail, one invariably found oneself."

Eve seemed to relax. "Exactly."

But I had to wonder. Perhaps the Grail *was* the world's first urban legend. But legends, I'd learned, quite frequently had their origins in the shadows of truth.

Look at the Marians.

"There it is," Eve said, before I could question Catrina further about the explosion that may have bridged myth and reality. I turned to see her pointing to a waterfall cascading from a high outcropping. "Isn't it beautiful?"

Against the late afternoon glare, I lifted a hand to my brow and felt my breath catch. A silvery ribbon streamed down against brown rock, dropping into a thermal pool we could not yet see. But the promise of it gave me a burst of energy despite my injured ribs.

"Stunning," I whispered, fastening another button of my denim jacket. The temperature was dropping—I suspected it couldn't be more than ten degrees Celsius. I hoped the pool Eve spoke of was as warm as she'd indicated. "How much longer?"

"Thirty minutes. Less if we hurry."

We did just that, picking up our pace until we came to a narrow stream. Catrina lingered there, letting the flow of water rinse the mud from her boots. Once we reached the other side, I reminded her she'd mentioned there were several theories as to the explosion.

"And none of them matter," Eve said. "I was there." This was at least the third time she'd said that. "No matter what those bastards say, I know for a fact the Adrianos used that laboratory to manufacture the virus that decimated an entire Swiss village."

I tore my gaze from the waterfall and looked at Eve, found in her eyes the same horror that twisted through me. And for a moment I was back in Saint-Tropez, staring at a chronicle of destruction. I hated to voice what I'd seen, but she and Eve needed to know.

"When I was at their villa, I found a stack of magazines about the outbreak." Beside me, Catrina sucked in a sharp breath. "And the Paris earthquakes," I added. "The blackouts— and the volcanoes." I'd written them off as human fascination with tragedy. Now I knew the truth.

"The apocalypse." That from Catrina. "Just as Scarlet warned." Then she let out an odd little half laugh. "We can only hope the eclipse is not upon us."

Steam rose from the secluded pool in a shimmering veil. All afternoon the wind had whipped at us, but at the base of the Pyrenees, with limestone cliffs on three sides, stillness permeated. There was only the sound of water falling from a steep ledge, and the smell of sulfur. Even the birds had quieted, as if they, too, realized this was a sacred spot.

Because instinctively I knew that it was.

Scarlet had known, too. Immediately I recognized the waterfall from one of the last pictures posted to my sister's Web site. She'd been here….

The pool was small, maybe five times the circumference of an average well. Water fell in a silvery curtain from all three sides of the rock face, creating a rainbow as it cascaded down like never-ending rain.

"Scarlet was big on ecliptics," Catrina was explaining as she shucked off her boots. I'd asked her what she meant by her comment about an eclipse. "It's an astrological philosophy—"

"I'm familiar with it," I told her, but the memory disturbed me. It was Olga who'd talked of ecliptics, the two to three thousand year intervals during which specific zodiac signs affected society. The pragmatist in me rejected the theory, and yet I could not deny phenomena such as the impact of Mercury going retrograde.

I'd had more than just my hard drive crash under Mercury's negative influence. I'd lost two fellow agents to a still unexplained plane crash.

Catrina tossed a muddy boot toward a scattering of small boulders. "Scarlet, of course, believed the Age of Pisces was drawing to a close," she said, tossing her second boot.

"She blogged about it," Eve said. I turned to see that she'd slipped out of her jacket and boots and was now working at her shirt. "She felt Pisces had been a restrictive era, a time that balanced progress with fear, advancements with closed minds. Duality. Haves and have-nots. Masters and servants."

"Paradise for the Adrianos." Catrina smirked.

I needed to spend some time with Scarlet's blogs. They were going to be as close as I would ever come to knowing my sister. "But bad for the Marians."

I stepped toward the pool, not quite sure where the words had come from.

"Exactement." Catrina shrugged out of her shirt, revealing a low-cut swimsuit. "According to your sister, the Marians realized they could not survive the Age of Pisces intact. Dark forces had already driven them underground. They knew the way of the goddess would never be accepted until the Age of Aquarius arrived. This is why they dismantled the Lady and sent her into hiding. They knew society would continue its decline, and if they did not take steps to preserve their way of life, the promise would be forever lost."

"It sounds far-fetched," Eve said. "But one must only look at history to realize the Marians were right. From the time of Christ on, books reflect the history of man, not woman."

And that's what the Marians had been. Powerful women whose vision for a future devoid of war and famine and oppression had threatened a male-dominated society.

Going down on my knees, I dipped my hand into the warm water simmering above a series of stone steps leading down into the depths. The sigh was automatic. The fear was not.

For most people, that would not have been a monumental realization. Slipping into a secluded lagoon or a tide pool, a thermal spring, is considered a decadence. But water and I have never gotten along, other than for drinking and bathing, or, after great discipline, in a swimming pool.

The dark rock forming the pool made it impossible to see what lay beneath, and yet, kneeling there beside the swirling water, I felt as I did while practicing yoga or meditation. The world around me shifted and blurred, thickened. Softened.

Time moved in circles, I'd always thought. There was no beginning, no end. Steam had risen from this heated pool for centuries, a constant in an ever-changing world. It was man and woman who came and went. Eve, Catrina and I were not the first to seek restoration in the warm waters, and we would not be the last.

"One of her last entries was about the Age of Aquarius," Catrina was saying. I felt more than saw her join me by the pool's edge, a mosaic of movement to my right. "She believed the coming age to be one of enlightenment and equality."

"Perfect for the Marians," Eve added, joining us.

I cupped my hands and brought water toward me, let it trickle down my neck and chest.

"Which means bad for the Adrianos." Catrina knelt beside me, but her voice seemed to come from much farther away. "Your sister discovered a school of thought that it is the time of transition when the world is most vulnerable to chaos."

As if in a trance, I looked toward the back of the pool, where water trickled down the rock. Something wasn't…right.

"Scarlet maintained that many ancient structures, such as Stonehenge, are aligned in accordance with ecliptics. When the planets align and the comet appears, when the sun goes into total eclipse, that is the moment their true power is known."

Dry-eyed, I stared at the never-ending supply of water spilling into the pool. There was no way out, I realized.

And yet the water level did not rise.

The misshapen pieces started to fall together, much as the

mosaic of the Lady was beginning to form at Catrina's farm-house.

"It sounds pretty woo-woo," Eve said.

Catrina agreed. "I did not believe her," she admitted. "But there was a definite connection between the solar flares and the earthquakes. Ever since I heard a recent news report about a rare alignment of the planets, I find myself looking toward the sky…."

Earthquakes in Paris, allegedly the result of ley line manipulation. Power outages. The outbreak in Switzerland, confined to a small village sitting atop a ley line. Seas rising. Volcanoes smoking.

The Adrianos chasing down the pieces of the mosaic, establishing a winery in the ley-line-rich region where the Marians' temple once thrived.

Tru's theory that the unusual configuration of gemstones and metals and other substances could create a magnifier.

The Age of Pisces drawing to a close.

The Age of Aquarius upon us.

Suddenly I couldn't breathe. It felt as if the weight of all those who had come before me—and those who would come after—was pushing down on me, urging me. Nudging.

Reminding me.

The secluded pool dissolved into a fractured picture, and though I heard Catrina and Eve's voices, I could not make out what they were saying.

There was only the water cascading down the craggy cliff, the gurgling warmth of the thermal pool—and the staggering truth.

Scarcely able to breathe, I pushed to my feet and dived.

Chapter 14

Swirling waters closed around me, not in hostility or menace like the frigid water in the cove along the Irish coast, but like the arms of a mother cradling her babe to her chest.

There was no darkness, despite the fact that I kept my eyes closed. Only shimmers of blue and streaks of white, like lightning dancing against a twilight sky. I relaxed and shifted into a strong breaststroke under the water. My fingertips skimmed the slippery rocks at the bottom of the pool, while the stringy remains of leaves and roots flirted with my toes.

The current increased toward the back, sucking me down. And still I swam, despite conventional wisdom that warned me to retreat. My lungs burned in protest, begged me to surface. But the shimmers of light seduced me deeper.

Farther.

I remember once, as a child, walking into the house and smelling fresh chocolate chip cookies. Eagerly, I'd started toward the kitchen in my muddy sneakers. My mother yelled for me to come back, but I scarcely heard her words. Even if they'd registered, I would not have cared, the promise of something fantastic just around the corner was so strong.

I didn't care now, either. Almost feverishly, I ran my hands along the slick boulders at the rear of the pool. The rocks were smooth, worn.

Then my hand slipped deeper.

I smacked against the wall, ramming my shoulder. The current kept rushing against me, fast and strong and eager, like water racing toward an emptying drain.

The desire to follow stunned me.

But the need for air punished—I'd been underwater for well over a minute.

Need won. Ripping myself away, I scissor-kicked toward the surface and burst into the mist, opened my mouth and tried to gulp in air, coughed instead.

"Nadia!"

"What are you—"

But I was under again, fighting the urge to cough as I shot back down toward the drain. This time the descent was quicker. Knowledge guided me. The flow of the water promised.

One by one, the women enter the small room. Minutes later, they emerge and scurry away. The ritual has been going on for days.

The chant of the elders fills the air. Drawn by the rhythmic pulsing of an old bamboo fountain, Naysa puts her hands to her rounded belly and waits her turn. The child is growing. At first she refused to believe the healer, who confirmed the elder's suspicions. That before he'd betrayed her, Joakim had left her with his child.

But with every day and week that pass, the truth grows within her. She carries life.

"We worry about you," the dark-skinned elder says when at last Naysa enters the small chamber. "Your sadness is not healthy for you or the babe."

She knows that. But no matter how much the priestesses try to console her, she knows she has let them down. She has failed.

"The rock that was taken from you," another priestess says. "How would you like the opportunity to replace it?"

Something inside Naysa shifts, like a weight sliding off her soul. "Replace it?"

"All is not lost, dear one," says the priestess who has cared for her so tenderly. "Time is still on our side." Her smile turns radiant, hopeful. "There is a way. There is a place...."

Using my arms, I glided through the opening in the rock and let the current carry me. Almost immediately the water grew cooler. And even though I was submerged, the sounds changed. Became lighter. Echoed.

I'm not sure what made me kick toward the surface. But I'll never forget the absolute euphoria that overcame me when I broke through the water and opened my eyes to the beauty of the cave.

I did not need Catrina or Scarlet or anyone else to tell me where I was. The truth surged through me, swirled around my soul.

After six centuries in exile, a Marian had come home.

On the outside, time had marched on, the world changing in ways that the priestesses who'd last bade farewell to their temple and each other, a way of life they'd treasured, had certainly been unable to imagine. During the time of Pisces, progress had been measured in terms of science and industry and technology, fact and theorem replacing intuition and instinct. Steel and concrete replaced trees and grass. Even our water we now drank from bottles, rather than streams.

But here in the cave the Marians had been forced to abandon, time stood still. The rocks may have shifted, water levels risen and fallen, new crystals formed, old ones crumbled, but I had no doubt that a Marian stepping forward through the centuries would have felt as at home among the stalactites and stalagmites of the present as she had hundreds of years before.

Not much light leaked through cracks in the thick walls, but not much light was needed. The cave shimmered and glowed on its own, hundreds of amazing formations glistening around me like a winter wonderland drenched in icicles and pearls and odd, amazing corals.

Water trickled and echoed around me, oozing down the walls and dripping into puddles, rushing quietly with the river that had carried me in—the river whose mild current the Marians had swum against to exit the temple after the main entrance had been destroyed.

Perhaps I should have felt like a trespasser, an interloper on hallowed ground. I didn't. There was only the incredible sense of…homecoming. The Marians had long since fled, but the temple they'd been forced to abandon remembered, preserving their legacy as fiercely as the women who'd scattered with the wind, carrying with them only tiles of the Lady and hope for the future.

The swirl of cool air against my damp body was unmistakable. I turned, fully expecting to see someone standing behind me. I didn't, of course. But that didn't mean she wasn't there.

"Scarlet," I whispered. And then came the tears. They dampened my eyes and spilled over, but I made no move to brush them away. There was no shame here in the lost temple, no need to be strong or brave. There was only an overwhelming glow of promise, and a shattering sense of loss.

She'd been so close. Scarlet, with all her quirks and seemingly far-fetched theories, had been extraordinarily near to finding the lost temple. She'd stood outside, in front of the waterfall. With Caleb. Maybe they'd slipped into the warm restorative waters, never knowing that the object of their mutual obsession lay so close at hand.

So close.

There were those who spoke of destiny and legacies, who debated whether free will existed at all. Like most things, I did not understand why there had to be an either-or, why destiny and free will could not live side by side. Scarlet had pursued her destiny with a joyous zeal few ever achieved. But in the end, free will led her into the arms of an Adriano.

Or had it? Had free will drawn her to Caleb, or had that, too, been destiny?

And what of my destiny? My free will?

Had it not been for Scarlet's death, I would have continued living in the dark, knowing nothing of my heritage, of the legacy that my ancestors had so carefully veiled. I would never have met Catrina or Eve. I would never have traveled to Ireland and found the Madonna Key, never have learned that my parents did not abandon me by choice, but by death.

I would never have seen a side of Joshua that made me doubt everything I'd once feared, and yearn for a future I'd never imagined possible.

And I never would have been standing on the bank of a tranquil underground river in a spacious chamber of dazzling crystal and shimmering beauty.

Now I did lift my hand and swipe at the tears. The possibility that my sister had to die in order for me to fulfill my destiny disturbed me on too many levels to count.

Blinking against the salty burn, I patted my hands against my cargo shorts—while Eve and Catrina had stripped down to their swimsuits, I'd been too focused on the steamy pool to do so. I'd dived into the water fully clothed, with my keychain penlight in a pocket and my 9 mm strapped around my hips.

It was the penlight I reached for, the same light that had guided me through the castle only a few days before. My hand found the cool cylinder and I twisted on the light, saw the pouch.

At least, I thought it was a pouch. Stooping on the slick gravel leading to the water, I picked up the leathery object and realized it was a water skin, the kind carried in the distant past. Dropped there, no doubt. By a Marian.

I swiveled on my feet and panned the light around the cave, saw the majestic archways. There were three of them, fanning out in the shape of a crescent. One of them had been blocked by a rockslide. Perched up against the limestone, carved stone angels supported sconces for torches. But now they stood empty.

Archaeology had been a favorite pastime of my father's, and though I'd never accompanied him on a dig, I had seen photographs. And instinctively, I realized the cave was most likely an outer chamber.

The true temple, where the Marians had worshiped, lay beyond the shadows, through one of the three passageways. I could almost hear the echo of their chants, set against a faint, rhythmic thumping from within the darkness. Beckoning.

Promising.

Living still, after all this time.

I was stepping toward the center arch when I saw three skeletons—two large, one fairly small. Shrouded in the tattered remains of robes they no longer needed, they lay at the base of one of the walls, one of the larger giving shelter to the smallest one, and I could not help but see a mother and her child. They'd been running. Toward the river. Away from persecution and toward the promise of freedom.

They'd never made it.

Lexie, I thought, and my throat closed up. Through the vestiges of a time long gone, I could hear the mother cry out, feel the hard rhythm of her heart as she fought to protect her child. Some things were universal, knowing no bounds of time or place or creed, like a mother's fierce love for her child. There was no greater bond. Death was a small price to pay. I would accept it unflinchingly, if I knew my daughter would live on.

Shaken, I started toward them, but the sound of a loud splash had me spinning, reaching for my 9 mm.

Until I saw Catrina.

She rose from the water like a drowned goddess, her hair splayed against her face, mascara smeared, mouth set in a mutinous line. "Do you have any idea—" The furious words died as shock darkened her eyes. *"Mère."*

Her voice was quiet now, drenched in reverence and awe. *Mother,* she'd whispered, and somehow the one word said it all.

Some would call the cave a tomb. It was cold and damp, filled with the remains of a time and people the ages had left behind. But for Catrina and myself, stepping into the underground sanctuary was like stepping back into a mother's welcoming arms.

There was peace, and hope. And promise.

The columns guided us. There were hundreds of them, carved with unparalleled beauty, not by man or woman, but by nature. There'd been no need to adorn or embellish. The hand of man could not compare to the hand of God.

Stalagmites streaked with quartz or amethyst rose into pillars, meeting stalactites that swept down from natural gothic arches, framing a portal leading into the darkness. The stones' uneven, increasingly thick crystalline bands refracted the beams of our flashlights into rainbow prisms along the rock floor, seducing us closer to the source of the eerily rhythmic echo.

There were no words. Talking seemed sacrilege. Neither Eve, Catrina nor I had said as much, but we hadn't needed to. We'd fallen into silence the moment we entered the middle passageway. Catrina walked ahead of me, regal despite the way her wet clothes clung to her body. I glanced back at Eve, saw she still clutched the animal skin flask she'd reached for as soon as Catrina had led her into the cave. The color had returned to her face, at least. For a moment there, when she'd pulled herself from the river and reached for the flask, her eyes had been like dark pools against skin unnaturally pale. Now she simply clutched the flask in one hand, the penlight from the bag she carried with her everywhere in the other.

Maybe I should have been cold. It must have been chilly in that damp narrow corridor, so deep within the earth. And I was wet from my swim through the hidden entrance.

But my body felt much as it did when I held myself in the pose of a warrior, with my muscles warm and my blood pumping.

Maybe I should have been frightened. We had no idea where the narrow passage of stalagmites and stalactites led. The muffled thumping grew louder the deeper we progressed, as if something were alive in the heart of the cave. Waiting.

But I thought of my sister, my mother, my grandmother, and all those who'd come and gone before me, and there was no fear.

Back in the other direction, we explored several passageways, finding in one a weaving of stone that seemed to suggest it had once been the main entrance. So did the armor-clad skeletons. Clearly there'd been some sort of struggle. But now only great piles of rock remained, blocking our progress.

As the corridor narrowed, the rhythmic sounds shifted into more of a low, double thump, repeating several times per minute. I could almost hear the chant of a forgotten sisterhood leading the way.

Destiny, I thought again, and as the passageway spilled into a crescent chamber, my breath caught.

Many years before, for my tenth birthday, Olga gave me a geode. It had been cut in half, revealing twin chalices of shimmering crystals. Hundreds of small violet prisms and pyramids had jutted up from the bottom, bunched together like a miniature, never-ending mountain range, and when the sun glinted against them, I saw an enchanted kingdom.

That geode had fit into my hand. Never had I imagined that one day I would emerge from a narrow passage deep within the earth, into a chamber the size of a modern movie theatre, and feel as if I were stepping into one of the enchanted kingdoms of my childhood.

"Mon Dieu," Catrina murmured over the hypnotic thudding. Thump, one, two, three, four, five, thump. Over and over. Pulsing around us. Steady but oddly hollow. Rhythmic, like the lullaby I'd played when Lexie was an infant, designed to mimic the soft, gurgling sounds of a mother's womb.

Thump, one, two, three, four, five, thump.

Slowly, I ran the beam of my penlight along the ancient walls of the temple, watched as the light of Catrina's lighter and Eve's penlight moved with mine, creating a waltz of light against darkness. Crystals glittered like stars. Against the far wall, a swell of rock resembling a frozen river of sparkling milk flowed from the darkness toward an intricately carved altar. Atop it sat a lone pottery basin, undisturbed and unbroken.

The fact that anything still existed told us that very few intruders had violated the temple's sanctuary before the rockslide closed it off permanently. And I had to wonder…had the rock-slide been an accident? Or the ultimate sacrifice on the part of the Marians?

Bits of dried flowers remained on the stone floor. Lavender, I thought as I inhaled the faint scent from another time. And sunflowers. The long-dried remains of the yellow that dotted the French countryside during the summer brought an odd splash of color to the room of shimmering pinks and purples.

"They left it alone," Eve whispered, stepping deeper into the inner chamber. Hypnotically, she lifted a hand to slide her fingers along a smooth formation jutting from the wall. Against the massive crystal, her hand looked like that of a doll's touching a full-length mirror of glimmering pink. She had that look in her eyes again, the same glassy, faraway gaze she'd had in the church in Paris, when she'd talked of the priestesses who'd been forced to abandon their temple. "They never reached the sanctuary."

No, but there had been a struggle. The evidence remained, vivid against the backdrop of sacred beauty. Clay pottery lay broken on the ground, stone benches overturned near a collection of carved pomegranates. Lilies, I recognized. And the lotus, the symbol of resurrection and rebirth. Incense burners remained on the cool stone floor, spilling small dark piles of ash. Frankincense, I guessed.

Yes, places held memories. People came and went, but their legacies lived on, etched invisibly into everything they'd touched. Little bits of them remained, the love and the laughter, the pain and the sorrow.

In this sacred, crystal-enshrouded temple, where the Marians had retreated to escape persecution, there'd been great love and reverence, a tranquility that survived despite the passing of eight centuries. But there'd been tragedy, too, fear and desperation, in those final moments after the sanctity of the temple had been breached.

From behind me, I heard a muffled sound break from Eve, and I turned to see the beam of her penlight exposing a stalagmite carved into the image of a mother and child. And another, exposed by Catrina's lighter, of a woman in a flowing robe, her arms stretched toward the heavens in a pose I instantly recognized as gratification.

Our gazes met. Understanding was silent, but intense. To the echoes of a long-silenced chant, I slid my light along the back of the chamber and found a third woman carved into ancient stone, on her knees with her head bowed and her arms extended, palms facing upward. At her feet lay a broken jug.

Violence, I thought again. Brutality had swept the French countryside in the thirteenth century, an unholy witch hunt designed to wipe out all who did not conform with those in positions of power. Whole villages were slaughtered. Legacies shattered. Ancient doctrines and beliefs buried.

But they lived on here in this temple, and in the blood of those who had descended from the women who'd fled through the underground river. Despite the chaos, the Marians had preserved their legacy.

Silently, Eve and Catrina moved about the small chamber, as did I. Everywhere my light shone, beauty glimmered. And everywhere beauty glimmered, hope lingered.

Movement to my right kicked my heart into a fast rhythm. I spun and reached for my gun, froze when I saw not an intruder, but a long, circular tube made of stone. The awe was immediate. So was the understanding.

The hollow cylinder sat atop a pivot, adjacent to a trickle of water emerging from the limestone. The gentle flow dripped into the stone tube, filling it with water. My breathing shifted as I waited for what I knew would come next: the weight of the water tipped the tube into a basin, thumping it against a rock on its way down, then again on its way up.

The heartbeat of the temple.

"Catrina, Eve," I whispered, and felt them join me. We watched, listening in silence to the steady thrumming of the ancient fountain, a rhythmic pulse that had beat for hundreds of years, long after the last Marian had fled. A beacon waiting in the darkness for the day when the Marians came home.

"Mère," Catrina whispered again, but this time her voice was different. Low and throaty and reverent, yes, but thicker, laced with the awe of a lost child swept from the darkness by the arms of her mother.

My pulse quickened before I even saw the wall exposed by her flashlight. Together we stood and stared at the vacant expanse of stone, framed by jagged, crystalline tiles.

"She was here." Eve was the first to step toward the cool stone wall and put her hand inside the frame, where the mosaic of the Lady had once watched over the Marians like a shepherdess watching over her flock.

Catrina went down on one knee, whispering in French.

I felt the overwhelming desire to move my hand over my forehead and chest in the sign of the cross.

She'd been beautiful. I knew that; we all knew that. But nothing prepared me for seeing the gaping emptiness of the wall, where the Lady had worked her magic. Nothing prepared me for the jagged edges that remained, the broken tiles on the floor, the stone chisels scattered at what should have been her feet.

More memories came, belonging not to me, but to this place, this time in the past, when the Marians had first assembled the Lady, when they'd let her guide them, when they'd raised her up so her light could purify the world.

When they'd been forced to destroy her, tile by tile, so that she did not fall into enemy hands. It had been the only way to ensure there would come a day when she could be whole again, and her light could once again shine.

Destiny, I thought again, skimming my finger along the outside of the frame. Mine, Catrina's and Eve's. Scarlet's. Ana's and Tru's and the haunted woman named Aubrey who'd robbed the Adrianos of the tiles they'd spent centuries collecting. Lexie's.

The Adrianos. They could not win. They would not win. We had the majority of the tiles, access to the abandoned temple, half of the blueprint.

By the time the sun set on the morrow, I would have the other half, as well. And if the Fates decreed, I'd have something else. The truth, once and for all, about the man Joshua Adriano was, and the destiny that awaited us.

Not much light remained as we hiked along the rocky hillside toward Catrina's farmhouse. The sun had vanished behind the bank of clouds hovering over the mountains, leaving twilight in its wake. Facing us, a palette of pinks and purples streaked and swirled across the sky. Monet himself could not have painted a more picture-perfect vista.

Behind us, hazy gray deepened into darkness.

"Be careful," I advised, positioning my foot firmly against a slab of slippery limestone. The rain had stopped and the temperature might have actually risen a few degrees. But the wind continued to howl viciously through the graveyard of rocks.

We were not going back the way we'd come.

That afternoon, on our way to the waterfall, we'd walked through the tall, waving brown grass of the valley, affording anyone on the surrounding hillside a clear shot. We could have been picked off with ease—but then we'd sensed no danger.

Not so now.

Maybe my nerves were just wound too tightly. Or maybe my imagination was playing tricks on me, driven by the haunting images of the temple, the fountain that had tipped and poured for centuries, the lingering essence of frankincense and lavender, the remembered chant of the priestesses. The mother and child who had not made it to safety…

Maybe. But I'd been a spy too long to ignore the tingle that had whispered down my spine the second I'd emerged from the warm waters beneath the waterfall. I'd felt that way before, when an enemy watched me from afar.

The faint but large footprints leading from the water to the surrounding boulders had been real.

Someone had been at the pool while we'd been inside the temple. Someone had stood at the edge, gone through our things. And I was willing to bet that someone worked for the Adrianos—and continued to watch us. Cat and Eve had caught sight of him several times over the past few days.

"Still no signal," Eve said quietly, and I glanced over my shoulder to see her shoving her cell phone back into her pocket.

My heart thrummed hard. Our phones didn't work, but my 9 mm did. I held it in my hand, my fingers curled around the butt.

"Stay low," I advised. The boulders afforded protection, minimizing the chance of someone getting off a clean shot— if the Adrianos' man really was following us. As Catrina had pointed out, the Languedoc region is exceedingly popular with tourists. Anyone could have stumbled across the waterfall, seen our backpacks.

But that was not a chance I could take.

Nor was returning to the temple, now that we'd emerged. If anyone had been watching, and if they'd seen us come out, only to return, they would know we'd found something. They could have reinforcements in place and take the temple before sunrise, with us inside, while Ana and Rhys and the others slept. They would never know what happened to us—or what we'd found.

No, the only choice was to trudge back to the farmhouse,

grumbling loudly about the cold wet cave we'd spent the afternoon exploring in vain.

We all knew the chance we were taking. And we all agreed it was the only way. Once we hit the valley, we would fan out in three directions. If someone really was tracking us, and one of us went down, there was still the possibility of the other two making it back to the farmhouse.

"I cannot believe you made me do that," Catrina pretended to admonish as the wind pushed against our backs and bit through our damp clothes. "I did not enjoy—"

"Let it go," I pretended to fuss back. "Everyone makes mistakes."

"The mistake was believing the legend," she spat.

And I almost laughed. She really was quite good.

"We'll be home soon enough," Eve soothed in that gentle, maternal way of hers. She didn't have children of her own, I understood. Not yet, anyway. But she'd assumed guardianship of her sister's children. They were very lucky.

"Rhys is never going to let me hear the end of this." Catrina pouted, inserting some theatrical French into her diatribe. "He says I invite trouble."

Grinning at her antics as I was, it took me a moment for the scene to register. Then I rushed forward. "Catrina, get down!"

"It is not I who invite—" She stopped abruptly, as if she'd slammed into an invisible wall. Then she blinked.

I wasn't that far from her. Maybe three meters. But I could not cross them fast enough. In one of those disjointed, dreamlike sequences when everything slows, I saw her lift a hand to her chest, saw the bloom of red against her shirt. *"Merde,"* she whispered with a rueful laugh, then dropped to the slab of granite on which she'd been standing.

The moment released me, and at a dead run I tackled Eve as a volley of gunshots peppered us from higher in the hills.

"Stay down," I commanded, dragging my friend behind the safety of a boulder. Shards of rock flew against us, sliced into our arms. But I felt no pain. There was only Catrina, lying so horribly still on a slab of rock that looked hideously like an altar.

She was not a sacrifice we planned on making.

"Here." I shoved my 9 mm into Eve's hands. "Cover for me."

Her dark eyes met mine. "Always," she said, and I felt the vow shimmy through my blood. She was a healer, a woman trained to save lives. She'd taken an oath that sanctified life. But with Catrina lying so still, Eve took the gun in her hand and positioned herself behind the boulder, curled her finger around the trigger and aimed. "Tell me when."

"Now!" I instructed, and as shots blasted up the sparsely treed slope, I dashed to Catrina's body and crouched over her, saw her dilated pupils gazing blankly at me. "Hang on," I told her. Then, still ducking low, I dragged her to the safety of the big rock.

"Okay," I called to Eve, and as the echo of gunfire fell into silence, I saw her body sag, driving home the indelible courage required to go against every scrap of training she'd ever had. But just as quickly, she regrouped and crawled to my side, hovered over Catrina.

"Can you hear me?" she asked, and when Catrina blinked in response, Eve lifted a hand to soothe the dark-honey hair from her friend's face. "Good girl."

The fact that Catrina did not bristle at the endearment told me how frightened she really was.

"I can stabilize her," Eve said, laying her hands against Catrina's upper chest. "But we need to get her to a hospital."

Strength hardened her voice, but the concern leaked through. I twisted toward the hillside above us, knew that as long as the shooter had the higher ground, we could not carry Catrina to safety. Even if we hugged the rocks, the three of us would be an easy, clumsy target.

"I'm going after him," I said, scanning the slope for the least obtrusive path. "Here." Once again, I shoved my gun into Eve's hands. "If he comes near you, take him out."

Her hair was damp, slicked back from her face to reveal the horror in her eyes. "You can't take him alone."

"I'm trained for this kind of thing," I reminded her. I knew what I was doing. "Buy me time. Try to lure him into the open."

"Bastard," Catrina muttered. I turned to see her staring up at us, and even though pain glazed her brown eyes, determination glinted there, as well. "C-cannot let…th-them win."

"We're not going to." Then I leaned over this brave woman who'd loved my sister, and pressed a kiss to her forehead. "We're not going to."

Eve took my hand and squeezed. "Be careful." Our eyes met, but no more words were said. Silently, staying low, I darted from behind the boulder to another large rock. Then another.

I'd always considered darkness my friend, and now was no different. Few of the pink and purple swirls remained. There were only lengthening shadows, hiding me as I made my way up the slope. In firing his gun and taking down only one of us, the shooter had made a critical mistake.

He'd given away his locale.

"What did they promise you?" Eve called into the stillness of dusk. Horrified, I swung back to motion her into silence, but too many shadows shifted between us.

"Money?" Catrina's voice, thick and husky, was laced with pain.

No! I wanted to shout as their words echoed around me, their voices would draw our assailant as effectively as a flare.

But then I saw movement above and to my left, and realized what my friends were doing. They were covering me with words rather than weapons, luring my target into the open.

"Whatever it was," Eve said, as I reached for a large rock and pulled myself alongside it, "they lied."

Fifty meters up the rocky slope, the dark form of a man emerged from behind the side of a small cliff. The darkness stole detail, but not the semiautomatic slung over his shoulder. He was a slender man, and if we had passed him on the cobblestone sidewalk of one of the villages, he would not have drawn our attention. But as he worked his way toward my friends, the stealth of his movements gave him away as a trained assassin.

The carpet of rocks shifted, taking my feet back with them. "They're bad people!" Eve kept going as I lunged for the rock face to steady myself, wincing at the sharp edges slicing into my fingers like razors. "Surely you heard about the outbreak of Spanish flu in Switzerland—over a thousand people dead, one lone pharmaceutical company stepping in with an antidote."

Wiping my bleeding fingers against my khakis, I kept my eyes on the target working his way toward Eve's voice. Soon, we would be parallel. Then, with only a few more steps, we would change positions. He would be lower, and I would have the high ground—and the leverage. As shadows deepened into darkness, I scanned the hillside and found what I needed.

"What do you think would happen if the virus had not been contained?" Eve pressed, God bless her. There was no fear in her voice, no hesitance, only the strong, solid resonance of a woman who refused to give up.

Catrina had fallen silent.

"Have you heard of a pandemic? Do you know how many people die? Millions!" she answered quickly. "Sometimes within hours of falling sick. It happened in 1918. The same strain that struck Switzerland a few months ago killed almost forty million people back then."

The switch happened. I stepped higher. He slithered toward Eve.

"Do you think these people you work for would give you the antidote?" she asked as I made my way toward boulders stacked like pumpkins waiting for fall.

The man, obviously a professional, said nothing in response to the grim scenario Eve painted.

"If your mother was dying, or your wife or your child, do you think they would care?"

My throat tightened. Few things frightened me, not even this trained killer. But pandemic, you better believe it did. Not for me, but for my daughter, and as I positioned myself behind the boulders, I couldn't help but wonder what would happen if Eve's dark prophecy came to fruition, and I was left with no choice but to reveal my secret to Joshua. To tell him of his second child, of the daughter with his eyes and my smile.

To ask him for an antidote, to spare her life.

The thought of him withholding the medication—it was not a thought I could consider.

"The answer is no!" Eve's voice was stronger now, drenched with a horror I understood too well. Time was draining away. With each second that passed, so did Catrina's chances. "The Adrianos will not let you live," she predicted as he lowered himself around a rock and lifted a pair of binoculars.

"Not after you've done their dirty work."

He was within range.

So was I.

"No matter how strong and vital you feel at the moment," Eve added, oblivious to the fact that he was closing in on the boulder she crouched behind. Forty meters. Maybe thirty.

Timing was everything. There would only be a brief window when I could take him out, without endangering Eve and Catrina.

"You are already a dead man."

They were prophetic words. I bent low and shoved against the boulder I'd targeted. Pain sung through me, but I strained with all my weight until the rock shifted, and the slide began, spewing smaller stones in its path. They all joined to race down the hillside.

The roar was incredible. The whole earth shook. From my vantage point I saw the man twist around, saw him start to run. But by then his fate had already been sealed.

A rock the size of a volleyball caught him first. It plowed into the back of his legs and sent him staggering. Then came another small boulder, this one more like a melon. It smashed into his back. His arms and legs flailed out and for a moment he seemed to take flight. Then he slumped into the shadows surrounding him and I could no longer see him at all.

I half ran, half slid after him. "Eve!" I shouted. "Stay where you are!"

"Hurry!" she called back.

The rockslide acted like an eraser, clearing an oddly slick but incredibly dusty path. I ran coughing through the debris, pausing briefly when the light of a sky suddenly full of stars revealed the man, lying beneath a scattering of smaller rocks. I checked his vitals, found him in bad shape.

Still, I relieved him of his weapons, binoculars, identification and phone before running to find Eve.

She remained exactly where I'd left her, safe behind a large, sheltering boulder, kneeling over an unmoving Catrina. Damp hair falling into her face, she'd torn open Cat's blood-soaked shirt, had ripped off her own to hold the soft cotton pressed against the right side of Catrina's chest.

"I've done what I can," she said, and grimly, her eyes met mine. "Get Rhys—fast."

And as I ran down the hillside, toward the others gathered at the farmhouse, I couldn't help but wonder if I'd been sent to summon Rhys the lover—or Rhys the former priest.

Who could still administer last rites.

Chapter 15

Blue was supposed to soothe. I'd heard it called a cool color, one that denoted peace and serenity, perfect for use in interior design because shades of blue, in essence, invited nature into our homes.

But as I stared at the unnaturally blue sky melting into the glittering blue waters of the Bay of Naples, I found no peace or serenity. There was only the bleak desperation in Rhys's blue eyes when he'd caught up with me a kilometer from the house. I'd called the second I'd gotten a cell signal.

Rhys had been out the door before I'd spoken two sentences. "Catrina's been shot," was all I'd had a chance to say.

"Where?" he'd demanded. Then, "How bad?"

I've seen a lot of things in my life. I've seen the face of a mentor in the ashen moment he realized a bad decision had just cost the life of several colleagues. I've seen survivors walking dazed among the ruins of what had been an outdoor café only minutes before. I've watched a man post a picture of his sister on a board of the missing, while another searched a row of sheet-covered bodies for his wife. I've seen a child clinging to her mother's limp hand, not understanding that she wasn't just asleep. I've been present when highly trained soldiers dropped to their knees and reporters in search of the next big story wept. I've seen courage and determination, honor and love and devotion.

And in that moment I saw Rhys Pritchard running toward me, I saw all of that and more clashing in his eyes. Even now, sixteen hours later, I'm still not sure I've ever seen so much emotion on one man's face, the fear and the horror and the hope. The love.

Except maybe in my dreams.

Sometimes, on those dark, dark nights, that's how Joshua would come to me. Sometimes out of the shadows. Other times, I would swear it was smoke from which he emerged, and that behind him, the world was on fire.

But none of that ever mattered. There was only Joshua, and the violent emotion drenching his eyes—the same emotion that had consumed Rhys the night before.

My heart twisted on the memory, and I forced myself to look up from the box in my lap, toward the fortress perched on a cliff overlooking the Bay of Naples. *Fortress* was my word. The locals referred to the sprawling compound built atop the ruins of an old castle as Palazzo Adriano.

The Adriano Palace.

From the narrow road where I sat in my rental, the old castle towers remained visible, crumbling after God only knew how many years. Scaffolding surrounded one of them, evidence of the refurbishment project the family had under-taken following a series of small earthquakes over the past several years.

Joshua was inside. I knew that. And while part of me burned to throw the rental into Drive, zip down the curving road and demand to see Joshua face-to-face, the massive iron fence surrounding the compound prevented that. So did the guards. They would demand to know who I was. What I wanted. Why I was there. They would inspect my car, find my 9 mm. They would notify Simon or Caleb.

Chances are, I would not leave the compound the way I'd arrived. So I sat in my car and flipped through a box of Scarlet's mementos while I waited for Josh to leave of his own volition.

Catrina. She'd been unconscious when Rhys and I reached her. Eve had hunched over her, stroking the hair from her face and murmuring encouraging words. An odd intimacy had veiled them, as if Rhys and I had stumbled upon Eve infusing Catrina with her own life force.

And then Rhys…my God. Silently, the man he was and the priest he'd been joined forces and knelt beside her. He'd draped his jacket over her, taken her pale hand in his and drawn it to his mouth, pressed a kiss inside her palm. And then he'd started to pray. At least, I thought he was praying. He spoke in an ancient language I hadn't fully understood. Latin, perhaps. But comprehension had not been necessary. Everything he felt, everything for which he'd prayed, had been evident in the stark planes of his face and the thick resonance of his voice.

Quietly, Eve and I had backed away.

Only a few moments passed before the others arrived, Tru and her fiancé Griffin, a few trusted locals. Together, we'd transported Catrina to a valley at the base of the hillside, where Ana had arranged for a helicopter to ferry her to a hospital in Toulouse.

Local authorities had found the would-be assassin. They thought he would live, but I seriously doubted it. Once the

Adrianos learned of his failure, Eve's dark prophecy would come true. The man would be discarded like the pawn he was.

And the temple…Tru and Griffin had staked it out as the helicopter had carried away Catrina and Rhys.

So here I was, on very few hours of sleep, dark glasses shielding my eyes from the bright sun and a scarf tied over my head, sitting in a white Peugeot on the winding road overlooking Palazzo Adriano.

Josh said he wanted to help me. He claimed to be on my side, to stand with me rather than against me.

I was about to give him the chance to prove his words.

To the frenetic beat of a Euro disco tune, I checked my watch and my mobile phone, all the while reminding myself to be patient. Despite the glitz and glamour portrayed by the movies, intelligence work is often tedious. Patience was not just handy, but mandatory. I knew how to wait things out. I'd waited hours for a courier. Weeks for information. Months for a lead. It was all part of the hunt.

But sitting in the shadow of Mount Vesuvius, watching the stone compound beyond the gates and knowing Joshua was inside—maybe with his son, Benny; maybe with his recuperating *wife*—an odd restlessness shimmied through me. The breeze from the bay carried with it a warm energy, almost like electricity. It crackled around me, like the surge I'd felt at the ruins of Dunluce and the mob of stones at the Giant's Causeway. I'd felt the same vibes the night before in the old temple room.

Some places more than carried memories. Some places possessed a breath of their own, a soul that had been here long before us and would remain long after we'd moved on.

The Adriano compound, it seemed, was one of those places.

Coincidence, I speculated, lifting my high-powered binoculars to scan the Adriano holdings. No way. I hadn't been lying when I said I didn't believe in coincidences. If two and two appear to add to four, chances are they do.

Agitated, I lowered the binoculars and took a swig from my water bottle, returned it to the cup holder and resumed thumbing through the box of Scarlet's belongings. This was actually the first quiet time I'd had to reflect on what she'd stashed away. And the pictures charmed me. I saw my sister as a young girl, when she'd looked so very much like me, with long brown hair and mischievous hazel eyes. And later, as a teenager, when her quirkiness had begun to emerge, giving her an eccentric identity so very different from the one I'd forged as the daughter of a peer of the realm. But in all of them she smiled.

Even the ones with Caleb. I'd seen most of those before, on her Web site. Now, in retrospect, the photo of her standing in front of the waterfall chilled me.

It was the small white envelope that changed everything. Three letters were printed on the outside with what I guessed was a thick marker: W. I. B.

Instinctively, something inside of me started to vibrate. I lifted the flap and withdrew a stack of small photos, flipped them over—and went very still.

The woman was turning away from the camera. She wore a scarf over her head holding back long, dark hair, much like I did at the moment, with sunglasses concealing her eyes. A long leather jacket hugged her down to her thighs. Her pants looked equally tight—and equally dark. It was an action shot. Scarlet had caught the woman looking away.

Clearly, she had not wanted her photograph taken.

The rhythm of my breathing deepened. I jerked off my sunglasses and squinted at the picture, told myself I was wrong. That it couldn't be. That the familiarity slicing through me was just my imagination. That the woman—

The next picture stopped the thoughts cold. Scarlet caught the woman head-on this time, on a street corner in New York City, with two enormous skyscrapers that no longer stood in the background.

This time her hair was down, long and straight, whipping around her angular face. But it was black in this picture, whereas it had been blond every time I'd seen her before. Again she wore an outfit of slim-fitting black—a color at stark odds with the creams and yellows and roses she'd loved for as long as I could remember.

And the way she stood, so taut and rigid…it was a pose I immediately recognized, but not one in which I'd ever seen my nanny stand.

The chill cut through me with blistering speed, and I found myself dropping the picture, flipping through the others, seeing Olga over and over and over again—in New York. In London. In Lisbon. In Frankfurt. Dressed in black.

Watching Scarlet.

Everything inside me shook. Denial backed up in my throat, a pasty residue that erased every happy childhood memory, replacing them with a dirty truth I could not reconcile.

Hands shaking, I picked up that first picture, the one that looked the oldest, and flipped it over, saw Scarlet's writing: "Woman in black—seventh sighting; Edinburgh, Scotland."

The date I recognized. It was the same week my father had died. Olga had been away, as she so often was, caring for her spinster aunt.

Except there was no aunt, never had been. And her stories of caring for her were nothing more than elaborate lies.

I pushed open the car door and gulped in as much of the crisp, late morning air as I could.

"Scarlet thought she was being followed," Giselle the shopkeeper had told me in what seemed like another lifetime, but

in reality had only been a few days before. *"She kept looking over her shoulder, saying something about a woman in black."*

Olga, it seemed, had been following my sister for a very long time. And she'd been in Saint-Tropez when Scarlet had died.

Then she'd returned to Cornwall, where I'd left my daughter in her care.

Now I wanted to vomit.

Forcing myself to think rationally, I turned back to the pictures and laid them on the passenger seat, studied them in sequential order. Scarlet had labeled and dated them all. The most recent was dated six weeks before. In Switzerland. In it Olga stood outside a small mountain café.

The dark sunglasses were conspicuously absent, as if Scarlet had captured her in an unguarded moment. Even the scarf was loose around her neck, allowing thick dark hair to flow down her shoulders. And the look in her eyes—the look in her eyes would have broken my heart if I hadn't already known the truth.

She looked…resigned.

Then I saw the man caught moving toward her.

Duke Simon Adriano—Joshua and Caleb's father.

I don't know how much time passed before my mobile phone rang. Maybe minutes. Perhaps only seconds. I only know that it took effort to shove aside the vertigo and click the talk button, recognize the voice of Eric Carbodes, bodyguard to Joshua's son, lover to reformed thief Aubrey de Lune, and the Marian man on the inside.

"He is leaving," he said, and my gaze darted from the road leading from the palazzo, to the guard shack. "He took the back way out."

The Bugatti Veyron streaked down the winding cliff road, taking hairpin curves at suicidal speeds. In pursuit, I accelerated out of a bend and glanced in my rearview mirror, expecting to see an armada of *policia* hot on our heals. Joshua wasn't just driving fast. He was driving as if his life depended upon it.

But only a few cars traveled the narrow road, and all of them drove at a leisurely pace.

Heart racing, I squinted against the high noon sun and did my best to keep Joshua in view. In a crowded city, that might have been impossible. But on this lonely stretch of road leading south from Naples, there weren't many places to hide—and there was nowhere to turn, except into rock, or into the bay.

Below, sun glistened off the noticeably choppy waters. They ebbed and swirled and crashed, whitecaps boiling and rushing forward much like they had in Ireland. The clerk at the car rental facility had commented that the sea level was higher here, as well, the result of an insanely rainy winter. Several of the popular beaches now stood underwater.

Jerking my car around a scattering of rocks in the road, I could see Joshua a kilometer or so in front of me, whipping around the last sharp curve and accelerating onto the long stretch of road that ran adjacent to the shore.

I did my best to keep up with him.

After five or ten minutes on the straighter road, I found the countryside changed. Cliffs gave way to lush, rolling hillsides dotted by small vineyards. Just beyond, rising up to the west, old Mount Vesuvius lorded over the countryside like a deceptively placid patriarch. My first thought was of intense beauty.

My second was of utter destruction.

My third was of Max Adriano.

How fitting, I mused, that the Adriano family had established their compound in the shadow of the old volcano, presenting one magnificent face to the world, while something deadly festered inside.

Joshua turned so abruptly that, had I not been paying

attention, I would have thought he'd vanished. Gunning the engine, I floored it to the intersection where he turned and began my way up the hillside. At first I thought I'd lost him. But after only a few minutes I realized the patch of light brown in the distance did not come from a village. At least, not an occupied one. In the blinding sunlight, I could see the city that had once been here, before the world turned black....

The seaside town bustles with activity. The narrow streets are crowded, filled with merchants, chickens and the occasional chariot. Fountains dance, and a piper plays. Children throw a ball across a courtyard.

Awed, Naysa drinks it all in as she makes her way toward the glorious complex of Roman architecture—the forum and the baths and the theater; temple after temple; magnificent residences mixed in with shops. Beyond the city walls, the sea sparkles and the mountain looms, but within the heart of Pompeii, it is man who dominates.

With a hand to her swollen belly, she reaches for a flask and drinks deeply. She tires more easily now, needs to stop more frequently. The sun lashes at her. But she is determined. She has been given a mission. A second chance.

She will not fail again.

The Cult of Isis, she has been told, with its promise of salvation after death, is unique among the Samnite culture. Among its followers she will find an old woman—

"Naysa!"

There's no time to run. No time to hide. Everything inside her rebels at the sound of his voice, but before she can even turn he is there, reaching for her from behind, his hands on her body—just like they'd been that night five months before, when they'd conceived the child that grew in her womb.

Then, he'd been a boy. There'd been no lines on his face. Then, there'd been a light in his dark eyes.

The Joakim who faces her now is a man. She sees it in his face, the harsh lines that fan out from the corners of his mouth. And she sees it in eyes that bore down into her as if she is the one who betrayed him.

"What are you doing here?" he demands in a voice she's never heard from him, one as hard and tight as his body. And the realization strikes her that, in the span of months, Joakim has lived years. Hard, dark years.

"It is none of your concern." She tries to twist from him.

But his grip is strong, and he will not release her. "You must go," he says. "You cannot be here."

She glares up at him. "Remove your hands."

"You must listen—" he starts, but then his gaze finds her belly, and his eyes go a little wild. "Oh Deus, Naysa!" he says, and then he's pulling her into his arms and holding tight. "There is so much you do not understand," he mutters, and the thickness in his voice stirs something deep within her. "There is great danger here. My family—the rock I took from you— Deus, it cannot be explained." Drawing back, he takes her face in his hands and gazes down at her, slays what is left of her heart. "I was wrong, and now it is too late."

The old wall remained, proud and defiant, crumbling around the haunting city so out of place there on the verdant hillside, yet so utterly, horrifically at home. In the millennia since Pompeii had served as both seaport and resort, life had moved on for the people of southern Italy. But here on the lush slopes of Vesuvius, the city itself stood almost exactly as it had on the shattering morning the old volcano had shown her true colors.

Once a coastal town, the fabled city now stood a good two kilometers from the water, the result of Vesuvius's fiery march to the sea.

Cars and buses converged on the archaeological site,

dragging traffic to a stop outside the parking areas that had sprung up beyond the city gates. Far ahead, I saw Joshua whip his expensive sports car into a small, open lot opposite one the public used. Adriano privilege, no doubt.

I'm not sure where I expected him to go. To the airport, perhaps. To another villa located along the coast. Maybe to Rome or the Vatican. The family Adriano maintained a long history of aligning with—or hiding behind—the church.

But a crowded tourist destination? It made no sense.

Frustration coiled through me, but I could do little about the snarl of vehicles. By the time I parked and paid my admission fee, worked my way up the steep ramp leading to the main gate—the one used centuries before—Joshua Adriano was nowhere in sight.

The legend of Pompeii has always fascinated me. But as I walked the narrow cobblestone streets, the scope of the tragedy struck me. Pompeii wasn't just a scattering of ruins connected by crumbling roads. It was a town. Once a jewel in the Roman Empire. A town that had thrived. A town that had died.

Throughout history, war and famine and disease have taken a toll on mankind. But there are very few instances of an entire community perishing at one precise moment. Atlantis, perhaps, but the lost continent is viewed as legend more than fact.

Pompeii was very much fact.

It was impossible to walk among the old stone buildings, to see columns rising up toward roofs that no longer existed, to see incredible murals on the walls of empty houses, to see fountains that no longer ran and grass growing where there should be none, and not feel the stark sense of life interrupted.

Memories, I remembered thinking in the temple room. They lived here, in the streets and buildings of Pompeii, silent echoes of all who had died here. Men and women, the old and the young. I had a hard time getting past that thought, the reality that I was, in essence, strolling through a graveyard. Lovers had died together, while others had been heinously separated. I tried to imagine what it would have been like to be one of the lucky ones who escaped, whereas those I loved—a husband? A parent? God forbid, a child?—remained behind.

Rounding the corner, I took in the splendor of the old theater, with darkened arches leading toward the amphitheater. The guidebook talked of stunning mosaics on the walls inside. But I did not enter.

"Pardon," I said to an elderly couple who appeared to be of Anglo descent. "I'm looking for a man…." But I did not have a picture of him. Only a description.

My questions were largely in vain. The tourists crowding the streets were more interested in history than each other. Very few paid attention to more than their guidebooks and the ruins.

Until I found an elderly tour guide. The second I described Joshua, his expression turned solemn. "The Adriano?" he asked, and my heart bloody well skipped a beat. Not only had the old man seen him, but he knew where he was.

There was no time to dwell on why the guide would know so much about Joshua.

Following his directions, I made my way toward the outskirts of town, into what appeared to be a residential district, where fewer tourists ventured. Small houses occupied the same street as larger ones, with no visible delineation between the classes. Palm trees shaded them all.

At the fifth building to my right, I turned and saw the massive entrance to one of the houses. It stood by itself, two Corinthian antas supporting a molded architrave. Picked out in the marble on the floor was one word: *HAVE*. Welcome.

With a frenetic riff of my heart, I stepped through the portal and into another time. The ornate vestibule welcomed me, and despite the passing of almost two thousand years, I would have sworn I smelled the embers of frankincense.

But that, of course, was impossible. Vesuvius had not succeeded in erasing the beauty or Pompeii's architecture and art, but smoke and ash had erased all scents of the past.

Elaborate shrines flanked me, Corinthian columns on stucco pedestals built into the walls. I followed them deep into the house, drawn by the soft sound of a child's laughter.

Clearly, I was not the only one present.

I stopped the second I reached the atrium. The vestibule spilled into an enormous center room, where once the Romans would have held their feasts. There was only stone now, palm trees and other deciduous plants, a fountain on the north end with a dancing faun in the center—and the murals.

They surrounded me, large, ornate mosaics of another time long before the Roman Empire. Alexander the Great, I guessed, and though it was Joshua I'd come to find, the ancient battle scene drew me in. I crossed to it and lifted my hand, ran my fingers over intricately placed stones of all colors and shapes and textures, so very, very like those that made up the mosaic of the Lady. Completely preserved, buried beneath ash for centuries, painstakingly excavated. The murals remained long after the creators had perished.

More laughter sounded, this time softer, and as I spun toward it, it changed to weeping. I followed it through a maze of narrow stone corridors, my maternal instincts in full drive.

I saw him the second I stepped into the overgrown garden. Between two Ionic columns he stood with his back to me, his feet shoulder width apart, his hands curled around a crumbling, waist-high wall overlooking a sprawl of ruins below. He wore dark pants and a dark shirt, and his head was tilted, not down as if in prayer, but up toward the faded blue sky, as if in challenge or dare.

I'd never seen a human being look more isolated.

The urge to go to him warred with everything I knew about common sense and caution. I'd come in search of him, after all. I had a deal to make. A question to answer.

But touching him was not part of my plan. Because he would turn to me then, and I would see his eyes. And then there would be nothing but him, and all my plans would shatter and I would do the one thing I wanted to do, what I'd wanted to do since the afternoon in Cornwall when he'd taken me in his arms and kissed me as he did in my dreams.

It wasn't fair that out of all the men I'd ever met, it was Joshua Adriano I could not forget.

Could not stop wanting.

He was an Adriano, damn it. His grandfather had murdered my grandparents and parents. His brother had, in all likelihood, killed my sister. I should hate him. I wanted to hate him.

But I didn't.

So I just stood there and watched him, saw his shoulders rise and fall with his breath, felt the hum of his presence across the old stone terrace that separated us, and realized that I no longer heard a child laughing or crying—that there'd never been a child at all. Just the memories of the grand old house.

"Do you feel it, too?"

His voice, thick and hoarse, seared through me. He turned with the words, and just as I'd known would happen, everything around me pretty much stopped. There was no cool wind sweeping through the gardens, no scarred stone walls and crumbling columns, no broken statue of an ancient god. There was only Joshua, and the scorched look in his eyes.

We'd come a long way from the time of Zoe and Antonio, just three years before. A long way from the raw passion that had erased training and identities and agendas. For so long I'd tried to convince myself that our affair was something brief and fleeting, that my mad dash through the tangle of olive trees had been the end. That there was nothing left between us. Nothing open-ended. Nothing simmering.

But in that frozen moment I realized how wrong I was. *Nothing* had ended that night three years before. In an odd way…everything had begun. Not just my daughter's life, but the latest chapter in a more intricate legacy than either of us had ever imagined, a dark dance that had bound our families for generations.

Destiny, I thought again. For three years this man had existed only in the shadows of my memories. Now, I faced him for the fourth time in scarcely a week.

My eyes met his, but I did not answer his question. Not with words, anyway. They seemed grossly inadequate.

"My grandfather used to bring me here," he said in the same hoarse voice. "I was five the first time. It was just the two of us, an Adriano rite of passage, so to speak."

The image formed before I could block it, that of a young boy and an older man, hand in hand, walking the oddly empty streets. It seemed…normal.

"He said we should never forget what happened here, that it was a lesson to all of us, a legacy we must remember and respect." Frowning, Joshua opened his palm, letting a handful of small rocks fall to the flat stone on which he stood. "History repeats itself, he says. Those who learn and improve come out on top. Those who don't…perish."

The wind swirled just then, sending dried, yellowish leaves dancing between us. "Odd words from Max Adriano," I mused.

Josh frowned. "My grandfather…he is a complicated man."

"He is a murderer," I corrected.

The shadows around him seemed to deepen. "And for that he will continue to pay dearly. But he is also the product of his upbringing and a student of history."

I could not let either Adriano off that easily. "You are a product of the same," I reminded Joshua. "Do you really believe that means there is only one path you can follow?"

The possibility chilled me.

"There were three of us," Josh said in that monochromatic voice. "The heir, the spare, and the donation for the church."

The Adriano boys, anyway. Rumor had it there were sisters, but I'd never found anything concrete as to how many—or if they even existed. The Adrianos were a patriarchal family. Sons were valued. Daughters were...not.

As the youngest male, Josh did not need to say what his fate would have been. Men like Rhys Pritchard proved that not all disciples of the church had to be middle-aged and balding, and yet I could not imagine cupping my hands for communion and lifting my eyes to see Joshua Adriano gazing down at me.

Shaking off the unsettling image, I realized Josh had yet to look away from me. But then, I wasn't sure that he really saw me. Wasn't sure he saw anything.

To the average tourist tramping through Pompeii, I suspected, Josh would look devastatingly handsome standing in the shadow of that old column—black really was his color. But to my trained and frustratingly biased eye, there was something off. Something sad. I'd seen the reckless way he'd driven along the narrow cliff road. And now there was the emotionless tone to his voice and the bleakness in his eyes.

Resolved was an odd word to describe him. But it was the only word that fit.

"My father was obsessed with Aaron," he said, as the sounds of a flute from across town drifted in on the breeze. "They would go off together for long periods of time. Talk in soft voices and stop whenever someone else came near." Finally, the ghost of a smile touched Joshua's mouth. I suspected it stemmed from the ghost of a memory. "It used to drive Caleb crazy. He was convinced they were keeping something from us. That by being the oldest, Aaron was heir to more than just the family business holdings. Caleb insisted there was more to being an Adriano than money and privilege. He swore there was a reason every generation had to produce at least three sons, that there was some dark legacy the family had to ensure lived on."

Despite the thick leather of my jacket, I shivered.

"There are tunnels beneath our house. We all knew they were there, leftovers from the first castle. I never spent much time down there, but Caleb was obsessed with them, always believed they held more significance than anyone wanted to admit."

And according to Aubrey, young Caleb had been right. The Adrianos had not only stored the mosaic tiles they'd been amassing there, but in a small, dark oubliette, they'd some-times stored their enemies.

"Did he ever find anything?" I asked.

Josh's eyes went flat. "While Aaron was with my father and Caleb was in the tunnels, I would come here. My mother said my fascination with this place where so many died was un-healthy, but she wasn't around much, and there was always someone willing to drive me. By the time I was eleven, I was giving unofficial tours."

My throat went curiously tight at that revelation. Joshua and I had shared a lot since we'd met—passion, betrayal, then sus-picion. But secrets were something new. And while the agent in me knew better than to trust the rare glimpse into the boy he'd been, the youngest son, in essence a mere giveaway, the woman I'd become—the woman who'd born his child—felt only…

I did not want to think about what I felt. But it was strong, and it was warm, and instinctively I knew that it was as dan-gerous as the family from which this man had come.

"You?" The image forming in my mind struck me as something straight from a Dickens's tale, a boy of privilege leading tourists through the dusty streets of Pompeii, and abruptly I realized how the old tour guide had known so much about Joshua.

"No one knew who I was—or at least I thought they didn't. No one expected anything of me. No one told me how to act or what to think, what I should or should not do."

In other words, he'd been free of his family's shadow.

My earlier question came back to me: *Do you really believe that means there is only one path you can follow?*

The answer I was beginning to suspect did cruel, cruel things to my heart.

"One night when I got home, Caleb was different. I couldn't pinpoint it, but he seemed…drunk almost. Victorious. Like he knew some big secret no one else did."

"He found something."

"He never mentioned the tunnels again. Never worried about secrets between Aaron and my father. He spoke only of destiny, and having the courage to reach for it."

"And you?" I asked. "You did not look for what he'd found?"

"I was a kid. It seemed like a game. At the time, I had no idea that not all games are innocent."

My thoughts went to Lexie, and while I looked at the remorse in her father's eyes, I couldn't help but see the dazzling innocence in hers.

"And now?" I asked.

"Now I am a man," Joshua said, and for the first time since he'd turned to find me watching him, he started toward me. "And I know that innocence is just an illusion."

My denial was automatic. The ache was deep. "Not always."

The shadows abandoned him as he moved into the sunlight sweeping across the veranda. Then he crossed the last meter and stopped so close I could feel the warmth of his body.

When I saw his hand lift toward my face, I told myself to step back. He meant to touch me. But I could no more have moved than I could have abandoned my search for my family. I felt myself tense—but his fingers did not skim my face, as I'd expected. He took hold of my sunglasses and removed them.

"Why are you here, Nadia? Why did you follow me?"

They were simple questions. Logical ones, even, considering how hard I'd worked to stay out of his path not just for the past week, but for almost three years.

And yet the answer was far from simple. For my tiles, yes. To reconcile the blood flowing through Joshua's veins with the man I so desperately wanted him to be…

Arms…strong, sure. Around me. Lifting. Dragging me from the crackling inferno.

"You pulled me from the car," I said.

He neither acknowledged nor denied my words, simply lifted his hand once again to my face, and once again, I braced myself. But this time his fingers found the ends of my scarf, and untied it. When he slipped the silky fabric from my head, my hair went flying in the cool breeze.

"You brought me to France." This time my throat tightened on the words—and the truth.

Now he didn't touch, just stood there so close that the wickedly familiar scents of leather and patchouli whispered through me. Words, I thought again. Sometimes they really weren't necessary. Joshua had risked his life to save mine, and we both knew it.

"You asked me to trust you," I pressed, because now it was my turn. In telling me of his childhood, Josh had given me a piece of his past and an opening to the future. He'd given me trust—something we'd never shared before, but repeatedly violated. Now it was my turn.

"You said you could help," I added. "That you stand with me, not against me."

We stood in the sunlight. Around us, the wind swept through palms growing unabashedly in this place of death. Columns arched toward the pale azure sky. Statues crumbled. Josh, in his black shirt open at the throat and tailored pants, his outrageously expensive shoes and designer watch, should have looked out of place. But didn't.

"You want something from me," he said after a long moment of silence.

My wince was automatic. His words should not have hurt; he spoke the truth. But until that moment I hadn't seen it that way. I'd thought of my presence in his world in terms of what it was costing me. That to ask him for what I needed, I first had to give him something I'd never given him before. My trust.

But in a disjointed flash, I realized how mercenary my actions were, and not for the first time, I was reminded that something of great beauty, such as the crystalline tiles of the mosaic, could also cut to the quick.

"I do," I admitted, fighting the stab of vulnerability. "But I am giving you something in return."

For the third time he lifted a hand to my face, and this time, he touched me. But this time, I had not braced myself.

"I'm giving you my trust," I said as a warm current flowed through my body. His fingers traced the outline of my cheekbone, but I felt each stroke, each caress, far deeper. "If I am wrong—"

"What, Nadia? What do you want from me?"

My body screamed an answer of its own, straining to be

closer, to feel him again. "They took something from me," I said, past the thickness in my throat. "A small bag, when the men ran my car off the road." I hesitated before laying my cards on the table. "I want it back."

Against my face, his hand stopped moving. "I am sorry, but I cannot do that, *cara*."

It was not the answer I'd expected. The disappointment crushed in on a cold dark wave, and something inside me started to shake. Violently. "But you said—"

"They are gone." The finality of his voice killed my protest. The shadows were back, despite the glaring sunshine. Even the glittering green of his eyes went dark. "I destroyed them."

Chapter 16

He. Destroyed. Them.

The words slammed into me, tearing down all the ridiculous illusions I'd allowed myself to create about this man. He was an Adriano, I reminded myself. Only moments before he'd all but confessed.

Innocence is just an illusion.

I wrenched away from him and staggered back, tried to breathe. Everything inside me was tight and tangled and jumbled, a tense knot of hope and disappointment, promise and lies, trust and betrayal.

Love. And hate.

"I should never have come here," I hissed, as much at myself as at him. "I should have listened to the others. I should have known better than to trust—"

"Nadia."

He reached for me, but I jerked back before his hand could find my arm. "Don't touch me."

Something dark and volatile flashed in his eyes, and for a moment he stood unnaturally still. Then he muttered something in Italian—prayer or oath, I did not know—and moved with a speed I had not anticipated, taking my shoulders in his hands. "You are right to be angry with me, but you were not wrong to trust me."

My chin at a fierce angle, I glared up at him. "How can you say that? The contents of that bag—"

"Tiles," he said, stopping me cold. "For the mosaic."

From somewhere toward the center of town, the piper kept playing, creating an odd, lyrical soundtrack for the darkness pushing through me.

"My grandfather told me about them," he added quietly. "On the plane after I pulled you from the car."

Everything inside me stilled. "Your grandfather?"

"He is how I knew to come after you. He is why I was there in the first place."

"I don't understand." And yet the memory fluttered in the back of my mind: *A flash of white. And a voice. Not Josh's. But older. Strained with sorrow. "How is she?"*

"My grandfather has done many terrible things," Josh said. "That is true. But I was with him when he finally came back to us after the assassination attempt. I was at his bedside when he opened his eyes. His body was the same, older and frailer, but it was a different man who looked up at me. The man from my childhood, who'd taken a little boy to Pompeii and bought him ice cream, who taught him to sing ballads, and talked to him of the old ways."

I swallowed hard. "You believe his story about a near death experience changing his life?"

"It is not a story, *cara*. It is truth. Were it not, you would not be alive today."

The thought chilled me. "But—"

"I did not believe him at first, either. He would ramble on for hours with an odd, glassy look in his eyes, telling me about a dark legacy he had to end, a prophecy he could not allow to come true. That he had to stop what he'd started before it was too late." A painfully familiar light sparked in Josh's eyes. "For the longest time I thought he had gone mad."

It was a logical assumption.

"But then the earthquakes came, just as he predicted."

The wind whipped hair into my face. "Then why did you destroy my tiles?"

"I tried to keep you out of this, *cara*. But you are very…what is the word? Stubborn? And you would not listen."

Damn it, the small smile happened all by itself. "It's my birthright, too."

"So it is," he acknowledged. "But I could not just stand back and let my family do to you what they did to your sister."

The pain was immediate and sharp.

"I had to protect you."

"I'm a trained agent," I said, reaching for the satchel slung over my shoulder. Inside, my 9 mm waited.

Josh eased the hair behind my ears, and looked into my eyes. "What kind of man stands on the sidelines and waits when someone he cares about is in trouble?"

Until that moment, I'd been breathing quite fine. But my heart stuttered at the question, and my blood strummed hot and hard through my body. Neither of us voiced the obvious answer: a man like his brother.

"I had to try—that is why my grandfather slipped a tracking device into the envelope he brought you in Ireland. That is how I found you in England."

I closed my eyes.

"And that is where I was when my grandfather called to tell me you had been compromised. That my father's men had tracked down the pilot who flew you from Ireland and forced him to disclose where he'd taken you."

"But Leonard—"

"Has a wife and children whom he loves very much."

Josh didn't need to say more. I understood fully.

"Once he knew you were with MI6, Caleb had someone on the inside pull your file. The rest was quite simple."

Reeling, I twisted away before Joshua could see my expression. If Caleb had someone inside MI6...*Lexie!*

Thank God she was with her godfather. I had to call him immediately, I realized, fumbling for my mobile phone.

"I did not mean to destroy the tiles," Josh said as I crossed the courtyard toward what had once been a playful fountain. "We were in the car. I was trying to get away from the men shooting at us—and I shot back."

Through the haze I remembered the sound of tires screeching.

"One of the cars exploded and went over the cliff," he continued. "But it was not until I was in Naples and Caleb was ranting that I realized the car I'd destroyed carried your tiles. I contacted sources—nothing was left."

I stopped walking. In my satchel, my hand slipped against a stack of photographs. Almost numbly, I pulled them out and stared at the images of beautiful glossy tiles that had waited safely for hundreds of years, until the time was right to resurrect the Lady. Now gone. Destroyed in an instant.

I felt him before he spoke, felt the familiar rush surge through my blood. *"Dio mio."*

The invocation was hoarse, an odd combination of surprise and reverence. I started to glance over my shoulder, but there was no need. He was already there, standing behind me, his chest to my back, his arms around me. "Where did you get these?"

I'm not sure I'd ever wanted to relax against someone quite so much. "These were the tiles."

Slowly, he flipped through the photographs I'd taken in my Belfast hotel room. Then he turned me in the circle of his arms and cupped my face, kissed me hard. "Come, *cara*. There is something I need to show you."

"She's beautiful," I said, staring up at the marble statue. She leaned slightly forward, the thin veil clinging to her body illuminating her full breasts and rounded belly, the ancients' sign of feminine beauty. Once, she'd held something raised in her right hand, but that object had been lost, to time or early nineteenth century vandals, no one knew. In her left hand she held an ankh; an ancient symbol of life.

"Isis," Joshua said. "This is her temple."

Is, he said. Not *was.*

I gazed up at her, at the serenity in her exquisitely carved face, and felt the same peace flow through me that I'd felt upon finding the statues carved of stalagmite in the cave. By fluke or miracle, we had the temple to ourselves. There'd been a tour group inside when we'd entered, but they'd quickly left. Now there was only the sound of the wind rushing through the columns of the outer portico. Once, there would have been walls. And once, the chants of worshippers would have echoed through the curiously ill-proportioned temple.

"Egyptian, right?" I asked.

He gestured toward a faded mural on the opposite wall, depicting the court of Isis against an Egyptian landscape. "By all accounts, the cult should not have flourished here," he said, and I had to suppress the smile that wanted to form. But I could see him as he'd been so long ago, a boy of privilege dressed in pauper's clothes, giving tours of the fabled city. "Unlike the traditional Roman religions, Isis promised life after death."

Sunshine spilled in from the missing roof, creating an odd pattern of shadow and light among the columns. It didn't strike me as odd at all that Isis would have gained followers against such a bleak outlook offered by the Romans.

Given the option, most people always gravitate toward hope. I certainly had. I was, still, at that moment.

"This way," Josh said, taking my hand and leading me toward five arched doorways leading to the center of the compound.

"Is this what you wanted me to see?" I asked.

He squeezed my hand. "Almost."

Inside, a black mosaic floor stretched across the room, drawing attention to the exquisitely preserved frescoed walls. There were seven large panels, five depicting views of the Nile, one representing a scene of mythology, and the final one—well, it was the one that drew me.

She was beautiful. I know I already said that about Isis, but here in this sacred chamber, the broken color of the two-thousand-year-old fresco lent the goddess a haunting grace. She gazed down from the wall, her expression one of wisdom and serenity, despair and compassion, and above all, hope.

It was the same expression I'd seen on the torn vellum I'd found in Ireland, depicting the Lady. To my untrained eye, they looked identical. Even the pose was similar, a jug at each figure's feet, a babe at her breast. "Shouldn't there be a sword?"

Josh slipped an arm around my waist. Perhaps I should have stepped away from the intimate contact, but I didn't. It felt too…right.

"Not with Isis," he said. "She did not need violence to accomplish what had to be done." He hesitated before adding, "The violence came later."

Another understatement. Throughout history, more men and women had perished in the name of religion than in the name of hate. Somehow, that struck me as missing the point.

"She—" I broke off when voices violated the outer chamber.

"Come," Josh said. He took my hand and tugged, but for a moment I did not move. I didn't want to leave her, wanted to soak in every detail so I could remember her this way, before the violence came, when there was only salvation.

The voices grew closer—and Josh grew more urgent. "Now!"

I allowed him to pull me toward a smaller archway. On the other side sprawled another faded mural and, partially obscured by a barricade, an even smaller arch that reminded me of a mouse hole. But it was big enough for humans.

More voices. Louder. Closer. Men. But they didn't sound like the tourists who'd been here before. *"Male ditto."* Josh cursed, but so quietly I could barely hear him. "Hurry!" he said, striding toward the stuccoed wall. "We cannot let—"

A man barged through the doorway and stopped, his expressionless gaze falling on Joshua. Then he barked something in Italian and charged.

Josh met him halfway, the two going at it like gladiators who'd once fought to the death in Pompeii's coliseum. Joshua was a man of culture, but he was also a younger brother, and he knew how to fight.

He reared back and smacked his head into the other man's face, didn't give him a chance to recover before kicking him in the gut. The man staggered, and Josh went in for more.

A second man raced into the outer chamber, straight for Josh's back. I reacted instinctively, rushing forward and positioning myself between him and his target. He was younger, but equally swarthy. And when he saw me, he laughed.

Smirking, he charged me, and I could only assume it was his macho arrogance that made him so sloppy, because he gave me all the time in the world to spin out of his attack and catch him from behind. I slammed a foot into his back and drove him down.

Now he was mad. He rolled to his feet and came after me, more determined this time. "Nadia!" I heard Josh shout as I danced out of my attacker's way. That was my goal. Keep him focused on me, so Josh could fend off his own assailant.

With a foul grunt, he came at me again, and this time as I kicked out and spun, he caught my leg and I went down. The crack of bone against stone sung through me, but there was no time for pain, because he was reaching for me, dragging me toward him.

Anticipating his move, I didn't resist, but rammed into him, driving him into the wall. He slammed hard, but I gave him no reprieve, instead swung my knee into his gut. Grunting, he curled inward, giving me the chance to launch my foot against his jaw and thrust his head against the stone wall.

As he slumped, I saw his eyes go wide—then blank.

Struggling for breath, I spun just as Josh flipped the first man over his shoulder and headfirst to the hard stone floor. He writhed only once before going still.

"Nadia!" His nose bloody, Joshua ran to me and took my shoulders in his hands. *"Cristo."* His eyes darkened as he lifted a hand and touched his thumb to the corner of my mouth.

I didn't need a mirror to know what he saw. I tasted the copper. "I'm okay."

Josh murmured something in Italian, his touch so unbearably gentle it was almost worth getting hurt to experience the sensation.

"This is my fault," he growled, eyes glittering. "They are after me, not you."

The words hit me like a punch from one of the thugs. "After *you?*" I tried to reconcile the battered man standing before me, a cut beneath his eye and a bruise darkening his jaw, with the jet-setter I'd met three years before, the son of privilege who liked fast cars and expensive wine, who wore a tuxedo as sinfully as he wore nothing at all. Whose smile had the power to melt everything inside me.

"Who?" I asked as he pushed the hair from my face and grimaced. Then, more important, "Why?"

"We must hurry," he said, releasing me and running toward one of the unmoving thugs. He dropped to his knees and ran his hands along the man's body, came up with a semiautomatic.

I did the same with the second man. Heckler & Koch, I noted. MP5K. Sleek, state-of-the-art and professional. Not the weapon of choice for your average mugger.

With a quick glance toward the other room, Josh came back and took my hand. "Can you run?"

If the question hadn't been asked with such fierce concern, I might have been amused. "Of course," I said as he led me to the darkened passageway. He shoved aside the barricade and gestured for me to enter. "Hurry. We do not have much more time."

Once, not that long ago, I would no more have followed his instructions than I would have rung up the tabloids and told them the truth about Lexie's heritage.

Funny how much can change in a matter of days. Moments, actually. A look, a heartbeat, and life just…turns.

I dropped to my hands and knees and peered inside, saw the ladder. Turning around, I put my foot on the first rung and lowered myself into the darkness.

The world burns. Naysa runs through the streets, tripping, stumbling, staggering through suffocating darkness. The sun is gone. Everywhere she looks, there is only smoke. And fire.

Rocks pummel down from the sky like rain. Still she runs, knowing there can be no refuge, not from a mountain that won't stop exploding. "This way," the slave guide instructs, but even as she turns, she feels him go down. She drops to her knees and gropes for him, feels the warm stickiness against the side of his face and the stillness of his neck. The boy is gone.

"Joakim!" His name tears from her throat as she runs toward the gate where he'd promised to meet her. His words still burn through her. He thinks he's responsible for the mountain that has betrayed them. Because of the rock, he says. It was his brother who wanted the rock, his brother who found a way to use the rock—

Around her, buildings collapse and others blaze. From the rubble, men and women scream. Children cry. The urge to reach out to them is strong, but she cannot stop, not this time. The priestesses are counting on her. She must get the new rock back to the temple. And her baby. Growing so strong in her womb, Joakim's child deserves a chance to live.

"Naysa!" His voice rises above the chaos as she squeezes with the others through the city gates.

"Joakim!"

Through the insanity he finds her. Through the darkness he guides her. Coughing, she staggers, and then he's picking her up and holding her. Running.

"You must get far away from here," he pants. "South," he adds, shifting her from his arms into a chariot. "Do not stop. No matter what happens, do not stop."

Blindly, she reaches for him as a stone from the sky slices her forearm. "Joakim—"

He presses a pouch into her hand. "You must go!"

Her heart pounds and the baby kicks, but in that moment

everything freezes. Joakim is pulling away. "You can't go back!"

"I have to," he shouts, and though she cannot see him, she hears the desperation in his voice, and knows that his eyes are on fire. "I have to help the others—the children—"

"You cannot stay here!"

"I cannot leave. This is my fault," he says again, as he's been saying over and over, something about vibrations in the earth and a disruption in the sky. About rock and power and destiny. "I started this and I must finish it!"

Tears rip from her heart. "This is not your fault!"

His hands then, warm and wide against her belly. "Be strong, Naysa. For me, for the babe." Then his mouth, hot and damp against hers. "We will be together again," he promises, and what's left of her heart breaks. "Someday. I will find you again."

And then he is gone and the chariot starts to move, and through the darkness everything is racing and exploding. Holding the pouch against her belly, she twists around and watches the red glow fade into the unnatural darkness of a world gone mad.

Shaken by the memory, I stepped from the ladder into some sort of underground chamber and squinted against the darkness. "Where are we?" I asked, but no sooner had I spoken the words than I saw the altar.

"Another shrine," Joshua said. He stepped around me and lifted his hands to the stone, where he dragged his thumb along a seam. From somewhere above, sunlight squeezed through cracks. "This is where they kept the sacred water."

And behind us, it continued to flow through a rhythmic fountain almost identical to the one in the Marian temple.

"Whether it truly came from the Nile is up for debate," Josh mused as I stepped closer. He dug his fingers deep into the groove. "Here, can you help—"

I lifted my hands before he finished the request, and together we eased the smooth rock from the wall, revealing a vault. Josh reached inside until I couldn't see any of his arm, just the side of his body pressed against the stone.

It wasn't until my body protested that I realized I was holding my breath.

I knew the second he found what he was after. His eyes glowed with a light that could only come from within. Slowly, he pulled out his arm, revealing a silver coffer the size of a shoe box. It was perfectly preserved, with absolutely no tarnishing—hundreds of doves carved with an intricacy that spoke of perfection.

Josh held it out to me. "Open it, *cara*. I think you will be surprised."

Answers, I remembered in some hazy corner of my mind. I'd come seeking them. Somehow, though, I hadn't prepared myself for finding them.

For a woman who places such a high value on truth, I was unsettled to realize how much comfort I found in illusion. It was easier to believe Joshua Adriano was the enemy. That he was dangerous. Given the opportunity, he would destroy the life I'd so carefully built. I'd used those thoughts to make me strong.

But standing there in the shadowy basement shrine, with the pulsing of the old fountain echoing around us, I found myself considering an even more disturbing possibility.

What if I'd been wrong?

My throat went tight as I looked into his eyes, so naked and unguarded, glowing with an anticipation I did not understand. "Trust me," he whispered.

And finally, at last, the truth came out of hiding.

Taking a leap of faith, I looked down at the coffer and lifted my hand, removed the heavy silver lid.

And saw the obsidian. Black as the night and smooth as silk, completely identical to the look and texture of the mosaic tiles I'd found in Ireland.

"I am not leaving you alone tonight."

The words stopped me. Bone tired and craving a shower, I spun from the doorway of the small bathroom to see Joshua sliding the dead bolt into place. I'd just suggested it was time for him to move to his own room. From the small number of cars outside the motel, I was quite sure they had plenty to spare.

But from the harsh set of Josh's jaw, I was equally sure he'd only requested the one.

"Joshua," I said, putting extra emphasis on his name. "This is not a good idea." We'd been together over twelve hours, and with each one that passed, the walls I'd slapped between us crumbled a little more. If we spent the night together...

Fighting off an attack and running through the tunnels beneath Pompeii, emerging through an old well beyond the city into the cold of night, was one thing. We'd been in task mode.

Even when we'd sneaked back to the parking lot and seen two black Saabs parked near our cars, we'd slipped out of sight with an efficiency that came from adrenaline and a mutual desire to see the next sunrise, alive.

After Josh placed a call to someone he trusted, we'd hiked to a secluded back road, and waited. True, he'd put his arms around me, and true, I'd let him. Perhaps I'd even leaned into him. Vaguely, I thought I might have put my arms around him, as well. But that had been because of the cold.

And the long drive northeast across Italy? Again, necessity. We had only the one car. With morning, we would part. Before then, actually. While I fully planned on seeing the next sunrise,

I did not intend to do so with Josh. While he slept, I would leave, head back to France with the obsidian from the basement temple. I'd already called Tru. She was eager to see if replacements could be made.

But spending the night with Joshua? Alone in a hotel room? Even if there were two beds? No way.

There was an intimacy that came with the dark, quiet hours of the night that I could not allow to settle between us. Lying in my bed, listening to him sleep, to him breathe…

"There are plenty of rooms," I pointed out.

He crossed to the lone window and cracked the blinds to peek outside. "There are," he agreed. "But from them, it would be too late by the time I heard you scream."

The little rush of warmth was immediate and so bloody wrong it made me grit my teeth. "I'm a trained agent," I reminded him, moving toward the worn recliner, where I'd dropped my satchel. From it, I removed my 9 mm and held it up like a show-and-tell object. "I can take care of myself."

The transformation happened so fast I had no time to prepare. One second Joshua stood sentinel by the window. The next he was stalking toward me as if I'd callously poured salt into a wound.

"Do you have any idea," he growled, and the sudden thickness of his voice took me even more by surprise. I instinctively took a step back as he shattered my personal space, but the chair blocked me on one side, the wall on the other. "Any idea at all—" he asked, and this time he lifted a hand to my face and slid the hair behind my ears "—what it did to me to see you with my brother at the villa in Saint-Tropez?"

My heart kicked hard and my mouth went dry. "I knew what I was doing."

"You have no idea how dangerous he is."

There were many kinds of danger. The Adrianos seemed to

specialize in all of them. "Caleb wanted me to lead him to the key," I pointed out. "He would not have killed me."

Josh slid a thumb down my cheek, forcing me to bite back a wince. I didn't want him to know how badly the bruise I'd seen blooming in the mirror hurt.

Nothing prepared me for him leaning closer, feathering a soft kiss to the base of my cheekbone. "There are many ways to kill someone," he murmured against the side of my face. "Not all of them involve the body."

Everything inside of me went very still. "You do not need to tell me that." Because God help me, he'd been the one to teach me. In exquisite, painful detail.

"What if my brother had tried to seduce you?" he asked, pulling back. "What if he'd backed you into a corner and forced you to sleep with him, to prove you harbored no secret agenda?"

The thought was sickening. "That would not have happened."

"Did he offer you a drink?" Josh asked. "Do you realize how easily he could have slipped you something that would have made you as hot for him as he was for you?"

I cringed. "I did not drink—"

"I was already in the air when I got the call," he revealed, and now his hand cupped the side of my face, his fingers stabbing into my hair. I told myself to struggle, to get away from him, but the feel of his warm palm against my cheek shimmied through me like a forgotten song. "I was returning to Naples," he said, our faces inches apart. I could feel his chest expanding against mine with each harsh breath he took. "Foolish man that I am, I thought you had listened to me the night before. I thought you had heeded my warning and left."

"While I still could?" I tried to retort. But the words were hoarse and breathy, even to my own ears. And my hands wanted to lift, to curl around his forearms.

With effort, I kept my arms at my sides.

"*Sì,*" he snapped. "I tried to forget about you. To hate you. Even as I looked for you. But then there you were, in Saint-Tropez, of all places, impersonating a dead woman. Even then, I told myself I did not care." The harsh words were dulled by his careful English and lyrical accent. "The plane had just taken off when one of my men called and told me he'd seen you leaving the casino with Caleb."

The revelation slammed into me, and I stood there sandwiched between Josh's hard body and the equally hard wall, trying to process the new image that was starting to form. I'd wondered how and why Josh had arrived at the villa, when Caleb had specifically told me we'd have the place to ourselves. But I'd never imagined—my God. I'd never imagined Josh had ordered a flight turned around.

"I could have killed him with my own hands," he was saying. "The entire time I drove, all I could think of was you, going to bed with my brother, just like you'd gone to bed with me."

It was like a bucket of ice water. I recoiled and jerked back, lifted my hands to shove against him, which the wall prevented me from doing. "You son of a—"

He grabbed my wrists. "*Dolce Madre di Dio,* Nadia. *Perché?*" Why? "Do you think that is what I wanted to believe? What I wanted to see? Do you think—"

I twisted my wrists and slammed down my arms, breaking his grip. "Is that why you think I made love with you?" I demanded against the boil of emotion I'd tried to suppress. To deny. "As part of a case?"

He froze. It was an awesome sight, all six-foot-one of him going brutally still. A dark light glittered in his eyes, emphasizing the dust and blood that remained on his face. "How could I think anything else?"

It was the quietness of the question that got me most. The naked truth that punished. I wanted to rail at him, to blast him for desecrating what we'd shared.

But there was one fact I could not deny, and that was the truth he spoke. *"Josh,"* I whispered, and felt my heart break on his name. "When I found out who you really were—"

He moved so fast I didn't have time to finish. He dragged me to him, caught my face in his hands and brought his mouth down on mine.

Chapter 17

It was a hard kiss, dark and erotic and possessive, demanding in ways that made my blood soar. I knew I should pull back from him, break the contact, but the only movement I made was toward him, sinking into him and lifting a hand to the back of his head, tangling my fingers in his hair and opening to him, giving and taking and demanding, just like he was.

Three years was a long time to want. An even longer time to regret. To try and forget. But as he deepened the kiss and backed me across the room, all those days and nights between us fell away, and it was just us again, Zoe and Antonio, the man and the woman who'd come together in Portugal.

At the bed he lifted me and put a knee to the mattress, eased me down as he hovered over me. For a moment he just looked at me, his dark hair falling across his forehead, his eyes glittering. His lips parted, damp from our kiss. Then he muttered something darkly beautiful in his native tongue and swept his shirt from his shoulders, came down over me.

My whole body quickened in anticipation.

I reached for him, curled my hands around his upper arms and urged him down, felt my legs close around his. The feel of him—the strength of his muscles and the width of his chest, the ridge pressed against my belly—blanked my mind and heated my blood, made some place inside of me beg. So many nights I'd lain alone in my bed, remembering, trying to forget, telling myself that the stirring he'd kindled within me had only been my imagination. But now—now I knew it was my memory that had lied, dulling the intensity of what we'd shared, out of sheer desperate survival. There was no way a woman could allow herself to remember such blind passion.

I did remember now. I arched beneath him and felt the heat curl through me as his mouth slid from mine and down my throat, kissing and licking and nibbling toward my chest. My breasts peaked in anticipation. In all the days and months we'd been apart, there'd been no other man—

The thought stabbed through me with vicious disregard, baring a truth I'd somehow let myself forget. A truth I had not known three years before, but did now....

"*Cara,*" he whispered, working at the buttons of my shirt. "I dreamed of you like this...."

I went very still, even as the pain coursed through me.

"I have waited so long," he murmured against my breast, and even as I denied it, I heard the broken mewl rip from my throat.

It should not have been possible to feel hot and cold at the same moment. Pleasure and pain. It shouldn't have been possible to have him straining against his jeans and want to have him inside me, while at the exact same moment wanting nothing more than to shove him away and run, and run and run and run. To erase him from my life—and my heart.

I felt myself start to shake. I shoved him and rolled across the mattress, tried to dart from the bed.

Josh caught my arm and held me, looked at me as if I'd just slapped him. *"Cara—"*

"Don't call me that," I said, hating the way everything inside me unraveled. Even more, I hated the way he looked sprawled there, across the cheap floral bedspread we'd practically destroyed, his chest bare, his shoulders rising and falling, dark hair falling into his glittering green eyes.

But most of all, I hated the way my body ached to slide back against his, to be beneath him or above him, with him. "This is so wrong," I whispered.

His expression gentled. "I know you are scared—"

And I couldn't do it one second longer, couldn't stay there on that bed with him, looking at him, wanting him, pretending that making love with him wouldn't be the biggest mistake of my life. "You're *married,*" I cried, and with the words emotion swamped my eyes, and I felt the sting of the hated moisture.

But I did not let the tears fall.

Josh visibly recoiled, his big body going very still for one horrible second. Then he closed his eyes and hung his head, released his grip on my arm.

I swept from the bed and worked at the buttons of my blouse. "You have a child." Two of them, actually. One he knew about. The other he did not. "A son. Benny." I shoved my shirttail into my slacks. "I know, Joshua, okay? I didn't know three years ago, but I do know now. Her name is Pauline. She's beautiful."

Now his eyes opened. And they glowed with something dark and fathomless I did not understand. "She is also my father's mistress."

He might as well have shoved me against the wall. I felt

myself stagger, felt my mouth fall open before closing once again. He rolled from the bed but made no move to cover himself, simply charged toward the small table where the bottled water we'd purchased sat. He brutalized the lid as he removed it, then threw back the majority of the contents.

"I always knew he was fond of her," he continued, more quietly now. "That he wanted her to marry one of his sons. But I always thought it would be Aaron." The heir. "Then he went to university and fell in love with a girl from Ireland, refused to marry any other. That left Caleb—or me. Pauline picked me."

Arranged marriages. I knew they still existed—my mother had certainly wanted to arrange one between me and my friend Lex—but I'd seen the pictures of Josh's wedding. It was a dumb thing to do and I knew it, but after I discovered who he really was, after I was safely back in England, I'd found myself surfing the Internet, hungry for…

Hungry for anything I could find about him. "I saw the pictures." Impossibly romantic glimpses of a fairy tale wedding rivaling those of the royal family. "You looked happy—and in love."

A rough sound broke from his throat. "I looked the way the Adrianos always look for the camera," he muttered. "And she *was* beautiful. I did not love her, but she was my wife, and I wanted to be a good husband to her."

I didn't want to look at him. I didn't want to see the regret in his eyes. But I couldn't force myself to turn away. "You have a child together…."

Or did they? I saw pain streak through Josh's eyes. If Pauline was truly involved with his own father, could Josh be certain of his son's paternity?

"After Benny was born—" He closed his eyes, opened them a heartbeat later. "Pauline was not cut out to be a mother. She wasn't ready to give. She wanted only to receive, to be the center of attention."

Little fissures sprang up all over the place, allowing compassion to squeeze through where before there had been resentment.

"We...drifted," he said. "She would go to Rome for days—to visit family, she always said—leaving Benny with me. After a while, I...stopped caring." He hesitated before adding, "Then I met you."

My heart thudded hard at the words. During our time apart I'd forgotten how easily he could unravel me with nothing more than his voice, and his eyes.

"I knew being with you was wrong," he said, and finally he moved. "I thought my family was being targeted. I thought we were under attack. That is why I could not tell you my name. That is why I pretended to be Antonio...to find out who was after my family, and why. But then you came along," he whispered, and my heart bled. "And after so many years of feeling nothing, you made me feel alive. You reminded me what it was like to want." He took my hands and brought them to his mouth. "And to hurt."

Everything just kind of faded, leaving the two of us standing there, my hands in his, lifted to his mouth, where he brushed a soft kiss to the backs of my fingers. I wanted to be angry with him. I wanted to hate him, to feel all those dark, destructive emotions that had eaten me alive after I'd learned his true identity.

But all I felt was a swell of warmth, and the overwhelming desire to put my arms around him and hold on tight.

"You have every right to hate me," he said.

I felt my hand slip from his, made no move to stop it. My fingers found the hard line of his jaw, skimmed along the whiskers there. "I don't hate you," I whispered. And dear God, that was the problem.

His smile, slow and boyishly endearing, nearly broke my heart. "I do not hate you, either."

I almost laughed. I wanted to cry.

Slowly, he lifted a hand to my face and skimmed his finger along my bruised cheekbone. "I cannot lose you again, *cara.*"

The words whispered through me, shredding everything they touched. He made it sound so simple. So easy. His marriage was a farce. He still wanted me, and I'd never stopped wanting him. Now that the truth had been exposed, nothing stood between us.

If only that were true.

"Joshua…" I drank in the tenderness in his eyes, the way he looked at me, touching me deeper than flesh and bone. The temptation to forget about tomorrow was strong. To step into his arms and lift my mouth to his, drag him back to bed, take what we both wanted. But—

"Now is not the time," I forced myself to say, and with the words, I untangled myself from his arms. "It's late and we're both tired," I added as the light in his eyes dimmed. In only a few hours, I would slip from bed while he slept, and head for France.

It could be no other way.

He made no move to stop me as I turned and walked to the bathroom. And I made no move to look back at him, even when his quiet voice sounded from behind me.

"There will be a divorce," he said. "I have already filed."

I'm not sure how I stayed standing there, barefoot and burning, when all I wanted was to turn around, see his face.

"Slow is not something that comes naturally to me," he added with all the naughty charm that had first drawn me to him. "But it is what you deserve. So I will try."

Scarcely able to breathe, I found the strength to walk into the bathroom and close the door.

* * *

Water ran through the old pipes, an unwanted reminder that beneath the spray of the cramped shower, Joshua stood naked. I lay in the bed he'd set me down on earlier, when I'd almost let my need for him sweep away common sense.

Frowning, I turned from the bathroom and stared through the darkness, but did not close my eyes. Because then I would see him, naked as I knew he was, standing in that little porcelain bathtub, bending to fit beneath the shower.

It was an image I did not need.

Instead I forced my mind to more practical matters, such as the obsidian in my satchel. I'd asked Joshua several times who was chasing him, and why, but all he'd said was, "I have made some people very angry with me."

The water stopped, and within minutes the bathroom door opened, allowing light to spill into the bedroom. Then the darkness returned and I heard him move.

Shutting my eyes before he caught me staring, I held myself very still. I could no longer see him, but I could feel him, and I knew he had not crossed to his bed, but to mine. I lay there dying inside, wanting so badly to open my eyes and reach out. He touched me with feather gentleness, the backs of his fingers brushing against my cheek and easing the hair from my face. Then he whispered something in Italian, and I could only brace myself as he lowered his face—and pressed a soft kiss to the bruise on my jaw.

Killing me softly. I'd heard the song. Now I understood.

I had no way of knowing how much time passed, how long he watched me lying there. How long my body burned. It seemed like an eternity. But after a while I felt him move away from me, heard him pull back the covers of the second bed, climb in and punch the pillow. That, I supposed with prurient relief, beat several alternatives.

He tossed and turned. A while later, I heard him fumble for something on the nightstand between us. Then came his voice, quiet and in Italian, and I knew he was speaking on his phone. All I recognized was the name of his son, Benny, who, under his bodyguard's watchful eye, was with Pauline. "Papa loves you," he whispered, and my heart ached.

Then silence, broken only by his breathing. After a while it shifted into a heavy rhythm, and I knew he slept. Eventually I drifted, too, the darkness of my mind melding with the shadows of the past. Joshua was there waiting, holding out a hand to me. I reached for him, went into his arms. The warmth was immediate. And fleeting. Abruptly, everything flashed, white, then red, and as I tried to orient myself, I realized it was not Joshua in my arms, but a pillow.

Spinning, I looked for him, called out for him, but saw only the smoldering remains of the valley leading to the temple. The grass and trees had burned. The sky glowed red. Even the birds had fled. And then I heard him, calling out. He was hurt, I realized, running blindly through the scorched field. His breathing was labored, strained. "Joshua!" I cried.

And then I opened my eyes. By the faint light from the window I saw him in his bed, tangled in the sheets and thrashing against an unseen enemy. I lunged for him, reaching him as he breathed his brother's name.

He twisted, making it necessary for me to become more forceful, to pin him down against the mattress and climb on top, hold his arms down with my legs. "Josh," I said, horrified by the heat of his body, the sweat that dampened his sheets. "It's me. Nadia." Then, *"Zoe."*

He froze; there was no other way to describe it. He went utterly still, his big, mostly nude body unmoving beneath mine. His eyes were open, but through the shadows I could tell he did not see me. Did not see anything.

"Josh," I said again. "It's okay. We're safe. No one is here—"

He moved so fast I had no time to brace myself. He bolted upright and caught me by the arms. "They killed them," he rasped. "All of them. Even the children."

The suffering in his voice…it ripped through me in a dark wave. "No one killed anyone," I said as gently as I could. "It was just a dream."

Dark hair fell across his forehead, revealing the agony in his eyes. "I was there," he insisted, holding me so tightly I knew there would be bruises where his fingers clenched. But I did not care. "In Switzerland. Damassine."

Now it was my turn to reel. Eve had speculated, but— *"Joshua…"*

His eyes met mine, and finally I understood what he saw. The bodies. Row upon row of sheet-covered bodies. "I can see their faces," he said roughly. "Men and women, children. Guilty of nothing but living in the wrong village."

Horror swept through me.

"We tried to stop them," he said. "My grandfather—he knew, but we were too late."

I lifted my hands to his face and found his skin hot, damp. "Joshua," I repeated, with all the love in my heart. "It wasn't your fault."

"I didn't know." The words were dark, tortured. "I did not see the truth about my family until it was too late. But you knew. All along, you knew."

"Not this," I said. "I never imagined—"

"You were right." He released my arms and took my hands from his face, clasped them in his, "You were right to keep her from me."

That would have been a good place to wake up. But I wasn't sleeping, nor was I dreaming. I was awake. Sprawled on top of a mostly naked Josh. And he'd just yanked the world from beneath my feet.

Somehow, I found my voice. "Her?"

And now his eyes gentled. "Our daughter," he said. *"Alexandria."*

Chapter 18

Bombs exploded quickly. It was the aftermath that revealed itself in slow motion. I pulled back from Josh, tried to put some distance between us. But he would not let me go, just kept me exactly where I was, straddling his hips, while his revelation settled between us like nuclear fallout.

Alexandria. The way he said her name, caressing each syllable with his yummy accent, melted my core. I'd always wondered. I'd imagined. What would it be like to hear her father speak her name? To see his face as he did so?

Now I knew. And it was alarmingly…right. There was none of the anger I'd expected. None of the harshness, none of the accusation. Only the awe of a father meeting his newborn for the first time.

"You know?" The words cracked out of me.

He brought our joined hands to his mouth, where he

brushed a kiss on my knuckles. "Not for long," he said. "Only a few days. When I was at your house, in Cornwall."

Even before he said the words, I knew.

"I saw her picture."

I closed my eyes, bowed my head. After all I'd done to vanish, it all came down to a simple photograph.

"She is beautiful," he said, and with the words he put a finger to my chin and tilted my face. "She has your smile."

I looked into his gaze, felt myself start to drown. "And your eyes."

His answering smile bloody well stole my breath. "That is not such a bad thing, no?"

"No." Josh had amazing eyes, wide and almond shaped, heavy lidded, the most amazing color of green. When Lexie looked at me, I could not help but see her father. For the longest time, that reality had broken my heart. Now I found myself smiling through unshed tears.

"She is why I could not find you, yes? Why you vanished so completely. You went to great lengths to protect my daughter." The lines of his face tightened. "From me."

Something inside me twisted. "Yes."

Looking away, he shifted me from his lap and swung his legs to the floor, climbed from bed and strode across the room. At the window, he parted the blinds and looked into the night.

I wanted to go to him, put a hand to his back and find a way to make him understand. But I did not let myself move.

After a long moment he turned and shoved the hair back from his face. "The girl that Aaron loved? The one he met at university?"

Standing there, I braced myself.

"Siobhan was her name. She was on her way to elope with Aaron when she died in a car accident. She was pregnant. With a girl child, Aaron told me one night, when

I found him crying." Josh's eyes met mine. "A bastard, my father said.

"Aaron was blind with grief, couldn't accept that it was an accident. On the plane, when we brought you from England? My grandfather confessed that Aaron had been right."

"My God." I rolled from the bed and crossed to him, took his hands. "They had her killed?"

"She was not wanted in the family," Josh said harshly. "Not her, nor her bastard daughter."

The chill was immediate, and inside I started to shake.

"When I was at your house, when I saw Alexandria's picture, I was angry. I felt betrayed. I could not believe you had given birth to my child, and hidden her from me." The dark glitter in his eyes stole my breath. "But then my grandfather called to warn me of the danger you were in, and told me about Siobhan."

Before I could so much as breathe, Josh took my face in his hands, a purely Italian gesture he'd done many times in the days before Alexandria was conceived. It was as if he needed to touch me to ensure I did not slip away.

"The darkness that drives my family," he said, "it is bigger than you and me, Siobhan and Aaron, Scarlet and Caleb. It is bigger than just my grandfather. It is in the blood," he said. "And it has been going on for centuries."

Lifetimes. "Because of the Lady?"

"Because of the power," he corrected. "The Lady is merely a means to an end. My family is running scared. They see signs of a foretold change, and they are determined to make sure that out of the coming chaos, it is an Adriano who rises as deliverer."

"Deliverer?" The hypocrisy sickened me.

He jerked his hands from my face and held them up, cupped slightly, his fingers apart. "Do you see these hands?" he demanded. "Do you have any idea how much blood is on them?"

Shaken, I did the only thing I could. I pressed my palms to his and closed my fingers around them. "None," I said.

"But there is," he insisted, jerking free of my grip. "It is there and it cannot be erased. Do you really think it is an accident that my family has survived since the time of Christ? That we have grown and prospered, through famine and plague, when so many others perished?

"My family endured, *male detto,* because they cared not what they destroyed. They cared not *who* they destroyed, as long as they came out on top. Women, children, entire towns and villages, it did not matter."

"The ley lines," I breathed.

"*Sì.* The ley lines. How else could servant become master?" he asked darkly, and I felt my eyes widen. "The first Adrianos were slaves," he explained. "But they were also disciples of the ancient ways and students of the skies. Perhaps the first incident was an accident. Perhaps not. No one knows. But once my ancestors learned the power that came through chaos, they quickly ascended from slavery to supremacy."

"My God."

His chest rose and fell as he drew a jerky breath. "They destroyed anyone who got in their way, including a group of goddess-worshippers in southern France one of my ancestors tried to convert. He made the mistake of kidnapping their children. He thought he could bend them to his will."

"I'm guessing he didn't?"

"They sent his body back to Rome as a warning."

My breath caught. The horror of it was captivating. "The Marians..."

"Odd things began happening after that. Ley line experiments began failing, and the family grew scared. If they could no longer manipulate—"

"They would fall out of power."

"They blamed their turn of bad luck on the women, called them witches, hunted them relentlessly."

Witch hunts? The Marians?

"It did not stop with capture, though," he said. "When they caught a Marian, she was subject to great torture." Again he looked down at his hands, closed them into tight fists. "That is how they learned of the Lady. Of her power. That the Marian priestesses had built a filter, and it was this filter that was interfering with manipulating the ley lines."

It was so fantastical, it was hard to believe.

"Eventually, the Marians fell. But they vowed the Goddess would return, when the planets align and the comet appears—"

"—and the eclipse," I breathed.

"Sì." His expression darkened. "Some say it is fairy tale or legend, but my family has spent centuries trying to reconstruct the Lady. To make sure that when the time of transition comes, the power is in their hands and no other."

In my mind I could see her, the Lady, her tranquil expression, the babe at her breast. True, she had a sword, but her existence was not about violence. "The Paris earthquakes—"

"Practice," Josh said. "Mild in comparison to what will occur if my family gets their hands on the completed Lady."

"That's not going to happen."

"No," he said. "It is not. I will die first."

"That's not going to happen either," I said, and this time I reached for his hand.

He clasped mine. "I will stop them no matter what it costs."

I felt the glow move into my eyes. *"We* will," I corrected. "We will."

It was hard to sleep after that. We were both wound tight, adrenaline flowing, thoughts racing. Goddess worshippers and warriors and witch hunts, massacres and pandemics, a two-thousand-year-old prophecy drenched in blood and shimmering with hope…it was a lot to take in.

But in the shadows of the small, run-down hotel room, I felt closer to Joshua than I ever had, even when we'd made love. For a long time we just held hands, his so big and strong, stained by blood only he could see, curled around mine. He looked beyond me, his eyes focused on the soft peach wall, but seeing a darkness that made me ache for him.

Not reaching out to him was impossible. Without even trying, I found my breath shifting to the rhythm of his, and I leaned into him, bracing my forehead against the wiry hairs of his chest. Closing my eyes, I listened to the steady cadence of his heart and inhaled deeply, pulling the scents of soap and man deep within me. It was the most peaceful I could remember feeling in a long, long time.

But after a while even that was not enough. I slipped my hands from his and wound my arms around his waist, held on tight. When he did the same, something inside me wept.

He'd promised to take it slow, had said that was what I deserved. But it wasn't what I wanted. Deliberately, I stepped back and reached for his hand again, lifted my eyes to his as I tugged him toward the bed.

His gaze went dark, but he didn't move, just stood there, looking at me as if I were ripping his heart out.

I'm not sure I'd ever loved him more.

"It's okay," I whispered with a smile, and finally he came with me to the bed. I climbed in first, held the covers out for him to join me. He slid between the sheets and reached for me, and I put my head on his chest, my arm against his abdomen, and closed my eyes.

His hands settled against my lower back. And when we slept, it seemed like the most natural thing in the world.

* * *

I didn't leave. I'd planned to. I knew it was the wise thing to do, knew I should not bring him with me to France. But when I woke before sunrise, wrapped in his arms and warmed by his body, I simply brushed a kiss to my daughter's father's heart and closed my eyes, went back to sleep.

Shortly after seven, I woke again, this time to the soft beeping of my mobile phone. For a moment I was disoriented—I was not accustomed to waking snuggled up to a man with his arm slung over my body. And I so did not want to move. But then came the sharp blade of reality, and the magnitude of the decision I'd made in the watery light of predawn.

My heart kicked hard and my thoughts started to race. Beside me he stirred, pulling me closer. Torn, I fumbled for the phone, found it on the nightstand. I forced open my eyes and flipped it open, punched the talk button.

It was Ana. "Thank God," I said when she told me Catrina had come through a second surgery and that the doctors expected her to make a full recovery. We chatted a few minutes longer, concluding with my promise to be at the farmhouse by the end of the day. I did not mention Josh.

I felt the mattress shift behind me, knew he was listening. But I did not turn around, felt strangely awkward. We'd done nothing more than sleep together. I was fully clothed. But for some odd reason, I felt as if we'd spent the night making love for the first time.

"Would you like some coffee?" he asked, and the ridiculously normal question made my heart strum. "I can go get some."

"That'd be great," I said, then noticed the message light flashing on my phone. "That's odd," I said. The call must have come during the night, while we slept.

The adrenaline was as unexpected as it was unwanted. Phone calls during the night—they were rarely a good thing.

"Cara?" Josh sat up behind me, bringing his bare chest to my back. "What is wrong?"

I fumbled with the buttons, found that the message was not voice, but text:

The time for games is over.
You have something that belongs to me.
I have something that belongs to you.
We will trade, or she will die.
Check your e-mail for instructions.

Everything inside of me went stone cold. The phone fell from my hands and I started to shake. Violently. Because there was more, a file attached to the message. An image. A picture.

Lexie...

Swearing, Josh picked up the phone and pressed a few buttons, downloaded the file. Slowly, while we both watched, the photograph came into view.

The relief was so sharp I almost threw up. Not a little girl. The Adrianos did not have my little girl. But then reality slashed in, and I stared in horror at the picture of the woman heaped on the floor, her cheeks bruised, her mouth bleeding, eyes closed.

Olga.

I'm a trained agent. I know about emotional blackmail and shock value. I know the tactics the enemy employ to throw those who hunt them off balance. I know the goal. To blur focus and concentration, to force an opponent to act foolishly or rashly, to make choices based on emotion rather than fact or strategy. To take risks they would not otherwise take.

To make a mistake.

I know all that. I've been trained to wall off any hint of an emotional reaction and stick with the playbook. I've been taught some sacrifices are necessary. That the greater good, the endgame, must be preserved at all costs.

But as I stared at the picture of Olga, every ounce of training I'd ever received fell away. I tried to tell myself it was a trap. A game. The time had arrived for the Adrianos to use the spy they'd planted in my life so long ago. As bait. But as I looked at the frail, beaten figure in the picture, I did not see the mysterious woman in black, as Scarlet had called her. I saw only Olga, the gentle-hearted nanny who had been a fixture in my life for as long as I could remember, who'd sung me lullabies and read me stories, who'd sewn clothes for my dollies and hosted tea parties for my teddy bears. I saw the woman who wore shirts of soft pink, not scarves of black. Who'd taught me how to color, how to dream.

The woman I'd trusted with my little girl.

The hotel manager had Internet access, and for the price of a few euros, he allowed us to check my e-mail. Caleb's message was simple: I was to travel to Naples and surrender all the tiles the Marians had acquired to him. All of them. In exchange, he would free Olga.

If I did not cooperate, he would kill her.

The time and place of the exchange would be forthcoming. But in the interim, he suggested I visit a church, the San Francesco di Paolo. There, beneath the third pew from the front, I would find an offering. Its contents, he promised, might help me make up my mind.

"It is a trick," Josh said. "I know my brother. He is desperate. He is trying to lure you out of hiding."

"I know." But that fact didn't change anything. Calling the bluff would get me nowhere. My refusal to obey the summons would only force them to take more extreme measures.

Find a more valuable sacrificial lamb.

That's why Josh and I traveled to Naples, I told myself. That was why I headed for the beautiful old church. My decision had nothing to do with the emotion churning inside me, the awful questions that had gnawed at me since seeing the pictures Scarlet had taken over the years.

"It was her," I told him, as he steered the old car through a village outside Naples. "In black. Following my sister."

From behind sunglasses, he shot me a look. "She is familiar," he conceded. "I thought as much when I saw her in Cornwall. But I cannot place her."

Nor could his men. He'd e-mailed her photograph to Eric Carbodes, who had run her picture against several databases with no luck. His grandfather had yet to respond.

"Perhaps she was not planted by my family," he speculated, reaching for my hand. He slowed the car, stopping to allow three children and two mangy dogs to cross the narrow street. "But by *your* family."

The thought went through me with an odd little rush. "My family is dead."

"But someone had to have found you and your sister," he pointed out, and I noticed him watching the little girl. She couldn't be more than three, wearing a knit cap and a long coat, with rain boots several sizes too big. There was a longing in Joshua's gaze that seeped through my flesh and perilously close to my heart. "Someone pulled you from the wreckage and brought you to the orphanage, made sure you both found good homes."

We were moving again, slowly, leaving the children behind. I stared straight ahead, seeing not the Italian village, but the treacherous cliffside road described in the newspaper articles.

I'd not once stopped to consider just how it was Scarlet and I had survived. How we'd ended up in the orphanage. Who'd covered our tracks and led the world to believe we were dead.

Who'd given us a new chance at life.

"My God," I whispered. Emotion left me raw. From the moment I'd learned of the Adrianos' involvement in my sister's death, I'd been seeing the world through a dark lens, ascribing malevolent motive to everyone and everything—the complete antithesis to the teachings of the Marians.

And now Olga, the woman I had loved for thirty-two years, stood poised to pay the horrid price of my mistake.

"He will not win," Josh said again, lacing his fingers through mine. I squeezed and held on tight, wondered how it was possible that, out of the chaos, it would be Joshua who emerged to hold my hand. Joshua who emerged to stand by my side.

Joshua who emerged to show me darkness did not last forever.

The church was stunning.

Situated opposite the royal palace, the early nineteenth-century basilica, with its neoclassical facade and curving colonnade, dominated one end of a sweeping plaza. Tourists and locals walked and milled. Pigeons hobbled and fed. Lovers held hands and children ran. Life, as it always did, moved on, oblivious to small dramas being played out.

Hand in hand, Josh and I ascended the steps toward the entrance. We looked like lovers ourselves. Very few would guess that we each wore a Kevlar vest, and that within our coats, we each concealed a small arsenal. A rational man would never select such a public, revered locale for a showdown, but the Adrianos were no longer acting rationally. We had to be prepared.

Stepping through the wooden doors was like stepping into another world. The hush was immediate. The scent of incense. The stillness. I glanced at Josh, he at me, and we kept walking. In all likelihood, Caleb was here. Maybe even Josh's father,

Duke Simon. Watching. Josh's presence would be a surprise, perhaps throw them off balance, make them angrier.

The Adrianos did not tolerate defection.

Quietly, we reached the circular sanctuary, where a wide red carpet ran down a sea of white marble, with wooden pews on each side. Fluted columns circled the interior. At the center stood the high altar, breathtaking even from a distance. Above, a quartet of bronze angels looked on.

Squeezing Josh's hand, I started down the red carpet, toward massive statues at the front of the church. They were all of male saints. I did not recognize them, could not help but wonder where the women were. My palms started to sweat. My pulse raced. Through the quiet I could hear the sound of my breathing, and of Josh's. I wondered if he could hear the pounding of my heart.

As casually as I could, I glanced around the ring of columns to the small chapels flanking us on each side. A group of older women knelt in one set of pews. Toward the back, a young woman sat with her head bowed. There were no men in sight.

My question was answered, I realized. The men stood in dominance. The women bowed in prayer.

Quiet can echo. And quiet can scream. There in the massive, two-hundred-year-old cathedral, it did both. But we kept walking, and again I found myself grateful for Josh. For his presence. And his strength. And his hand, which held mine. I could have done this alone. But in that moment, I was glad I did not have to.

With each step I counted, until we reached the pew referenced in the e-mail. My hand itched to slide inside my jacket and withdraw my 9 mm. But it was not the time. Instead, we veered off the carpet and onto the marble, went down on a knee in an instinctive genuflection before entering the pew—and finding the box.

It was small. Nothing fancy. Rather like a lockbox used to preserve important documents in case of fire. I sank down on the kneeler and retrieved it, rocked back in the pew as I balanced the container in my lap. Beside me, Joshua put a knee to the bench.

It did not escape me how he'd positioned his body between me and the open expanse of the church.

While the angels watched, I put my hand to the lid and lifted. I'm not sure what I expected to happen. Lightning to strike or the organ to sound, something dramatic. But in the end there was only a stack of documents—and photographs.

Some of them I had seen before, such as my birth certificate and my parents' marriage license, the newspaper articles detailing the accident that killed them.

The adoption papers were new. So were the pictures of me and Scarlet as children. And the clippings about the antiquities exhibit where Josh and I had first met, the night an unknown assailant had attempted to assassinate his grandfather. There was a black ski mask. A gun.

And pictures. She wore all black in the first—tight black pants and a black turtleneck, a black ski mask like the one draped over my knee. It was impossible to see her face.

She was running in the next picture. Fighting in another.

In the fourth her mask had been ripped off and long dark hair scraggled against her face.

Until that moment, I had not known it was possible to live, after your heart stopped beating.

The picture slipped from my fingers, but there were others behind it. And through a vacuum of time and space I made my hands work, forced my fingers to lift them, my eyes to analyze.

There she was as a younger woman, on her wedding day. There she was pregnant. Beaming. Smiling. Holding her husband's hand, young and innocent and in love. With the babies, two of them. Both girls, judging from the pink bows in their newborn hair.

Then later, strolling with the infants through a park.

Vaguely, I was aware of Josh reaching for me.

But as I looked at that last picture of my young mother, as yet untouched by the horror waiting in the weeks ahead, smiling down at her giggling daughters—at me and the sister who'd died before I could know her—I drank in the sight of her eyes, eyes so familiar to me, and I started to cry.

Chapter 19

The basilica faded, the columns and statues and frescoes dissolving into the sea of white. Inside there was a tearing sensation, as if some fundamental part of me was being ripped in half. My throat burned. My heart bled. Shock is funny like that.

"Nadia," Josh whispered, but I did not look up at him, could not so much as move. Had I tried, I surely would have shattered. The truth, with all its stunning shades of brilliance and betrayal, swamped me.

All these years. All these years I'd wondered and longed and wanted. And cried. I was five when my parents first told me about my birth parents, and that's when the questions had started. And the dreams. I would wake from them, cold and shivering and crying out for a mommy whose face I could never quite envision. And sometimes during those long dark hours of the night, it was Olga who slipped into bed with me, my nanny. Olga who held me and rocked me, murmured soothing words in a foreign tongue, ran her hand along my hair and lulled me back to sleep.

Then, later, when I was a teenager and realized what adoption meant, when my thoughts turned darker and my imagination more tortuous, again it was Olga who would intervene with the calm voice of reason, quietly assuring that my parents had loved me. That they'd had no choice.

It was Olga who'd insisted that it was only my imagination playing tricks on me when I confessed that I'd dreamed of a sister. That I thought I had one out there somewhere, waiting to be found. It was Olga who had cried.

And it was Olga who had lied.

Josh dropped to my side and slid an arm around me. Mechanically, I was aware of leaning into him, but I felt nothing. Heard nothing but the rush of thoughts through my own mind.

"She was with me all along," I whispered as he pressed a kiss to my forehead. My mother had not died when I was a baby, as the newspaper articles had suggested. Nor had she abandoned me, as I'd always believed. She'd survived, sacrificing life as she knew it to create a new life for her daughters, one where, through the facade of death, Scarlet and I had been safe from the evil that had stalked our family for decades. All the while she watched over us, Scarlet from afar, ensuring the Adrianos never discovered we still lived.

I wanted to feel betrayed, and perhaps on some level I did. But in the curve of Joshua's arm, with the imposing angels looking on, other emotions swept through me, awe and gratitude, the realization that my mother had sacrificed everything for her daughters. A mother myself, I could only imagine the devastation she'd lived with every day since.

And now, because I'd doubted her, because I'd failed to protect her as she'd protected me, she'd fallen into Adriano hands.

I'm not sure what changed. I lifted my head and looked around, saw that the women no longer knelt in prayer. Even before I twisted to look, I knew I would see no tourists. No devout. There was a stillness to the church, as if all the statues held their collective breaths.

Slowly, I stood and moved around Josh, left the pew and walked toward the altar. "You can come out now," I called, and heard my own voice, strong and sure and drenched with loathing, echo through the chamber. Before I could so much as blink, Joshua was by my side, semiautomatic in hand.

A large wooden door opened. I saw Olga first. My mother. Her hands and feet were bound, a blindfold tied around her eyes, but I would have recognized her with a blindfold around my own eyes. She staggered into the sanctuary, followed by Caleb who, like the coward he was, held her in front of him as a human shield.

"I see you found my little surprise," he said blandly, as armed men materialized on either side of me and Josh. "Amazing what you can dig up when you know where to look, is it not?"

I tensed. Eyes on Caleb, I slipped a hand into my jacket and curled my fingers around my 9 mm. "Let her go."

He shoved her forward, smashing her shoulder against one of the columns. Then he smiled. "Perhaps," he said, looking and sounding every bit a son of privilege. His clothes, tailored gray slacks and a black silk shirt, looked to be straight from the cleaners. His tinted hair was neatly combed. "If you behave."

I'd never wanted to scratch someone's eyes out more. Clenching my jaw, I stared at Olga, at the dirty bandanna tied around her face. I longed to see her eyes, to promise her I would protect her as she'd done me and Scarlet.

"Take me instead," I growled, but when I tried to shove past Joshua, he stood like a mountain in my path.

"No!" he said harshly, and Caleb laughed.

"I should have known I would find you with her, *fratellino*. The weakest link is always the one to break."

Joshua tensed. "Your definition of strength is not one I share, brother."

"A man does what he has to. An Adriano does more."

"Perhaps," Joshua conceded. "But it is a coward who is unable to think or act for himself. And a coward who murders the woman he claims to love simply to please Papa."

Caleb went still. All but his eyes. They glowed with an unnatural light.

"She loved you." The words tore out of me. I stared at Caleb, saw the truth stamped in every line of his body. To think that, for a time, I'd actually entertained the notion that he could be innocent and Joshua guilty. "She believed in you. If you'd given her the chance, she would have led you to Ireland. She would have *given* you the vellum. You could have had them both."

"No." His fingers dug into my mother's arm. "You are lying, just as she lied. She never loved me." His voice broke on the words. "I would have given her anything, but she was just using me, as you are using my brother."

I felt my mouth fall open. "You are wrong—"

"I warned you," he said. "In Saint-Tropez. I told you what would happen if you didn't back off."

"The note," I whispered. It had been delivered by a woman in black...but authored by an Adriano running scared.

"But you did not listen." He turned to Joshua. "Do you not see what she has done? How she has seduced you with her lies, just as her sister tried to do with me? I—I was strong." But his voice wavered. "I stopped her before she stopped me," he said, his expression oddly twisted. "There is still time, *fratellino*. Return the Madonna Key to me. It is not too late. Together we can retrieve the tiles and assemble them—"

His litany ran together, all but three words. Confused, I looked up at Josh. "The Madonna Key?"

He didn't blink, didn't so much as flinch, just kept staring at his brother with hard, unyielding eyes. "Our family was the thief," he said coldly. "We took what did not belong to us. I merely returned the property to its rightful owner."

"Idiot!" Caleb roared, lifting his arm to reveal a handgun, which he pointed at Josh. "It is time—"

"Stop!" called a voice from the back of the church, and as Caleb's eyes narrowed, I twisted to see Max Adriano walking up the aisle with surprising authority for such a faded old man. As always, he wore only black, the severity of the color offset by the flowing gray of his hair and beard, the light in his eyes.

"Grandfather," Caleb stated. "You are not looking well."

Max passed us with the slow, measured steps of a man who has walked the wasteland of his life and emerged on the other side. "I am doing far better than you, Caleb. Put down the gun. This is not the way."

"But it is!" he roared. "You taught me so yourself. Nothing can stand in our path, that is what you always said. We have only to focus on the goal, and it will be ours."

"I was wrong," Max said, nearing him. "Your father is wrong."

"No." Caleb's voice dropped to a hiss. "It is too late for turning back. The wheels you put into motion have been spinning for too long. Not even you can—"

Maximillian Adriano stopped in front of his middle grandson. "It is never too late."

Incredulity lit Caleb's eyes. "You cannot be serious."

"I have seen things no man should ever see," Max said, his gaze steady. "Done things. I have betrayed those who trusted me, destroyed that which I cherished, killed the one I loved. As have you."

Olga thrashed against Caleb's hold, and Max's expression gentled. "And I will pay the price, in this life and the next."

Caleb shoved Olga to the floor. "Do you not know who this is, Grandfather? Who I found for you? This is the woman from Portugal, the assassin whose image was captured on surveillance cameras. She shot you in cold blood and—"

"—in doing so saved me. Yes, Caleb. I know who she is. I have always known."

"Saved you?" Caleb spat. "She *destroyed* you, turned you against your own flesh and blood just like—"

I watched the drama between grandfather and grandson, all the while trying to reconcile the fact that dear, gentle Olga, the woman who'd raised me, who had given birth to me, was in fact the assassin who'd nearly ended Max's life three years before.

"Caleb, you do not understand," the old man insisted, putting a hand on his grandson's shoulder, and in doing so stepping between him and Olga. "Your father will never love you. But Scarlet did. And I do. Some of the damage can be undone—"

But it could not. That was evident from the desperation in Caleb's eyes. I saw him lift his gun, saw Max try to grab it from him. "No!"

I lunged. There was a small distance separating me from my mother, no more than a few meters, and as I reached her, I heard Joshua shout my name, and the gunfire erupt.

I knocked my mother free of Caleb and pushed her to safety. On blind adrenaline I took position behind the jeweled altar, squinted through the smoke and lifted my own gun.

Men lay sprawled against the bright red carpet, red of another kind pooling against the cold white marble. From the back of the sanctuary I heard shouting, and saw people running. Vaguely I was aware of crawling, of calling out for Joshua. Of seeing him, slumped over his brother at Max's feet.

In that moment everything stopped. Then raced forward. I saw everything. Felt everything. There was the past, the night we'd met, the slow dance of seduction, the game of cat and mouse. The first time he'd taken me to the villa in Saint-Tropez, when we'd put an end to the wanting, and taken. Then the second time, when I'd learned his true identity, and fled.

I remembered the day I'd discovered I was pregnant with his child. The shock and the horror, the dull ache that had claimed my heart. The mix of pain and joy as my belly had grown, as I'd writhed in labor and given birth to his daughter. As I'd seen her for the first time, looked down into her perfect face and seen his perfect eyes gazing back at me. I remembered crying and holding her to my heart. Telling her it would be okay.

The dreams and the nightmares, the dark fantasies and even darker realities. Every time I'd stumbled across his photo on the Internet or in a newspaper, how I would touch my fingers to his face, and remember. And want.

Saint-Tropez. The Irish coast when he'd warned me to back off, the Giant's Causeway when he'd risked his life to save mine. In my bedroom in Cornwall, when he'd kissed me within an inch of my life. And Pompeii.

In a heartbeat it all flashed, and burned, and then I was there, kneeling over him, clawing him back from Caleb to find his eyes open and coherent, but glazed.

"Nadia…" My hands kept running over him, searching for where he hurt. "I am fine," he said, drawing them to his mouth. "Caleb…"

Was not. I knew that the second I looked at his unmoving body, his eyes glassy and fixed. I jumped when his bloody hand closed around my arm and pulled me closer. But I did not resist. I hovered over him, let him lift a hand to my hair. *"Scarlet…"*

And then he was gone.

* * *

The gusty cry fills the small chamber, and everything else fades—the desperate journey from Pompeii; the devastation discovered when the earth stilled and the sun returned; the search for the impossible; the cold realization that Joakim had been wrong. He will not see her again. He will not find her.

He will never know his child.

"A girl," Sarah, the dark-skinned elder, pronounces. Holding up the wriggling child, she smiles. "You have a beautiful daughter."

They did. She and Joakim.

And finally the tears come, tears she has not let fall since the night the world blurred. They stream down her face as she takes her daughter from Sarah and brings her to her chest, cradles her to her heart. Her child. Hers and Joakim's.

"Welcome," she whispers, as her daughter gazes up with a wisdom and compassion that cannot be possible for one only minutes old. Her eyes—Naysa swallows hard as she looks into her daughter's eyes, so dark and Roman and deeply set. Just like her father's. "Narella," she says, smiling over her daughter's damp dark curls to Sarah. "We shall call her Narella."

And because of her father's bravery, she will live here in the land of the Gauls, among the safety of the Marians. She will live, grow, thrive. She will see things Naysa has only dreamed of. She will be there when many priestesses return from their far-off journeys and the mosaic takes form. She will see, and teach, all because a woman named Naysa and a man named Joakim had lived, and loved, and died.

Destiny. The word drifts through her as Narella latches on to a breast and begins to suckle. She is exactly where she is meant to be. And while she will not see the end to the darkness, one day, one of her descendents will....

* * *

"I wanted to tell you. So many times…"

Sitting next to Olga—*my mother*—in the front pew, I lifted the handkerchief Max had given me and wiped away a smear of dried blood. "You've been through hell," I told her. Not just since Caleb had nabbed her, but from the day she'd made the wrenching decision that the only way to protect her girls was to give them up. "Just rest. We can talk later."

Tangled hair fell into her face. "I wanted you to know that you were loved—"

"I did know," I assured her with a soft squeeze of her hand.

"And Scarlet," she said. "It killed me to be apart from her, but I could not risk us all being together. The Rubashkas were good people. They gave her a good home—"

I couldn't even imagine the strength required to do what she'd done. There'd never been a frail aunt, I now realized. Only a mother and a daughter. "While you loved her from afar."

Her eyes filled. "I did."

Pulling her into my arms was the most natural thing in the world. I held her, much as she'd done for me as a child. Around us, the Naples police had moved in. Joshua and his grandfather were talking to the officer in charge, while beneath Joshua's and Max's jackets, Caleb's body remained at the base of the altar.

Gradually I became aware of a slow warmth moving through me, and I looked up to see Joshua watching me.

"Go to him," my mother said. "He needs you."

"I don't want to leave you."

"You are not leaving me. You are joining him."

And in the end, it was as simple as that. I stood and walked toward him, felt my heart strum low and hard and deep. I'm not sure I'd ever wanted to put my arms around him more. "Joshua—"

He lifted a hand, drawing my attention to a black satchel he'd been carrying with him. "This is for you."

I accepted it, but did not look inside, could not look away from the isolation in his eyes. In the end, he and Caleb had seen the world differently, but once, they'd been little boys getting into mischief together. Josh had loved him, I knew, even as he'd held a gun on him. It was a blessing we would never know who fired the fatal shot. "We'll be able to get out of here soon," I said, reaching for him, but he stepped back from me.

"There is much I need to tell you," he said. "Much I need for you to understand. I know how everything must have looked to you—I promised you I stood with you, and yet I seemed perfectly aligned with my brother."

The hoarse words threw me back to the beach at Saint-Tropez, when he'd warned me to leave Scarlet's death alone. Leave *him* alone. "You were trying to protect me," I pointed out.

"My grandfather and I thought it best to fight our family from within," he acknowledged. "But after Caleb killed Scarlet, after he tried to kill you..." Josh lifted a hand, let it fall agitatedly to his side. "Everything changed. I could no longer pretend. I had to go back. I had to stop him, to take this from him," he said, glancing toward the satchel in my hand, "and bring it to you. To your sisters."

Sisters. Only a week ago I'd been an only child. But Joshua was right. Now I had sisters.

I'm not sure why I turned around, but I did, to find Max Adriano kneeling before my mother. Whatever had been transpiring between them, they now watched Joshua and me. Max's old eyes were glowing. My mother's were bright with emotion of another kind.

Scarlet was right. A time of change was upon us. Slowly, I looked down and slid my hand inside the black leather.

"You asked who was after me," Josh stated. "What they wanted." He paused while I withdrew a long tube. "It was my brother," he explained. "Caleb. And this," he said as I removed lid, "is why."

Even before I looked, I knew.

"It has been in my family for decades," he added. "But it belongs to you."

To all of us, I silently amended. The Marians. Those who had walked before us and those who would walk after us. Because this time, we'd gotten it right.

And with that, into my hands slipped the missing half of the ancient vellum Madonna Key.

Epilogue

Her name was Scarlet, and she was my sister. With Joshua on one side and my mother on the other, I carried the perfume-bottle-shaped urn through the glimmering semidarkness of the underground temple. Torches guided us. The muted heart-beat of the centuries-old fountain drew us toward where the others would be waiting—even Catrina.

Around my neck, I wore a simple silver chain with two keys—Scarlet's and my own. Technically, we'd been separated as infants. And technically, we'd been reunited only through death. But in my heart, I knew she'd been with me all along. I'd dreamed of her. And in those dreams we'd laughed and loved and lived. Our lives, so diametrically different to the casual observer, had run parallel paths. We'd both been driven by the blood of our Marian ancestors. Every step we'd taken had brought us that much closer to fulfilling the prophecy of our birth.

And now she was coming home. To the temple she'd dreamed of, the network of caves she herself had found. This was where she belonged. Where we belonged.

"It is beautiful," Olga whispered. After so many years of thinking of her as my nanny, perhaps I should have found it difficult to think of her as my mother. But she'd loved and cared for me my whole life. I could not have loved her more had I known her true identity from the start. Perhaps I had.

Leanb mo croide, she'd always called me. Now I knew what the Gaelic words meant. *Child of my heart.* "Yes," I whispered.

"Natalia would have loved it," she said in a voice more heavily accented than usual.

"She does," I corrected, because Scarlet was not gone. She was there with us, her incredible life force and zest for all things Marian responsible for shattering the lies and bringing us together. All of us. Not just me and my mother, but me and Joshua, as well, and the others who waited in the temple, those who'd entered through the waterfall, as well as those who'd come through the second, even more benign, entrance that Tru had located.

Joshua had been understandably quiet since leaving Naples. We'd spent the better part of a day with the local police, answering a litany of questions. In the end, Max had used his remaining clout to satisfy the inquiry, while the rest of us were allowed to leave. My last sight of him still haunted me.

I worried how the others would react to Joshua's presence. The last time an Adriano had entered the temple had been one of destruction. But this was a time of reunion. Tomorrow we would travel to Paris, where I would meet little Benny. But today was about another introduction.

"Almost there," I said, glancing up to see the oddest light gleaming in Joshua's green eyes.

"Perhaps I should have waited—"

"You have waited long enough." We both had. In so many ways. But soon his divorce would be final and we would wait no more. Until then, I could give him this, my trust, and a gift of even greater value. Just as he had given me the other half of the Madonna Key.

"Trust me," I said. "All will be fine."

His smile was tight and tentative, and in that moment I'd never loved him more. He'd always been bigger than life to me. Privileged and charming and completely untouchable, a man of private planes and luxury yachts, fine wine and priceless art. Confident. Intelligent. Fearless.

But walking through the crystal-shrouded passage in wet hiking clothes that clung to his body, with his dark hair slicked back from his face to reveal the awe in his eyes, he was just Joshua. A man. And I was just Nadia. A woman.

And a mother, I amended as we stepped through a glimmering arch and into the ancient temple room. I saw her immediately, standing next to my dear friend Lex in front of the rhythmic fountain, staring in fascination at the play of water.

Lex and I had carefully orchestrated their arrival. With the time of transition less than one month away, Joshua and I could not take chances. We were being watched—Lex was not. Traveling only as a man and a little girl, he could move freely. He and Lexie had used the second entrance; Joshua and I the waterfall entrance. As insurance, armed operatives posed as hikers throughout the hills. For the moment, there was nowhere safer.

I'm not sure what tipped Lexie off. But before I could even speak her name, she turned and ran. "Mommy!"

My heart swelled with more love than I'd imagined possible. Vaguely, I was aware of Olga taking the urn from me, but then I was on my knees and my little girl was in my arms. I held her close and buried my face in her silky dark hair, noticed the scent of watermelon. That was new. But everything else, the pink tie-dye hoodie and her soft skin, the way she wiggled even as she clung to me, was classic Lexie. My little girl—mine and Joshua's—whom I'd dreamed of since the moment I'd sent her to safety.

I became aware of Joshua, standing so still beside me. Throat tight, I glanced up and saw his eyes, slumberous and green, the exact shape and color of his daughter's. Except in his I saw tears. And in them I saw my future. *"Josh,"* I tried to say, but my voice didn't work.

Silently, I held out my arm. And silently, he took my hand and went down on one knee. "Alexandria," I whispered, easing her back from my chest. "There is someone I want you to meet."

* * * * *

Don't miss the next instalment of this series.
Seventh Key *by Evelyn Vaughn*
is out in May 2008!

*Turn the page to read an exclusive extract from
bestselling author Beverly Barton's*
Raintree: Sanctuary.

Available in May 2008!

Raintree: Sanctuary

by

Beverly Barton

Sunday, 9:00 a.m.

On this extraordinary June day, only a week away from the
summer solstice, Cael Ansara watched and waited as the
conclave gathered in their private meeting chambers here at
Beauport. He and he alone knew just how momentous this day
would be for the Ansara and the future of their people. Two
hundred years ago, his clan had lost *The Battle* with their
sworn enemy and been all but annihilated. The few who
survived had found solace here on the island of Terrebonne
and, generation by generation, had grown in strength and
numbers. Like the proverbial Phoenix, the Ansara had risen
from the ashes, stronger and more powerful than ever.

One by one, the members of the high council came
together this Sunday morning as they did once a month,
speaking quietly among themselves, comparing notes on the

family's various widespread enterprises as they waited for the Dranir to arrive. Judah Ansara, the all-powerful ruler who was respected and feared in equal measure, had inherited his title from his father. From *their* father.

What would the noble council say, what would they think, how would they react, when they learned that the Dranir of the Ansara was dead? As soon as word came in that Judah had been killed, Cael knew he would have to act fast in order to take control and secure what was rightfully his. Naturally, he would pretend to be as shocked as everyone else, and would make a great show of mourning his younger half brother's brutal murder.

I will even swear vengeance on Judah's behalf, promising to hunt down and kill the person responsible for his death.

Cael smiled, the corners of his mouth curving ever so slightly. Even if several members of the clan suspected him of being behind Judah's murder, no one would ever be able to prove that he had sent a skilled warrior to eliminate the only obstacle in his path to ultimate power. Nor would they be able to prove that he had been the one to bestow a spell of ultimate strength and cunning on that warrior so that he would be equal, if not superior, to his opponent. All would soon learn that Judah the Invincible had been defeated.

At long last, after a lifetime of being the bastard son, of waiting and plotting and planning, he would soon take his place as the Dranir. Was he not the elder son of Dranir Hadar? Was he not as powerful as his younger brother, Judah, perhaps even more so? Was he not better suited to lead the great Ansara clan? Was it not his destiny to destroy their enemy, to wipe every single Raintree from the face of the earth?

Judah claimed that the time was not right for an attack, for all-out war, that the Ansara clan was not ready. At the last council meeting, Cael had confronted his brother.

"We are a mighty people, our powers strong. Why do we wait? Are you afraid to face the Raintree, my brother?" Cael had asked. "If so, step aside and I will lead our people to victory."

At the very moment he had confronted his brother, Cael had already made his plans and had been preparing assignments for the Ansara who looked to him for guidance. He had endowed each young warrior with protective spells. First, the most fearsome of his followers—Stein—would kill Judah. Then Greynell would strike a deadly blow to the very heart of the Raintree, in their home place, the land that had been the family's sanctuary for generations. After that, Tabby would eliminate the Raintree seer, Echo, to prevent her from "seeing" what devastating tragedies awaited her clan.

Unfortunately, only one member of the council had agreed with Cael. One of twelve. Alexandria, the most beautiful and powerful female member of the royal family and third in line for the throne, was his first cousin. She had once been Judah's faithful supporter, but when Cael promised her a place at his side if he were to become the Dranir, she had secretly switched allegiances. What did it matter that he had no intention of sharing his power with anyone, not even Alexandria? Once he ruled the Ansara, no one would dare defy him.

"It is unlike Judah to be late," Alexandria said to the others now.

"I am sure there is a good reason." Claude Ansara, another cousin, had been Judah's closest confidante since they were boys. Claude was second in line to the throne, right after Cael himself, his now deceased father a younger brother to Cael and Judah's father.

Rumblings rose from the others, some concerned by Judah's tardiness, others speculating that undoubtedly there had been an emergency of some sort of which they were not aware. The Dranir had never been late for a council meeting.

Why has there been no telephone call? Cael wondered.
Why hasn't the news of Judah's death been made known?
Stein had been given orders to disappear immediately after
killing Judah, and not to resurface until Cael was irrefutably
in charge of the Ansara and could give him permission to
return to fight the Raintree. Soon. On the day of the summer
solstice.

Once the Raintree had been destroyed, the Ansara would
rule the world. And *he* would rule the Ansara.

Suddenly the chamber doors burst open as if a mighty
wind had ripped them from their golden hinges. A dark,
snarling creature, his icy gray eyes surveying the room,
stormed into their midst. Clad in black boots, black pants, a
bloodstained white shirt and ripped black vest, Judah Ansara
arrived, growling like the ferocious beast he was. The wall of
windows facing the ocean rattled from the force of his rage.

Cael felt the blood drain from his face, and his heart
stopped for one terrifying moment when he realized that
Judah had survived the assassination attempt. He had been
able to defeat a warrior fighting under a spell created by
Cael's incredibly powerful magic, which meant that Judah's
powers were undoubtedly far greater than Cael had realized.
But that wasn't of key importance right now. Even the fact
that Stein was dead was unimportant in the wake of a far
greater concern. What Cael needed to know was whether
Stein had lived long enough to betray him?

"Lord Judah." Alexandria rushed to his side but stopped
short of touching him. "What has happened? You look as if
you've been in a battle."

Whirling to face her, Judah narrowed his gaze and glared
at her through sharp, shadowed slits. "Someone within my
own clan wishes me dead." His voice reverberated with the
throaty intensity of a man barely controlling his anger. "The

warrior Stein came into my bedchambers at dawn and attempted to murder me in my sleep. The woman who shared my bed was his accomplice and had thought to drug me last night. But they were both fools to think I would not sense danger and act accordingly, despite the strong magical spell that had been placed on Stein. I switched drinks with the lady, so she was the one sleeping soundly, while I was dressed and ready for battle when Stein slipped in through the secret passage to my quarters that only you, the council, even know exists."

Cael realized that he must speak, must react with outrage, least suspicion fall immediately upon him. "Are you implying that someone on the council…?"

"I imply nothing." Judah speared Cael with his deadly glare. "But rest assured, brother, that I will discover the identity of the person who sent Stein to do his dirty work, and when the time is right, I will have my revenge." As Judah rubbed his bloody shoulder, a fresh red stain appeared on his shirt.

"My God, you're still bleeding." Claude went to Judah, his gaze thoroughly scanning Judah's big body for signs of other injuries.

"A few knife wounds. Nothing more," Judah said. "Stein was a remarkable opponent. Whoever chose him, chose well. Only a handful of Ansara warriors have battle skills that equal mine. Stein came close."

"No one has your level of abilities," Councilman Bartholomew said, as he and the other council members surrounded Judah. "You are superior in every way."

"If your battle with Stein was at dawn, why are you still bloody and disheveled?" Alexandria asked. "Couldn't you have bathed and changed clothes before the meeting?"

Judah laughed, the sound deep, coarse and mirthless. "Once my men disposed of Stein's body and the body of his accomplice, the whore Drusilla, I intended to bathe and make myself presentable, but a telephone call from the United States—from North Carolina—interrupted my plans. What I learned from the conversation required immediate action. I spoke directly with Varian, the head of the Ansara team assigned to monitor the Raintree sanctuary."

The council members murmured loudly, and then elderly Councilwoman Sidra spoke for the others. "Tell us, my lord, was the call concerning the Raintree?"

Judah nodded; then again cast his gaze directly on Cael. "Your protégé, Greynell, is in North Carolina."

"I swear to you—"

"Do not swear a lie!"

Cael trembled with fear, all the while hating himself for cowering in the wake of his brother's fury. Squaring his shoulders and looking Judah directly in the eyes, Cael faced the Dranir's wrath. He reminded himself that he was an equal, that he was the elder son and deserved to rule the Ansara, that the failure of his most recent plot to dethrone his brother did not mean that he was not destined to rule. Regardless of what Judah said or did, he could not stop the inevitable. Not now. It was too late.

"Did you know that Greynell had gone to North Carolina?" Judah demanded.

"I knew," Cael admitted. "But I didn't send him. He acted on his own."

Judah growled. "And you know what his mission is, don't you?"

Cael wished that he could destroy his brother here and now and be done with it. But he dared not act. When Judah died, his blood should not be on Cael's hands.

"Yes, my lord, I know that some of the young warriors grow restless. They don't want to wait to wage war on the

Raintree. A few have taken it upon themselves to act now instead of waiting until you tell them the time is right."

Judah swore vehemently. The windows shivered and cracked. Fireballs rained down from the ceiling. The marble floor beneath their feet shook, and the walls trembled.

Claude placed his meaty hand on Judah's shoulder and spoke softly to him. The shaking council chambers settled suddenly, the fires burning throughout the room died down, and the broken glass windowpanes jangled loudly as they fell out and hit the floor.

Judah breathed heavily. "Greynell is on a mission to penetrate the Raintree home place, their sanctuary."

Cael swallowed hard.

"Who is his target?" Judah demanded.

Did he lie and swear he did not know? Or did he confess? Cael could feel Judah probing his mind, searching for a way to penetrate the barrier he barely managed to keep in place. If he himself were not so powerful, he could never withstand his brother's brutal psychic force.

"Mercy Raintree." Cael spoke the name with reverence. The woman might be a Raintree, but her abilities were legendary among the Ansara as well as her own people. She was the most powerful empath living today.

Judah's nostrils flared. "Mercy Raintree," he said, his voice deadly calm and chillingly restrained, "is mine. I claimed her. She is my kill."

A deadly truth...

When Victor Holland comes flying out of the night, he runs straight into the path of Catherine Weaver's car. Having uncovered a terrifying secret which leads all the way to Washington, Victor is running for his life – and from the men who will go to any lengths to silence him.

Victor's story sounds like the ravings of a madman, but the haunted look in his eyes – and the bullet hole in his shoulder – tell a different story.

As each hour brings pursuers ever closer, Cathy has to wonder, is she giving her trust to a man in danger or trusting her life to a dangerous man?

Available from 18th April 2008

www.mirabooks.co.uk

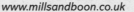

Celebrate 100 years of pure reading pleasure with Mills & Boon®

To mark our centenary, each month we're publishing a special 100th Birthday Edition. These celebratory editions are packed with extra features and include a FREE bonus story.

Plus, starting in February you'll have the chance to enter a fabulous monthly prize draw. See 100th Birthday Edition books for details.

Now that's worth celebrating!

15th February 2008

Raintree: Inferno by Linda Howard
Includes FREE bonus story Loving Evangeline
A double dose of Linda Howard's heady mix of passion and adventure

4th April 2008

The Guardian's Forbidden Mistress by Miranda Lee
Includes FREE bonus story The Magnate's Mistress
Two glamorous and sensual reads from favourite author Miranda Lee!

2nd May 2008

The Last Rake in London by Nicola Cornick
Includes FREE bonus story The Notorious Lord
Lose yourself in two tales of high society and rakish seduction!

Look for Mills & Boon 100th Birthday Editions at your favourite bookseller or visit
www.millsandboon.co.uk

0108/CENTENARY_2-IN-1

4 FREE

BOOKS AND A SURPRISE GIFT!

We would like to take this opportunity to thank you for reading this Mills & Boon® book by offering you the chance to take FOUR more specially selected titles from the Intrigue series absolutely FREE! We're also making this offer to introduce you to the benefits of the Mills & Boon® Reader Service™—

- ★ **FREE home delivery**
- ★ **FREE gifts and competitions**
- ★ **FREE monthly Newsletter**
- ★ **Exclusive Reader Service offers**
- ★ **Books available before they're in the shops**

Accepting these FREE books and gift places you under no obligation to buy, you may cancel at any time, even after receiving your free shipment. Simply complete your details below and return the entire page to the address below. You don't even need a stamp!

YES! Please send me 4 free Intrigue books and a surprise gift. I understand that unless you hear from me, I will receive 6 superb new titles every month for just £3.15 each, postage and packing free. I am under no obligation to purchase any books and may cancel my subscription at any time. The free books and gift will be mine to keep in any case.

18ZED

Ms/Mrs/Miss/Mr ....Initials ....
BLOCK CAPITALS PLEASE

Surname ....

Address ....

....

....Postcode..

Send this whole page to:
UK: FREEPOST CN81, Croydon, CR9 3WZ

Offer valid in UK only and is not available to current Mills & Boon® Reader Service™ subscribers to this series. Overseas and Eire please write for details and readers in Southern Africa write to Box 3010, Pinegowie, 2123 RSA. We reserve the right to refuse an application and applicants must be aged 18 years or over. Only one application per household. Terms and prices subject to change without notice. Offer expires 30th June 2008. As a result of this application, you may receive offers from Harlequin Mills & Boon and other carefully selected companies. If you would prefer not to share in this opportunity please write to The Data Manager, PO Box 676, Richmond, TW9 IWU.

Mills & Boon® is a registered trademark owned by Harlequin Mills & Boon Limited.
The Mills & Boon® Reader Service™ is being used as a trademark.